Just About a Rake

Ladies Who Dare
Book Five

Tanya Wilde

ARE YOU SIGNED UP FOR DRAGONBLADE'S BLOG?

You'll get the latest news and information on exclusive giveaways, exclusive excerpts, coming releases, sales, free books, cover reveals and more.

Check out our complete list of authors, too!

No spam, no junk. That's a promise!

Sign Up Here

www.dragonbladepublishing.com

Dearest Reader;

Thank you for your support of a small press. At Dragonblade Publishing, we strive to bring you the highest quality Historical Romance from some of the best authors in the business. Without your support, there is no 'us', so we sincerely hope you adore these stories and find some new favorite authors along the way.

Happy Reading!

CEO, Dragonblade Publishing

Additional Dragonblade books by
Author Tanya Wilde

Ladies Who Dare Series
Almost a Scoundrel (Book 1)
By No Means a Gentleman (Book 2)
A Knave By Any Other Name (Book 3)
A Little Bit of Hellion (Book 4)
Just About a Rake (Book 5)

Chapter One

"I'M IN A crisis," Lady Leonora Heart declared to one of her good friends, Harriet Hillstow, now the Marchioness of Leeds, amidst the crowded ballroom of Lord and Lady Haversham's event.

"You're in a what?" Harriet asked, concern on her face as she glanced over at Leonora.

"A crisis," she repeated. A big one.

"Here? Right now? A crisis of what sort?" Her friend lowered her voice. "*That* sort?"

Leonora waved her hand dismissively. "No, not *that* sort. A *moment* sort."

Harriet blinked, confusion crossing her face. "Then I'm not sure I am following . . ."

"I need a moment, Harriet. A. Moment."

Harriet arched a prompting brow.

Leonora fought for a way to explain, for she herself couldn't quite pin down the specifics of the moment she sought. Only the magnitude. Presently, her life felt unmoored. Something essential felt *missing*. Every smile she gave, every laugh she laughed, every dance she shared seemed almost hollow, as though she were an actor playing the part of herself, rather than living as herself. It was disheartening, this vague sense of lack.

"A moment to rule all moments," Leonora declared.

"Well, that doesn't sound ominous at all." Her friend cocked her head to the side, studying her. "Why do you need a moment to rule all moments?"

Leonora stared at her empty—by choice—dance card with a small frown. "Because I'm tired of waltzing to the same tune. I've been swaying to the same melody for a whole season. I need something else. Something more."

"So choose another song."

"But it should be *the* song."

Harriet leaned over to peek at the card. "I can hardly believe your card is not full of all London's rakes and rogues tonight. I believe you—you are in a crisis."

Leonora pursed her lips. "Tonight is different."

"Did something happen to bring on this sentiment?" Harriet asked.

Yes. Something had happened, yes. *Nothing* happened. Well, not *nothing* nothing. She supposed it had actually started with her brother reading the paper and him doing nothing. Just reading the paper. But it was a hard sentiment to convey to someone whose nothings were still full of the person they loved.

"You are married," she said to Harriet, "so you will not understand."

"Perhaps you are right. I cannot understand your thinking. But don't you usually revel in dancing? Especially when you are dancing with rakes? You once said it's delightfully exhilarating."

"Yes, but even that has lost its appeal." With one notable exception. Her gaze tracked the crowd for a certain, tall, blue-eyed rogue. *He* remained the only breath of fresh air in an otherwise stifling landscape.

"Really?" Harriet murmured with blatant curiosity. "And this is why you want a moment to rule all moments?"

Leonora gave a single nod. "Exactly."

"Interesting." Harriet slowly fanned her face in thought. "What if what you need is not a moment to rule all moments but a dream to rule all dreams?"

"A dream? I believe they belong in my sleep." And moments belonged to waking life.

Harriet scoffed. "No, a *dream*. Like love." Her eyes narrowed on Leonora. "You want a love match, do you not?"

Love? "I haven't given too much thought to the future, to be honest. As you know, I'm more of a woman who revels in the present."

"Well, you should consider it. Perhaps you can try your hand at reforming a rake."

"Don't be ridiculous." Her eyes tracked the crowd again, searching. "I have no intention of reforming any rake. If anything, my future husband shall have to reform me."

"Goodness. Very well then, but you can still make love your dream."

Leonora shrugged. "I don't know. Love is a consequence not a dream."

"A consequence of what, exactly?"

"Finding your soulmate." Leonora grinned at her friend. "You should know better than I do about that."

Harriet matched her smile. "So find your soulmate."

Leonora wanted to scoff. "If only it were that easy."

"Perhaps you make it harder by flirting with rogues. What if you worked your wiles on a different sort of gentleman? You know, like a *gentleman*."

"Rakes are gentlemen," Leonora defended. They were more fun, and in a way, safe. "They're just *wild* gentlemen."

"I cannot understand your fascination with them."

"What can I say? There is just something about teasing a man who so clearly wants something you know he could never have."

"How diabolical," Harriet said dryly. "In any event," she continued, "if you won't change the tune, you could change the dance floor. You can always try dancing in different settings. Such as the garden. A dirt road. Places like that."

Leonora nodded thoughtfully. *Not a bad idea.* But . . . "Whether on a dance floor, dirt road, or a garden, it's still a dance. It's still a tune." The *same* dance. The *same* tune. "Unless I find myself a dreamlike man like you found in Leeds."

Harriet's gaze flicked fondly to her husband in conversation with the Duke of Calstone and back again. "Perhaps you shall when you stop flirting with rakes you have no intention to reform."

"But I can't help myself," Leonora said, then laughed. "I'm drawn to them like a bird to the sky."

Harriet rolled her eyes heavenward.

"Go on and say it," Leonora murmured. "I am hopeless, I know."

"You *are* hopeless. But at least you are aware of the fact." Harriet tapped a finger on her chin. "What you need is a new sort of wild man who can help you experience dancing or whatnot in a refreshed way."

A new sort of wild man? Other than rakes? What sort of wild would *that* be? "You mean like a country man?"

Harriet pointed to the Duke of Calstone. "Like him."

Leonora followed her friend's gaze to the man next to Leeds. "The duke? What's so wild about him other than his wildly coveted title?"

"He is the *good* sort of wild," Harriet pointed out. "Not rakish at all."

"Good sort of wild?" Whatever sort of wild he may be, it didn't call to her in the slightest. Nothing about him seemed destined to result in a moment to rule all moments. Nor did he appear to be the sort that might lead to the stirring of a dream— not in her, at least. "Anyway, he is not my type."

"*Rakes* are your type, then?"

Leonora grinned at her friend. "Hopeless, I tell you."

Harriet snorted. "This is not about what your type is and what it is not. This is about a new experience. He might be the tune you are looking for."

"Fine, shall I just dance with him, then?" Leonora offered, then teased, "It seems awfully lackluster, though, just dancing with a duke. How about I steal a kiss from him?"

Harriet laughed. "I'm sure you shall shock the trousers from his body."

"Why? Is he a prude?" That would be a rather intriguing prospect.

"Your tone is terrifying, you know." Her friend shook her head. "You are aware that you are going from one extreme to another. From chasing after rakes to being fascinated by the thought of a prude."

"The middle is exceedingly boring, don't you agree?"

"No, I don't. Boring is beguiling, my friend."

Leonora laughed. "If you say so. I, on the other hand, prefer the thrill. The thrill of making the most of every moment." *For you never know when the privilege of those moments might be taken from you.* And perhaps that was the crux of her crisis. Even the thrills were becoming less and less thrilling.

"I daresay you should have been born a man."

"Now wouldn't that have been wonderful! Though I can still accomplish all I want being a woman."

Things certainly would have been different if she had been a man, though. And it wasn't that Leonora didn't have dreams. After all, when one thought about it, dreams were just moments that had been properly seized, weren't they? And she had many, many moments she wanted to pursue. At the end of her life, she wanted no regrets, no matter how regretful certain circumstances may be.

Otherwise . . .

The face of her older brother flashed into her mind, a reminder of the scandalous secret regarding her family circumstances she'd discovered on her fourteenth birthday. Which was why she had vowed from that young age to savor the pleasures of the moment and, where there were no delights, create them herself.

Nothing in this world of hers was guaranteed. Only the present moment and how she chose to claim it.

"Speaking of chasing rakes, what happened to your Lord Dare?"

Leonora scoffed. "He is not *my* lord anything."

They'd been flirting for the whole season, true, skirting on the edges of crossing the proverbial line. However, it was just a spot of fun. She delighted in teasing him. He enjoyed teasing her.

But he was a rake. Moments—lots of moments—of fun, but not her dreamlike man. Her lips curved upward as her eyes darted past Calstone, sweeping the crowd, hunting for that fun.

Ah, Leonora! Did the root of her crisis lie there?

She hadn't lied. She had no plans to civilize a scoundrel—not even that one—though she loved flirting with him. In any event, if it were that easy to tame a rogue, wouldn't there be reformed rakes prancing all about London? No, Leonora wanted those moments of fun. She wanted to collect tons of marvelous memories, but that was all. She didn't want to bleed from her wrists in an effort to refashion a man who was resistant to change. What sort of amusement was that?

Harriet's soft laughter rang in Leonora's ear. "Ah, Calstone," she called for the men's attention. "You have been formally introduced to my friend, Lady Leonora, correct? Doesn't she look lovely tonight?"

Harriet! What was her friend up to now?

"Yes of course," Calstone answered, directing a grin her way. "You are a true vision."

Leonora resisted the urge to shoot a glare Harriet's way and returned the man's smile. Might as well seize this moment, even if she hadn't exactly chosen it. "You look quite handsome yourself, Your Grace. A star amongst this tedious crowd."

He opened and closed his mouth, blinking a few times. Her smile brightened. Admittedly, the man could be considered no less handsome than Leeds. But he lacked the calm charm the marquess possessed. But then he surprised her, just a bit, by leaning in conspiringly and saying in a lowered voice, "What a terrifying prospect for our host. Don't ever let word of their lackluster guest list get out to them, I beg you."

Leonora laughed. She was all for men who did not raise their brows at a spot of playfulness. Add a dash of flirtation, and she had her man—at least for a little while. Calstone might be closer to matching this recipe than she'd thought, though still not a perfect match, to be sure.

"Ah, well, perhaps the night holds a bit more promise now."

"I have no words," Harriet muttered from the side. "Now that I think about it, do not let Leonora set her claws in you, Calstone," she said in a louder tone. "Dukes are not her usual type of gentleman."

Leeds arched a brow.

"Do not fret, my lovely Lady Leeds—"

"She's not your lovely lady anything," Leeds interjected flatly.

Leonora bit back a smile and she could see Calstone do the same.

"I have skin as thick as an elephant. Claws cannot penetrate me." He turned to Leonora. "Try your best, my lady."

"Well, I cannot claim I have claws to try with, so do not get too excited, Duke. Besides is that term even the appropriate one?"

"Then what would you call it?" Harriet asked, cocking her head to the side.

"Sights." Leonora grinned. "Isn't that what everyone is doing these days—setting their sights?"

"Dear God, please don't do that," Calstone lamented. "Please don't set any sights on me. The prospect is most horrifying. Most horrifying."

The tension Leonora had borne this past week eased a degree. She cast a mock-offended glance at Harriet. "I heard right, didn't I? He did call me horrifying? I've never been called horrifying before."

Harriet laughed, placing her hands over her lips.

"That is certainly not what I meant," Calstone said, unflustered. "I, Duke of Calstone, will never call a lady horrifying. The idea that one has set her sights on me, however . . ."

"Ah, so it's my *sights* you find horrifying." *What a refreshing change of pace!*

"Perhaps I should have phrased that differently," Calstone said.

Leeds nodded in agreement. "Agreed."

"Leeds," Calstone pleaded. "Help me, old chap."

"My apologies," the marquess said without a beat of hesitation. "But now my level of intrigue is so much greater than it was before."

Leonora laughed, and her head lifted to lock with a pair of eyes that burned into the very soul of her. A ripple of tingles spun from the palms of her hand to the tips of her fingers.

There he was.

A spark of heat bloomed from the depth of her chest, lifting her mouth into a grin that mirrored the unfolding sensation. Ah, yes, only one man made her come this alive.

Unfortunately, his name was Dare.

Harriet grinned at them. "I can see you and Calstone will get along just fine. I had hoped so."

"Hope," Calstone murmured, "is but mere disappointment one has yet to discover."

Leonora blinked, then cast a glance at her friend. "I'm not sure what to make of *that*."

"Oh, pay half of his words no mind," Harriet said with a shake of her head. "The duke is prone to exaggeration and dramatics."

Leonora tilted her head ever so slightly and regarded the man. "I suppose rather than spending one's time hoping this and hoping that, it's best to just act."

Harriet dipped her head in agreement. "I second that. Action is good. Great."

Leonora nodded thoughtfully. Quite right. She never did like that word. *Hope.* Especially not when it came to the grand scheme of a person's life. Which was why she preferred to actively seize her moments rather than just hope they seized her.

"I say," Calstone said abruptly, his air of teasing replaced by a pensive glance. "I don't know if I've mentioned this before, but you've always looked oddly familiar to me, and I suddenly remember who you remind me of, Lady Leonora."

Leonora arched a brow, curiosity piqued. "Oh? And who might that be?"

"The Widowed Duchess of Crane."

Leonora gave a light shrug. "I can't say I've ever met her."

"Me neither," Harriet supplied.

"Oh, she hasn't frequented London in years," Calstone said. "Uncanny resemblance, really, though."

An uncanny resemblance? If it were any other resemblance, Leonora wouldn't have paused. But uncanny? Her heart stuttered. The phrase echoed back and forth across her mind, startling her into speculation. Could the Duchess of Crane be . . .

Could she be . . .

Her real mother?

SOMETHING WAS WRONG with that little temptress.

Rake Sloane, the Earl of Dare, tracked Lady Leonora's movements from across the ballroom. The saucy flirt hadn't danced once this evening. She had also barely conversed with anyone but her friend. Yet most unsettlingly—a realization which was unsettling in itself—she'd neither sought him out.

He narrowed his eyes on her and pursed his lips in thought.

Yes, something was very, very wrong.

It shouldn't bother him.

And it didn't.

Not a lot.

Though he could admit he adored her teasing. If brandy were made from her charm, every man in London would be drunk on her. A night without a daily dose of her laughter seemed a loss.

He couldn't look away from her.

That bothered him, too.

But not a lot.

He knew better than to let it. Just like he knew, more than anyone else in the world, who he was and who he was not. Well, perhaps his father had known, too. Why else would he have named him something so fitting, something that bound them together in reputation and reality? The irony was not lost on him. But that didn't mean he'd follow in the man's exact footsteps.

Dare pulled a face.

His father had created difficulties Dare did *not* intend to repeat.

Period.

Like naming his children.

The beguiling temptress, on the other hand, was a bright spark, though she was one that didn't dare linger long with a jaded rake. Not that he allowed his own thoughts to linger in her direction, either, but even he, drunk on the brandy that was Lady Leonora, couldn't help but be drawn to her light, evening by evening.

And she was keeping her distance from him. Or so it seemed.

His brow furrowed.

A throat cleared from beside him. Loudly. "You've got that look."

Dare gritted his teeth and glanced at Knox, his longtime friend, as he approached. More formally known as Brent Madden, the Marquess of Knoxley, he was also arguably Dare's only friend. "What look?" His view returned to Lady Leonora.

Knox followed his line of sight. "The look you get when you're about to stir a pot full of trouble."

Dare scoffed. "That's just my face."

"True. But there is something else in this look. Something worrying."

Dare's fingers twitched. Knox could read him like the latest issue of the *London Times*, flipping through each of the pages as though he had damn well written the content himself.

So yes, this look of his probably conveyed how his fingers wanted to grab hold of something—anything—like the sandy swirls of Lady Leonora's curls outlining the soft profile of her heart-shaped face.

He clenched his hand.

Or just *her*.

But he could never reach that far. He could only dig his nails into the palms of his hands and draw sense from the sting.

"Don't be absurd. It's nothing."

Knox arched a brow. "Doesn't look like nothing. Looks like an awful lot of something."

A woman, Dare heard what his friend hadn't uttered. *That woman.*

But whatever conclusion Knox had come to, he had it wrong. Their teasing and flirtatious remarks could never amount to whatever the tone his friend's voice implied. That was outlandish. Blasphemous, even.

His brows knit together when he spotted Lady Leonora laughing at something the Duke of Calstone said. Calstone . . . a duke. A proper gentleman. A perfect match.

The exact opposite of him.

"She's just innocent fun," Dare murmured offhandedly even though those two words had certainly never been used by anyone else to describe anything he did.

Knox's brow line spoke volumes, but he said nothing. He supposed he should be thankful his friend hadn't laughed outright, and yet, even those two words could be considered laughable coming from his mouth, it was the simplest, and oddly truest way to describe his interactions with Lady Leonora.

"Your cousin is in town," Knox suddenly said.

Dare looked at Knox. "Drake is in London?" He was the only cousin worth mentioning.

Knox nodded.

The furrow in Dare's brow deepened. Drake loathed London

and hardly ever left Brighton. For him to be here, something big must have lured him. "You've seen him?"

A nod. "He requires your help with something."

"Oh? This is going to be interesting. Why send you? Why not come to me himself?"

Knox shrugged. "You'll have to ask him that."

Dare shook his head. No point. Drake wouldn't set foot in Mayfair or any part of town he considered belonged to the pompous and wealthy. But was a note too damn much to ask? "What's this help he requires?"

"The Duchess of Crane has returned to London. She has something he wants."

Dare gave his friend an astonished look. "What do you want me to do about it?"

"*I* don't want you to do anything. I'm just telling you what Drake told me. He didn't say anything about the what or the how."

How very Drake. "Damn lunatic." His gaze returned to search for the one face that never failed to lift his mood. "What exactly does he want from the duchess?"

"A deed of land."

Interesting. "Then he can get it himself."

Knox chuckled. "You know he won't set foot anywhere near nobility. He'll erupt in welts."

Dare's smile turned sly. "Then let him break out in gushing sores. I don't care. I'm not doing God knows what he wants me to do to get his hands on that deed. I'm not one of his boys."

"In any event," Knox continued, "even if you were to help him, I've heard she has yet to shed her black, so your . . . methods of persuasion will likely be wasted on her."

As if he would seduce her anyway. He wasn't some dog in heat. Most of the time. "Hasn't the late duke been dead for two years?"

Knox spread his hands, palms up. "What can I say? The widow apparently refuses to come out of mourning."

"Then what does that devil Drake want me to do?" Dare muttered more to himself than Knox.

"Not sure, but aren't you a master at slipping in and out of houses undetected?"

Not entirely true, though Dare *had* mastered the art of slipping in and out of the bedchambers of ladies. They did, however, generally leave a door open for him.

"You are a better master than I," Dare pointed out.

A scoff. "I'm not family."

Dare sneered. "Count yourself lucky." And just what land did the Duchess of Crane have in her possession that Drake wanted, anyway? What property would have him even step foot in London of all places?

Though in reality it could be any one of the Crane properties. It was no secret that Drake was one of the late duke's bastard sons. His mother was sister to Dare's own mother, and yet Dare was the only one in his family who recognized his cousin and aunt as family. So ostracized, Drake may well feel entitled to a bit of inheritance now the old duke was dead.

"You can tell Drake to seek me out himself to tell me what he wants. And I won't be his burglar, if that's what he thinks. Besides, if the woman is still in black, it's best to let her be."

"It's my impression that he has been waiting until she steps out of mourning, and he is growing impatient."

Sweet laughter spilled into his ears from across the room, causing his shoulders to tense up. His gaze found Lady Leonora again. He couldn't help but scowl. Just what did she find so funny in the Duke of Calstone's conversation? "Damnation, this night is all but ruined."

Knox let out a low laugh. "I suppose your cousin believes you have the charm or some tricks to lure a woman out of her mourning drab."

"What utter nonsense," Dare snapped. "I don't have *techniques* for these sorts of situations." If that were true, what a horrifying thought it would be. It would involve some form of comfort, would it not? And that would mean tears might be shed. The thought of a weeping female gave him chills.

"I'm sure he will be disappointed."

Good. "I'm sure he will get over it."

Knox arched a brow. "Has it ever occurred to you that he might merely want you to mediate since you and she are of the same world?"

"No. It didn't." Not even the slightest. "Let's change the subject, shall we?"

"As you wish," Knox said. "You still have a rather troubling look about you. Why don't you ask some chit to dance?"

"Not in the mood." The only chit he enjoyed dancing with stood across the floor flirting with another man.

Little temptress.

And too breathtaking for her own good. Everything about her radiated beauty. Even her gown, a soft, silky green, reminded him of a misty morning in the garden before the sun broke through the haze. Her eyes were probably sparkling like twin drops of water as she smiled at Calstone.

Christ, Dare. You sound like a poet.

But if this gut feeling was right and she was keeping her distance tonight, just what had he done to deserve being sidestepped by her?

"You've changed," Knox remarked quite unexpectedly.

Dare flicked an incredulous look at his friend "Me? Impossible. Birds can't change their feathers."

Knox lifted his shoulders in a small, careless shrug. "They can pluck them out and grow new ones."

"They will still return as the same color."

"Nothing returns as the same color. It's always a bit more dull or a bit more vibrant."

"How wise of you," Dare remarked dryly. "I wonder if my color will return uglier or prettier." Probably uglier.

"You haven't plucked out all your feathers, so I really can't say."

Dare snorted. Well, no matter. He didn't mind the way he was anyway. Though he wouldn't deny his path was a rather lonely one. His house at night, for one, had the feel of a silent graveyard. Who the hell could sleep in a graveyard? He certainly struggled. Which was why he attended these events and sought out a bit of light.

Her light, if he was honest. It drove away the shadows of exhaustion. At least for a little while.

It was a damn miracle she hadn't been infected just by cavorting with him. But then, she was such a presence that no one could ever doubt her glow. She was a woman so bright he could never taint her with his darkness.

And she came to him openly. Publicly. That was even more tempting to him. She didn't want to hide her teasing. Her flirting. She didn't want to hide *him*.

That was dangerous.

Dare sighed, his eyes hunting her down again.

It was for the best then if she were to finally get smart and stay away from him. Best that she kept her distance. Best that she captured herself a duke.

Chapter Two

LEONORA STEPPED UP to the table full of tarts and other confections, surveying the fashionable horde as she snatched up a lemon cake. Should she go and claim her nightly dose of Dare's charm or continue to keep a bit of distance? Honestly, she had not meant to avoid him. However, Dare could never be part of the moment to rule all moments that she sought.

He was a rake.

And her time was precious. Far too precious to waste on taming a man. And truth be told, she quite liked him wild. A reformed Dare? The very thought was laughable. Like declawing a lion or trimming the wings off a hawk—why ruin something so gloriously untamed? Besides, a man could only reform himself. If Dare wanted to be good, he would choose to be good. If he wanted to stay wicked, he'd choose to stay wicked.

And that brought about a spot of excitement to her thoughts.

She sought his familiar tousle of brown hair amongst the men. Always styled nine parts fashionable for one part scoundrel. Oh, why is it *so* hard to resist this bit of thrill?

"Looking for someone?" a low voice drawled from behind her.

Leonora whirled, cheeks bulging with cake, and met the gaze of the most devastatingly swoon-worthy man, in her blunt opinion, in the whole of London. Perhaps even Britain. Dark-blue eyes stared back at her. They reminded her of the depth of the ocean, an intriguing contrast to his rather shallow character.

But that was the charm of Dare.

His handsomeness wasn't subtle. One didn't have sneak looks at him. Once you looked, you couldn't look away. He was *that* beautiful. He knew this, too. The knowledge hung on his smile and echoed back into his posture.

Ah yes, there it was—the smile he was directing at her now, his gaze brimming with sparks as a wayward lock of hair fell over his forehead.

Leonora's lips tugged upward until they fully matched his. It was also one of those things one couldn't help in his presence. His smile had a way of luring the corners of even his opponents' lips to draw upward bit by bit, until one smile matched the other, and neither person could tell who had won and who had lost, but they were grinning at each other like fools.

Like right now.

Leonora swallowed the cake. "Who would I be looking for?" Ah, certain excitement was just as eager to seek her out as she it.

"Perhaps a certain ruffian that you love to jab with teasing remarks?"

"Ruffian?" She laughed. "There are many men such as that."

"So harsh," he murmured, the perfection of his smile never slipping. "Have I been cuckolded by my little beauty?"

Leonora gave a less-than-perfect eye roll. "I'm not even going to begin to explain all the things wrong with that statement."

He chuckled. "I saw you conversing with the Duke of Calstone earlier."

Her ears perked. "Jealous?"

"Exceedingly. The duke is a much better man than I. Not a ruffian at all."

"Is that something to be jealous about when your reputation is one of your own making?"

"A man can be jealous of all sorts of things, even when he is not quite in the right."

"Not quite in the right, you say?" Leonora laughed. "Well, when it comes to prospects, I dare say most men are better than you in that regard. But do not fret, Lord Dare, you still have your roguish charm that sets *you* apart from most."

"What a comforting thought."

Leonora laughed. He didn't look comforted at all. Neither did he look offended. This was what she loved about Dare. He didn't put on airs, and if he did, it was so obvious that she couldn't help but be amused.

He picked up a lemon cake of his own for inspection. "I noticed you haven't danced once tonight."

He'd noticed that? "You should try it," she said, motioning to the lemon cake. "It's good." She turned to survey the dancers. "And you are quite right. I haven't danced."

"Why not?" He bit into the cake, nodding his agreement after a moment. "It is good."

She smiled. A rake indulging in something as sweet and simple as a lemon cake. There should be a headline about that. "I'm not feeling the music tonight."

"How strange. You love dancing. I know at least that much about you."

"I suppose"—her gaze flicked over his face—"I'm bored."

He dusted off his hand after finishing the cake. "Bored? This is a grave problem. What shall happen in the years to come if you're already bored?"

"I expect I shall have someone by my side to relieve my boredom in the future. The present moment is the challenge."

He inclined his head, eyes sweeping the room. "I suppose after the excitement of this season so far, a good, old-fashioned ball would seem boring."

"Are you blaming the heiresses and the scandals following the lost betting book of White's for my boredom?"

"Is it not at least partly responsible?"

"If that were the case, I would be as well off staying home and reading a book." She couldn't tell this man about her woes. That wasn't what they did. Her gaze moved to the lemon cakes. "But then I wouldn't have been able to taste these cakes. They must be the highlight of the evening."

"Ah, so my charm can no longer hold a candle even to lemon cakes?"

"Well, they are particularly sweet tonight, the dash of lemon just right."

"Nevertheless, it's only natural to discover that there is more to life than beauty and dancing, although most young ladies don't discover it this young."

"Two *youngs* in one sentence." She cast him a humorous glance. "You are talking as though you are an old fox."

"I *am* an old fox."

"You cannot be older than thirty."

One brow lifted high. "Thirty is still much older than you. What are you, eighteen?"

"*Twenty.*"

He seemed surprised. "Ah, eleven years my junior. A mere sprite."

This sprite will bite you. "I take that back," Leonora said. "You are old. And not the good kind of old either."

"And just what is this good kind of old?"

Her smile turned sly. "Eleven years older but not eleven years wiser."

He clutched his chest in a mocking gesture. "A direct blow to my heart. You have a saucy mouth, you know, Lady Leonora."

"Well, what can I say?" Her smile widened. "You are here with me, at a table full of tarts, flirting with a sprite eleven years your junior, making it absurdly easy."

"I'm not sure why, but I now feel the need to point out that youth is just state of mind."

"Of course. And how many times has that sentence alleviated the heaviness in your mind?"

He puffed out a breath of laughter before admitting, "More times than I care to admit."

She laughed.

"By the by," Dare continued, "where is that surly brother of yours? He is rather slow tonight, is he not? Usually, he'd have burled through the crowd to drag you away from my unsightly presence."

"You exaggerate." But Leonora felt a prickle of discomfort skittering down her spine.

"Exaggerate?" Dare scoffed. "An infant could tell he doesn't like me."

Well, it was true that Logan Heart, heir to the title of Marquess of Heartly, had a way of sniffing out whenever she engaged in a bit of flirtation with Dare and promptly whisked her away. It was though he possessed a sixth sense where Dare was concerned. But then, Heart was so very much older than she was, so he had accumulated more worldly experience, she supposed.

And yet, for all his overprotectiveness, their relationship wasn't as simple as it seemed. For he was her brother who was *not* her brother. It wasn't that they weren't blood. They were. Just not in the way everyone believed.

She bit down on her lip, her thoughts flashing back to Calstone's off-hand remark about her resemblance to the Duchess of Crane. Could the duchess be the other half of her secret? A secret Leonora had stumbled upon on her fourteenth birthday. A secret that she instinctively understood contained within it many more.

Of course, neither Heart nor her parents had any idea she knew, and she'd always wanted to keep it that way, even as her own feelings about it settled and unsettled. Most people would call it a dark, shocking secret, and perhaps it was. But not for Leonora, at least not entirely. Her family had provided her with so much love and care that bitterness or resentment had never found a place in her heart. Instead, there was only a quiet, calm understanding about their actions. She had even vowed to take the secret to her grave, for her family had acted out of a desire to protect. However, a growing curiosity had started to bloom within her recently. Who was the woman who had given birth to her? What was she like? Did she think about Leonora every so often? And could Leonora truly keep the vow she had made as a child to keep the secret?

She glanced over at Dare. She wondered what secrets lay buried beneath the surface of his family. Given the man's reputation, it was probably best not to wonder. In any event, secrets were part of the fabric of their society.

"See?" Dare broke through her thoughts. "You are not saying anything, which means I am right. Your brother despises me."

"Not true," Leonora tried to appease. "He merely doesn't approve of you."

"Isn't that the same thing?"

Leonora chuckled. "Don't sound so sour. Most men don't approve of you." Her gaze skipped over his face. "For obvious reasons."

He assumed a thoughtful stance, studying her. "*You* seem to always ignore these obvious reasons."

"And because I ignore them so regularly, our peers," *except for Heart,* "don't bat an eye anymore when you and I converse at the table of *treats.*"

"Damnation, woman, do not say 'treats' in that tone."

"Why?" She smiled sweetly. "Don't you like *treats?*" She laughed at his flat look, and teased, "I'm not even sure why I enjoy conversing with you so much."

He leaned in close. "Because I'm charming."

Amusement bubbled. "I want to deny it, but I cannot."

A commotion broke out on the margins of the dance floor, drawing both their gazes. Not a big one, though—it seemed to be a small tiff between a lady and her gentleman.

"What do you suppose that is about?" Dare asked curiously.

Leonora craned her neck to get a better look. "Why ask me? You should know it better, should you not?"

"*Me?*"

She grinned at him. "With all the wisdom and experience of

that eleven years of age you have on me."

"Saucy wench."

"Old rogue."

He clucked disapprovingly, but his voice still held cheerfulness. "Perhaps he commented on the color of her dress? Green is such an unflattering color."

Leonora glanced down at her own gown and back at him, raising a brow.

His gaze flicked to her bosom—of all places!—and back to her face. His face transformed into a smoldering rogue look complete with the playful arch of his brow. "I meant *that* shade of green on *that* woman is very unflattering."

Leonora laughed. "That face won't work on me, and I doubt a comment on the shade of her dress was enough to spark the anger plainly displayed on the lady's face." A righteous storm gathered there, and the small tiff seemed to be growing. "Seems the night is about to turn interesting."

His gaze returned to the couple. "I suspect you are right."

"Perhaps she discovered a wager."

"Perhaps," Dare drawled. "We should move along from this spot. It seems they are heading in our direction."

To be precise, the woman was marching their way and the gentleman was trailing behind her, all the while pleading for her forgiveness.

"Are you sure? We have the best spot to witness the drama unfolding."

"Do you want to observe it or be part of it?" Dare asked dryly.

Leonora paused. Not part of it, of course.

A hand settled on her lower back to guide her a few steps away from the oncoming tempest even as a slap echoed through the ballroom.

Too late.

The storm had arrived.

Rebellion was the mood of the hour.

"HELL AND DAMNATION."

The foul words blew past Dare's lips while several more echoed in his head. He'd had a bad feeling the moment those two chose a direction that would collide with him and Lady Leonora, and that feeling was downright ominous now.

He wanted to snatch Lady Leonora up and make a dash for it, but she had turned her incredulous gaze to the couple—whom he now recognized as Lord and Lady Hamish—and was thoroughly snared by the drama.

"You lowly cockroach!" the woman shouted. "Unless you tell me who the harpy is, your marriage bed turns cold tonight and every night hereafter!"

Strong words. Rather terrifying, actually. And they were too close to the eruption.

He leaned over to mutter into Lady Leonora's ear. "We should retreat." They were too close for his comfort.

She glanced between him and the couple and then nodded.

Dare moved to guide Lady Leonora away from the spectacle but was stopped cold when his eyes momentarily locked with that woman's. He felt the horror unfolding within him as her finger pointed straight at him. "You!" she screeched. "It's libertines like you who cause the rot in our society!"

His face darkened. "Madam, I am not your husband, so do not drag me into your theatrics. Don't vent your anger at innocent bystanders."

She swelled like a round pufferfish. "Innocent? You are a libertine, just like him!"

Did that give permission to attack him? He wouldn't give this harpy any satisfaction of being too bothered, so he smirked, picking at his jacket. "Come now. I'm an honorable rake."

"Honorable! Can there be such a thing amongst libertines?"

"Well, yes, honorable rakes don't play with a lady's feelings.

They rather abhor them, in fact."

"You—you infamous rogue!"

Lady Leonora stepped forward. "Lord Dare is right, Lady Hamish. If you wish to take your anger out on someone, it's best to do so on the person who offended you, not a man who was simply enjoying the host's treats."

Dare glanced at Lady Leonora. There was that word again. Nevertheless, all his annoyance melted away.

When Lady Hamish's eyes narrowed on Lady Leonora, Dare stepped to the side to block her view. Hell hath no fury and all that. "Like I said madam, do not drag others into your argument. It's bad sport."

"Quite right, quite right," Lord Hamish said, finally stepping in. "Camilla, let's take this to a more private setting!"

"Why?" she exclaimed. "You weren't private in your affairs, so why be private with the consequences?"

Poor fool.

Dare didn't mince his actions with words. He turned on his heel and ushered Lady Leonora away before the little temptress said anything else and Lady Hamish dragged them even deeper into her affairs. How bothersome that a simple meeting of gazes could spiral into a nightmare. Was this the new world they lived in?

He flinched as another slap echoed through the ballroom. At this rate, between Lord Hamish's drink-inflamed cheeks and all the slaps, his face would be swollen to a sphere tomorrow.

And they'd had the nerve to drag him into the mess.

"What a disaster," Dare muttered. He could still hear her cursing at his back, but at the very least—a sweep of the room confirmed—all eyes remained on that woman's chaotic performance.

"Are you all right?" Lady Leonora asked, sending him a concerned glance. "I cannot believe you were a target for Lady Hamish's ire."

"I cannot believe you inserted yourself into said ire," Dare countered, still mired in some disbelief that she would do such a thing. When last had anyone stood up for him in such a manner? Not in years. Certainly not in his adult life.

"Why not?" She waved a hand. "If I hadn't defended you, I'd not have been defending myself, now would I?"

Dare spotted a nearby pillar and pulled her over behind it. "Your logic has flaws as deep as underground mines." He stopped to make sure they weren't being noticed. "Let's wait here for a bit."

"*Hiding* is your solution?"

"Being caught up in that disaster will bring nothing but more disaster to you, Lady Leonora," Dare said, the hairs at the back of his neck prickling with awareness. "My reputation can survive any calamity, but yours cannot." And no shadows should taint the woman beside him, not even his, as large as they loomed. But even if his shadows lacked the ability to taint her all on their own, if she stepped any closer and fully entered the darkness that shrouded him, she might never recover from that. And yet, he couldn't bring himself to regret this flirtatious thing they had formed between them.

Regret couldn't touch its brightness. Yet.

She lifted to her toes to peek at the ongoing commotion. "Well, we are out of the blast range now, though it seems Lord Gibsy and his wife have been dragged into their tiff instead of us."

Dare followed her gaze. Lady Hamish was indeed pointing a finger at Gibsy, who had turned red, purple, and blue all at once. It seemed the woman was determined to blame any man passing for her husband's indiscretions. At least it wasn't just him.

"He looks like he wants to throttle Lady Hamish," Lady Leonora murmured.

"I want to throttle her," Dare muttered. And that was saying much. This was the first time in his life such an urge had overtaken him where a woman was concerned.

He glanced at Leonora.

And it was because of her.

Not because Lady Hamish had dragged him into that spectacle—Dare could handle drama—but because she had done so while Leonora was at his side.

"I pity her," Leonora murmured. "She's had a shock."

"Of course. It's how she treats the bystanders that I object to."

Leonora nodded. "Agreed. There are a thousand different ways to vent anger. This is quite something else." She paused. "Tell me, Dare,"—she sent him a speculative glance—"has a woman ever slapped your face?"

"No, I have been fortunate there." He didn't much care for pain.

"I find that hard to believe. Don't all infamous rakes have a slap or two to boast?"

"Should a lady be speaking about infamous rakes *to* an infamous rake?"

"Are you avoiding the question?" she countered while avoiding his.

Dare shook his head, chuckling. "Only the rakes lacking in charm get slapped. And let me assure you, a slap is nothing to boast about, even for men who have been labeled rakes."

"Then your charm must indeed be quite something."

"Haven't you experienced that for yourself?"

"I suppose I've gotten a slight glimpse."

A throat cleared behind them. "And just what glimpse have you gotten from him? And why in everlasting damnation am I always finding the two of you together?"

Dare sighed, turning to see Leonora's brother. The sun seemed to have set on their coquetry. "Your sister is speaking of charm, Heart, just as she is charming. Does that appease your curiosity?"

"No, it doesn't. What are the two of you doing behind this pillar?"

"Well, depending on your perspective, we are not behind it," he replied.

The man scowled. "You always have a blasted answer for everything, don't you?"

"That is *my* charm."

"Heart," Leonora said flatly, claiming her brother's attention. She pointed at the couple over yonder. "We are just observing a bit of a commotion between Lord and Lady Hamish from a respectable distance."

Dare clasped his hands behind his back as Heart stepped forward to follow his sister's line of sight.

"Oh, that," Heart muttered, his gaze flicking between the two before stepping back again. "I heard Lady Hamish learned about her husband's affair tonight. She must not be taking it well if she is publicly causing such a ruckus."

"Would any woman take such a thing well?" Leonora demanded from her brother.

Dare flinched, pushing back a memory that tried to resurface. Indeed, no woman would take a philandering husband well. His own father had been an ill-famed scoundrel. But his mother's distress had been the exact opposite of Lady Hamish's public lashing out.

Leonora made a dismissive gesture. "Forget I asked."

Dare glanced at the man. Both he and Heart carried reputations that could shame any ordinary rogue. Heart was even more notorious than him. Though, twenty or so years ago, if gossip could be relied upon. Still, it would explain why Lady Leonora couldn't so much as blink in his company without her behavior being noted but could also hold her own with any teasing remarks.

If Heart truly was as black as the rumors claimed, she'd been standing in a rake's shadow since birth, though Dare doubted she had knowledge of her brother's previous or current exploits.

"No, I can't imagine any woman would respond favorably," Dare murmured.

Heart cut him a nasty look. "Come, Leonora, we're leaving."

She scrunched her brows. "Leaving, as in you are dragging

me away to another pillar? Or leaving, as in going home?"

"Leaving, as in going home," Heart bit out between clenched teeth.

Dare chuckled, a ray of sun breaking through the shadows once more. Ah, how temptation beckoned for him to step into the full brightness of her light, but he would resist. It would be a repeat of the past, a past that destroyed his family, and he refused to allow that to happen again. Leonora should always shine bright.

"What do you find so amusing?" Heart demanded.

Dare shrugged. "I merely wonder how I would fare if I had a little spitfire for a sister like yours."

The man took a threatening step forward. "Do not call Leonora a spitfire."

"*Heart.*"

Dare winked at her, almost laughing at her glowing eyes, the same blue of a clear summer sky. "What should I call her then?"

He caught her soft sigh.

Heart jabbed a finger at him. "Don't call her anything if you know what is good for you. Stay away from her."

"Gentlemen," Leonora said exasperatedly.

"But what if your sister is good for me?"

"Oh, dear lord," she muttered, rolling her eyes.

Heart sneered. "Are you saying she can reform a hardened blackguard like you? Don't make me laugh."

"I never said anything about reform."

Leonora cocked her head to the side, suddenly interested in the content of their jabs, and he caught the sparkle in her eyes, the mirth. "Good for you how?"

His eyes met hers. "Your smiles brighten my evening."

"That's it," Heart growled. "We are leaving, Leonora. Now."

She returned his wink even as her brother all but hauled her from the ballroom. Dare tracked her until she was out of his sight before chuckling and shaking his head, any traces of a smile quickly fading from his face. He counted to sixty before lazily striding through the room to the cloakroom to retrieve his coat. There was no point in staying any longer.

None of what he'd said was a lie. Leonora Heart *was* good for him. She brought a spark to his evenings more and more with each encounter. He accepted his coat from the attendant who rushed over, flicking a coin to him.

"Thank you, my lord."

Dare gave a curt nod, shrugging into his coat.

It wasn't enough. *More*, something in him cried out at every one of her smiles. Was tonight's sparse glimmer enough to tide him over to tomorrow's ball?

Stop with the foolishness, Dare. You know . . .

He scowled, striding through the main doors of the Haver-sham residence and descending the stairs.

Yes, he did know.

While she was good for him, he was no good for her.

Chapter Three

LEONORA LAUGHED AS her horse flew over a fallen log in the park. She had snuck away to ride, and she loved these early morning gallops. Especially on misty mornings when the crisp air brought a flush to her face. She hadn't gotten much sleep last night after a certain rogue's parting words and her brother marching her from the ball, but she was hoping the exercise would help finally clear her mind.

She was good for *him*? Her?

Leonora grinned as she spurred Lightning faster. Ah! Why did such a simple thing bring such a thrill to her? It wasn't that much of a compliment, and she would never read more into it given its owner, but the thought of being good for someone brought her a touch of delight.

In addition to Dare's words, she had a certain duchess on her mind as well. She should have questioned Calstone more and rather regretted that she hadn't seized the opportunity.

"Whoa!" a voice called.

Leonora's head whipped to survey the vegetation from whence the shout came. She brought her horse slowly to a halt, every nerve going on alert. Her morning rides weren't exactly proper, since she wore breeches beneath her skirts and rode her horse astride. Plus, she was a lady alone. Fortunately, the mist hung low today, obscuring her a bit to onlookers.

She patted Lightning's neck. "Who could that be, do you think?" Her gaze tracked the parklands. "Let's just be on the outlook. Luckily, we have the skill to outride just about anyone, isn't that right, Lightning?"

These rides were the only time she could unpin her hair and ride as though she were a breeze in the park. No restraints. No worries. No nagging Heart breathing down her neck. But continuing to enjoy these moments was contingent on them staying secret.

The galloping hooves of a horse approached, and Leonora bit her lip while she gathered the hood of her cape and shrugged it over her head, burrowing deeply into the shelter it provided. But there was no helping it—she would have to make a hard run for it. She sent one last glance over her shoulder before readying to spur Lighting into to run.

And froze.

Leonora blinked at the rider emerging from the mist like some mysterious phantom. Only, he was no phantom at all.

Dare?

Think of the rake and he shall appear.

He sat atop his thoroughbred as though he might as well have sat atop the world. Imperial, that's what he was. He wore a white shirt with a black coat and no hat, his hair falling in wild disarray, giving her a rare, intimate glimpse of a side of him she hadn't seen before. The ties of his shirt were fastened only up to his collarbone, offering her a view of the full breadth of his neck. A glimpse of his strength. One part elegant and nine parts rogue.

Undeniably handsome.

He brought his horse to a stop when he caught sight of her. "Greetings," he said in a low, gruff voice. "Is all well, madam? Do you require some assistance?"

Oh, right. He probably didn't even recognize her with her cloak pulled close and her hood up, and here she was, staring in his direction as if she'd never seen a man atop a horse before! But, Lord, oh Lord. What a delightful surprise! She grinned beneath her hood and pitched her voice low. "All is quite well, sir. In fact, my morning has taken a turn for the better."

Surprise crossed his face before his gaze narrowed on her in a very obviously scrutinizing way. "You sound strangely familiar. Do I perhaps know you, my lady?"

"Who says I'm a lady?"

"I have a distinct ear for voices," he said slowly.

Hah! "That does not mean I'm a lady."

"Your speech gives you away."

Leonora chuckled. He had, in all likelihood, already guessed her identity. "I'm indeed a lady, and yet at the same time I am not."

"Fascinating words coming from such sweet lips."

"Sweet lips? Well, I suppose it has been suggested that I am the delight of a certain gentleman's evening."

"I'm sure the man who said that was no gentleman at all." His voice had a hint of a smile in it.

"Well, he is a bit rakish."

He cocked his head to the side. "Only a bit?"

She shrugged. "From my experience, yes, although the same cannot be said about his rakish reputation. That is somewhat big."

He laughed. "Only somewhat, Lady Leonora?"

Leonora pulled the hood of her cape back from her head, her eyes sparkling at him. "What brings you out and about so early in the morning, Lord Dare? Don't rakes play until dawn and rise only at twilight?"

He scoffed. "What a cheeky assumption." He nudged his horse forward to approach her. "What about you, my lady? Riding this early all alone in the woods? Is that wise or is it reckless?"

"Can it be both? The morning air clears my head."

"You should be careful," he admonished, though no sting clung to his words. "Danger lurks in these woods."

Her gaze swept over him. "I can see that."

"Then you should know if we are discovered together that—" He cut off at the sound of more hooves hitting the ground echoed in the distance, approaching fast.

He cursed.

Her sentiments exactly. "The woods seemed to be fully occupied this morning. Should we find a spot to hide?"

He nodded, his gaze flicking over their surroundings. "Put your hood back on. We can't be found together like this."

Leonora pulled the hood over her head again. He didn't need to tell her. She was all too aware that while she boldly flirted with this man in the presence of the *ton*, her reputation would never survive *this*. Well, it might, but that depended on who it was who was approaching them, whether they would be recognized, and whether any newcomers could be convinced that it was a mere coincidence that she and Dare had met here today. Unlikely.

"Come." Dare dismounted and led his horse behind a patch of thick bushes. Leonora followed suit. "This should do."

"First a pillar and now bushes," Leonora murmured. "I daresay I'm learning all sorts of hiding spots from you. Is this bush an old haunt of yours?"

"Ridiculous."

Soon two riders came to a halt a few feet away beneath a big tree. Neither dismounted. Leonora squinted to peer through the bushes, her sight partly obstructed by the mist but not enough to completely obscure her view. Inadvertently, they had found the perfect spot. One of the riders was cloaked, not unlike Leonora, but the other was not. The uncloaked rider was clearly a woman, and judging by stature and bearing, the cloaked person seemed to be a woman as well.

"A secret meeting?" Leonora whispered.

Dare leaned in, his face almost touching hers as he too peered through the spot she found.

"Well, what do you know . . ." he said, his voice a barely audible murmur.

"What?" Leonora asked in a hush. "Who is it?"

"I believe that is the Duchess of Crane," he whispered back, nodding toward the uncloaked rider.

The duchess! What were the odds?

"Are you sure that is the duchess?" Leonora asked softly.

"No doubt in my mind."

Leonora turned her head to look at him and started when her lips grazed his upper cheekbone.

Slowly, his head turned to meet her gaze.

"I mean . . . that . . ." *Dear Lord.* "That was an accident." So awkward! She quickly changed to topic. "I've heard she hasn't been in town for years. Have you met her by any chance?"

His eyes probed her before once again peeking through the spot. "Yes. Fleetingly, right before the duke's death."

Really? Leonora swallowed her heartbeats and glanced at the duo again. What a brilliant coincidence. Both people she'd thought about this morning had now appeared before her. "Who is the person with her, do you think?"

"I'm not sure, but it's most certainly a woman. These woods seem to attract a lot of those."

Leonora smiled at his mocking tone. From this distance, while she could see the duchess, so many nuances were lost to her. But she could tell by her posture that she was tall and slender, poised, and she should be about Heart's age, or perhaps a few years younger. Her dark hair, the exact opposite color as Leonora's, was swept up in a delicate twist, and her riding habit— a rich green—blended with the trees of the parklands. She couldn't help a small grin, recalling Dare's comment about the color the night before.

She wished she could get a closer look. And a listen. "I wonder what they are talking about."

"Why are you so interested in the duchess?" Dare asked.

"I have my reasons," she said softly.

"Are *you* by chance acquainted with her?"

Leonora glanced at him. Something in his tone struck her as odd. "No. Why?"

Dare arched a brow. "I have some interest."

That surprised her. "In what? The duchess? Whatever for?" What was this pinch in her chest? "Or perhaps I shouldn't ask. A rake showing interest in a woman can't mean too many things."

He arched that smoldering brow at her. "Tell me your interest and I'll tell you mine."

She might be my mother.

But Leonora couldn't reveal such a shocking thing. That would expose her family's secrets and open them up for scandal and scrutiny. Neither did she have any other explanation that Dare might find plausible. But perhaps a half-truth would do. So, she answered in a faint voice, "She has knowledge about a family member I'm curious about."

"A family member?" He nodded thoughtfully. "So it's information you are after?"

Leonora nodded.

"Well, then, our interests are the aligned."

"You want information, too?" Her curiosity bloomed.

"Yes. Well, not precisely. The duchess is in possession of something that an . . . acquaintance of mine wants."

Fascinating. What did the duchess have that someone Dare knew could want? "And you are helping them retrieve this something?"

He shrugged. "I haven't decided yet."

Mmm. "Is it rightfully your friend's?"

"My friend believes so."

"I see." Leonora could scarcely wrap her head around the idea that the woman she was curious about was equally of interest to Dare. What a strange, strange coincidence.

"What exactly is this information are you looking for?" Dare nearly pressed his lips against her ear as he whispered. "Perhaps I can be of help."

Leonora shivered, biting her lip. Could he? If she told him, would he put two and two together? No. It was just too unbelievable to guess at. And she had to admit, the weight of trying to discover all these hidden truths, while looking as though she weren't trying to discover anything, sat heavily on her shoulders.

She could use a friend.

She could use a bit of help.

Her eyes met his. "I want to know if she ever had a daughter."

DAUGHTER?

Dare's mind raced as he stared at Lady Leonora. So many questions flared at her admission. Why would she want to know if the duchess had a daughter? Could the duchess be connected to the Heart family? Wait . . . Heart, the rake of old. Did Leonora wish to know if she had a niece? All that her words implied rather stunned him.

Heart, Heart, Heart.

Always acting like he was better than Dare. *Just what have you been up to?*

Of course, it could be information about another family member that Lady Leonora sought, but somehow—call it instinct—that didn't ring true.

It was remarkable that he had encountered Leonora on his ride morning ride at all, which he usually took an hour later in the morning, but now he'd learned possible news that he was perhaps better off not discovering. He should have slept later.

"You have questions, I presume," she whispered when he remained silent.

Dare scratched his head. "It's none of my business." He should never have offered his help in the first place. It moved them beyond shallow flirtations into deeper territory, and Dare didn't do deeper territory with a woman. Ever.

"Oh? I suppose that is smart of you," she said a touch teasingly. "So, do you know whether the duchess ever had a daughter?"

"I know she has a stepson, the current duke."

"Oh, yes, I hadn't even thought about him."

Why would you? No, Dare. It is none of your business. Keep it at shallow flirting. "I can ask around."

Dare, damn it.

To his surprise, she shook her head. "No need. That might just raise questions."

Ah yes, true enough. "If you require my help, all you have to do is ask."

"Likewise." She didn't smile, but the promise of a one hovered on her lips. "Help from a rake, now wouldn't that be thrilling?"

"I wouldn't know," he said dryly.

She did smile then. "I'm curious. Does it not bother you that people—that I—blatantly call you a rake? I'd imagine most rakes are in denial and don't care for the term."

Dare shrugged. What was there to mind when he lived the very definition of the term? "Most are; I am not. And you forgot infamous—I am an *infamous* rake."

"Well, I daresay you shall have to marry one day."

"A wife is inconvenient." He lowered his voice even more. "And having me for a husband would be even *more* inconvenient."

"But you've never been a husband, so how can you know?"

"Trust me, I just know."

She picked at a leaf. "Oh? Heart says the same thing, so my mother always scolds him, saying that *inconvenience* is just another word men use to justify skirting their duties."

Well, what could he say to that?

Duty had always been a double-edged sword for him. It conflicted with his desire for freedom—freedom from the past. But he'd rather not give history the chance to repeat itself in any way or form. Just look at his father. He had been optimistic about breaking the cycle of rakish forefathers, but he had failed over and over again.

And who was Dare if not his father's son?

Being as self-aware as he was, he would never deny this. Denying it would mean countless tears and heartbreak in the future. It wasn't that he was against duty or marriage. No, he was against love. The best sort of marriage for him would be an arrangement where neither expected anything from the other beyond producing an heir and then moving on with their lives however they wished.

Dare had yet to meet a woman with those expectations.

"Your brother must smart from such scolding."

She gave a tiny snort. "Oh, no, he's got quite the thick head."

On that, they agreed. "I would still like to argue that an inconvenience is inconvenient."

"And what a stellar argument, if a bit dull."

Well, hell. "No woman has ever called me dull."

"How fortunate that I am the first." She paused. "Look. The cloaked woman is leaving . . ."

"Dare peered through the bush at the same time the cloaked woman turned in their direction. The breeze caused her hood to flutter, offering them a glimpse of her face.

"Lord above, is that your mother?" He glanced at Leonora, who had gone still beside him, her gaze fixed on the marchioness. And the plot thickened. "I suppose whatever you wish to discover, you are on the right path."

"I . . . this . . . she is supposed to be in Wales with my father. Did she return, or did she lie?"

His brow inched upward. "She hasn't been home?"

"No . . ."

What an interesting turn of events, then. "Why don't you ask your mother for the information you seek?"

"She doesn't know that I am seeking it, and for now, I'd like to keep it that way."

So complex. There must be more to the secret that he didn't know. Didn't *need* to know. He watched as both figures trotted off, remaining silent at Leonora's side until they were well out of sight and he could no longer hear any echo of hooves.

"We should leave, too," she finally whispered.

Dare caught the note of disbelief still lacing her voice and glanced at her. The little temptress had not expected the other woman to be her mother, and he couldn't tell if she believed it a good thing or a bad thing or if she was just stunned.

"You know," he said after a moment, "I find it quite interesting."

Her eyes met his. "What?"

"The duchess hasn't frequented the circles of London for years. Now she suddenly appears, all stealth and intrigue, with multiple people showing interest in her. What a mystifying woman, don't you agree? So many secrets."

Her lips quirked.

Ah, there is that smile. "Lady Leonora, all mixed up in mystery, and here I thought you were just a simple lady."

Her smile widened. "I am the very epitome of simple."

I don't believe you, minx. Leaves crunched, and Dare went on alert. His gaze tracked his surroundings, but he couldn't find anything suspicious.

He reached out to adjust Leonora's hood, drawing it down farther over her head. He placed a finger over her lips, wishing he hadn't worn gloves so that he could selfishly indulge in their softness. He cursed in his mind. Another rustle of leaves, this time closer to them.

Both horses shifted restlessly.

"It's probably just a mouse," Lady Leonora murmured.

A mouse? His back stiffened. He'd prefer anything else over mice. "Then we should leave before the mouse makes its appearance."

"I don't think mice do that. They just scurry about." Her eyes widened. "Why? Are you afraid of mice?"

"Let's just say they are not my favorite creatures in the world."

"But they are just little mice, and you are a big, scary, intimidating man," she teased.

"Scary? Intimidating?"

"For the mouse."

He gave her a flat look. He should have told her he was concerned about their horses. "Did you know you have a talent for speaking nonsense?"

"Oh, I'm very well aware. Heart never misses an opportunity to inform me of my nonsense. Shall we go?"

Dare nodded and mounted his horse alongside her. Fortunately, they hadn't been caught by the duchess and Leonora's mother. Just the thought brought a slight shiver up his spine. They waited a few more moments, listening carefully to the silence, before she smiled at him and gave a nod.

"I'll be off then."

Just like that? Why did it feel so abrupt? As though they'd shared a monumental moment, and now they parted ways? "I'll escort you home," he said before he could think better of it. Had he forgotten they could not be seen together? He must have lost his damn head.

She laughed. "Accompany me? Why not race me?" More nonsense. "Or are you going to tell me women shouldn't race?" she asked before he could answer.

"I'm not the sort of man to tell a woman what she should or should not do."

Her laugh turned merry. "No words of wisdom for me?"

"Wisdom? No." Just look at him.

"Then race it is! The first one to clear the woods wins." She spurred her horse into a run.

"Prepare to lose," Dare called out after her, urging his own thoroughbred, Flash, into a run after her.

Utter madness.

He loved it.

He would be skinned by her brother if they were caught, but so be it. He'd chase her light like a determined shadow. And while he didn't rightly know what possessed him to race against her, he did know he might never get the chance to do so again.

And when it came to this woman and all her brilliancy, he wanted to grasp every chance before the inevitable conclusion of their acquaintanceship came about.

For it was just a matter of time.

Chapter Four

LEONORA WAS AMBUSHED the moment she stepped into the house. She couldn't say she was surprised. Thir race hadn't ended when they'd cleared the park—they had raced all the way to her house, caught up in the thrill. But the man had fulfilled his wish and escorted her home. Her only regret was that her morning rides were now exposed to Heart. A botheration.

"Didn't I tell you to say away from that man?" her brother demanded, following on her heel into the dining room.

"You speak as though Dare is this monster that might suck out my soul."

"He is a rake, Leonora. Do you not understand what that means?"

"It means he loves women."

"So you are aware, yet you continue to consort with him."

Leonora turned to face Heart's thunderous countenance. "As long as I am not seduced by him, can he truly harm me?"

"His mere reputation—"

"Yes, yes, can slice mine into pieces." She arched a brow. "Why is everyone so theatrical when it comes to rakes? He is still just a man." A devastatingly handsome one. "As a man, he has feelings, too, you know. Behind the reputation there is a person."

"I don't know if you are being serious or mocking."

"A bit of both."

"Then do you have a fantasy to reform him? I'm telling you now, that will never happen."

"A fantasy?" This time she sent him a mocking glance to accompany her tone. "I've no intention of doing anything of the sort."

"Then what the hell are you doing, Leonora? And thinking, for that matter. Did the two of you arrange this morning's little ride? Did he?"

"I met him by pure coincidence."

"You expect me to believe that after finding the two of you flirting behind a pillar last night?"

She shrugged. "Believe what you will. Dare is a friend. We have fun conversing with each other. We met each other by accident this morning. That is all."

"Riding with a *friend?*" Disbelief flashed across his face and straight onto his tongue. "You cannot be friends with a rake, Leonora."

She tilted her head to the side, smiling. "Why not?"

"You are a woman. He is a rake. Do you need more of a reason?"

She rolled her eyes. Yes, she did. "It is only a chaste friendship."

"Don't talk nonsense. What does that even *mean?*"

Well, she did have a knack for speaking nonsense, didn't she? However, this was not it. "It's not nonsense. A man and a woman can be friends if they have no interest in forming anything beyond friendship. It's the mark of wise adults."

"For you, that might be possible," Heart growled. "But not for him."

"Casting stones a bit too hastily, aren't you?"

He dragged a hand through his hair. "It's strange and you know it. I can only assume that your true aim is to make me miserable, in which case you could have used anyone else. It didn't have to be *him.*"

But you would not be half as miserable as you are now. But that had never been her aim. "What is this antipathy, Heart? Why are you so sensitive on the subject of Dare and rakes? Are you perhaps recalling the memories of your youth?"

He flinched.

"I see that I'm right. By the by, instead of harping on the subject of my friendships, why don't you find a wife," she locked onto his gaze, "and produce an heir?"

"That has nothing to do . . ." He trailed off as she arched a brow.

"I'm your brother, Leonora. Does my concern mean nothing to you?"

She almost snorted, stepping up to take a seat at the table spread with an assortment of bread, cheese, and tea. Her brother followed, placing himself square across from her.

"Didn't you once dream of a fairy tale prince?" he continued. "Dare is not a prince. Why not focus on your prince?"

Her prince? Ah yes, she did recall such memories, but that had been before her fourteenth birthday when she'd discovered the truth of her birth. She could never marry a prince. Having grown a bit wiser, she didn't want to either. Instead, she rather enjoyed having fun with a prince of a rather different kind all the while seizing moment after moment. This morning's race with a rake, in particular, had been a delightful one.

She buttered a scone. "*Prince* is just a metaphor, Heart."

"Nevertheless, it's an admirable ambition."

She shot him a flat look. Truly? An admirable ambition? "And what about you, *brother*? What admirable ambitions do you have?"

"Helping you marry a prince."

"What a commendable brother you are." Or not a brother at all. In fact, the word had long since become a discomfort on her tongue. But the alternative was impossible. Yet, he served as a perfect example of how many things in life could simply be taken for granted. But this was her life, these were her choices, and she didn't want to miss out on anything and only to have regrets later, much like the regrets she oftentimes sensed from Heart.

No, he was the last person who ought to lecture her. Plus, she'd heard all the rumors. Apparently, the red-faced fellow before her had once been quite the heartbreaker.

He poured two cups of tea and pushed one over to her. "Listen to me for once, I beg you. Stay away from Dare."

She reached for the sweet preserve. "I'm curious. Did you have a falling out with the man?"

He started. "What?"

"Why are you so against him? Is it only because of his reputation?"

"I don't need another reason. That's enough."

"Not for me." She bit down on her scone, chewing while studying him.

"Damn it, Leonora, if you don't stay away from that rogue, I shall be forced to take alternative measures. And while we are on the topic, these secret morning rides of yours are done as well."

"Heart!"

He sat back and smirked. "Do I have your attention now?"

"Stop it, Heart. Are you my father? Do not think to threaten me."

His smirk drooped, but instead of feeling sorry for him, Leonora felt only satisfaction. She motioned to the spread on the table. "You should eat something. One shouldn't pick fights on an empty stomach."

He scowled but still reached for a scone and butter. "I've never understood your habit of taking breakfast at this ungodly hour."

She shrugged. It was a routine that had developed from riding early in the morning. This was her space in the morning where she could collect her thoughts.

"I like the silence."

"What nonsense. You thrive with clatter."

"I like silence in the *mornings.*" She reached for another scone.

"Is that what you call your frolicking with that blackguard—

silence in the morning? Your definition of silence is rather suspect. If I hadn't witnessed it firsthand—"

She cut him off with a scoff. "Peering through the window hangings doesn't suit you."

"I just happened to look," he bit out. He cleared his throat, plainly intent on changing the subject. "I received word from our parents."

Her ears perked up. "Oh? How are they enjoying Wales?"

"They are staying another three months. Father has a bit of a cough."

Interesting.

And at least one part lie.

She studied Heart. Was he aware their parents weren't in Wales? That their mother had participated in a clandestine meeting in the park not even an hour ago? Leonora was convinced—not only that her family was steeped in secrets, but that she had only glimpsed the tree, not the roots.

She itched to dig them all out.

Finishing her second scone, she reached for another, dabbing a generous amount of preserves on this one. The sweetness would settle her sudden annoyance. She could, if she wanted, argue that all her life she had lived a lie. Or, at the very least, part of a lie. This was why, like this morning, she looked at other people's actions rather than their words.

"Well," Leonora said, successfully hiding a note of sourness, "as long as they are enjoying their trip."

"I have no doubt that they are—they love that place." He stared at her from beneath his lashes. "How about you? Have you any news?" Heart suddenly asked. "Anything of note?"

"Like what?" Was he referring to their mother? The duchess, perhaps?

He shook his head. "It's nothing. Forget I asked anything."

Leonora gave an inward snort.

You expect me to do that? What do you take me for, Heart?

No, she would not forget. She would not let this drop. Keeping her circumstances a secret was one thing, but the duchess—potentially half of that very secret—had returned to London, apparently putting Heart on guard and luring her mother from Wales. She'd only been curious before, but now she was determined. Determined to get to the bottom of this family, Heart, and her real mother.

Everything.

"DULL HAS NEVER been used in a sentence to describe anything I do." Dare leaned back in his chair, lifting his gaze to Knox while ignoring the distaste clawing up his throat. He hated the stench of cheap taverns. Stale ale, unwashed bodies, and the acrid reek of God knows what clinging to the floorboards. "Have I turned dull? This can't be, can it?"

"I'm not sure. However, if I were to reflect upon it—"

"Please don't."

"She does have a point."

"And how is that?"

Knox sneered. "You have now asked us three bloody times whether or not you've turned into a bore. You tell us."

"When last did you indulge in pleasure?" Drake asked, motioning a server to bring them each another ale, the very picture of a relaxed ruffian in their secluded corner of a tavern called The Rose—a recent purchase of his.

It was the only reason Dare set foot here in the first place.

Drake Fury.

A cousin that no one in his family recognized except for Dare. Also one of the seven bastard sons of the Duke of Crane. A long, ragged scar ran down the length of his face, making him look particularly fierce. It never ceased to amaze him, that scar.

"Does that matter?" He hadn't *indulged* in weeks. Not that he hadn't tried to indulge. He would arrive up to the moment of the deed, and then . . . nothing. No urge. No desire. No . . . *fire* in his loins.

"Suppose not," Drake drawled lazily. He inhaled his unlit cheroot. "If you're dull, then what are we?"

"The dullest of the dull," Dare stated.

"In that case," Knox swallowed the last of his ale, "the whole damn world is dull."

Dare cut a dirty look at his friends. Were they even his friends? Enemies in disguise more like.

Knox nodded as the server brought their ale. "How did you react when she called you a bore?"

"I raced her home. To *her* home," he added before they gave a pestering remark on that as well.

Drake chuckled. "Well, that's a new one, I'll grant you."

A new one? It wasn't meant to be. He hadn't meant to race her that far either. "Don't start with me, my head must still have been full of fog to do something as reckless as that."

Drake chuckled. "Her family must have been thrilled."

"I didn't stop to take stock." Instead he had continued on like the devil nipped at his heels.

"The chit certainly has no fear consorting with you," Knox said before emptying a quarter of his glass and letting out a belch, patting his chest.

Dare shook his head. Could he argue with that? The little temptress possessed a bold quality that was infused with a bit of oddness. How else to explain her fearless interactions with him? "If she were a man, her reputation might even be more infamous than mine."

Drake took a slow swig from his beer. "Seems to me like the girl enjoys playing with fire."

More like she *was* the fire.

"Don't go too far if you don't want to end up leg-shackled," Knox advised.

"Lord, no." Dare relaxed into his seat, trailing a thumb over his glass. "There are some lines even I won't cross."

"You should stop flirting with the chit altogether," Knox said.

"It's dangerous territory you are venturing into, my friend."

"I shall try my best." Like hell he would. But that didn't mean he would be too reckless about it, either. He studied Drake for a moment. "What about you? What's your excuse for sending Knox to me as a messenger? You didn't even send word you were in Town."

Drake shrugged. "I have business with Knox."

"But you want to do business with me, too? Do you still want my help?" His attitude toward being involved in his cousin's venture had quite changed over the last few hours. He was more than happy to help now that Leonora had questions about the duchess as well. He couldn't deny he was curious—about her business if not Drake's.

"I'm looking into something first," Drake murmured, removing another cheroot from the inner pocket of his jacket and dragging it beneath his nose.

Dare took a swallow from his ale, pulling a face. As bad as the first one he hadn't finished. "Let me know when you require my aid, and I shall consider it. But I am curious, why not ask her directly for what you want? You're her late husband's son, after all."

Drake shrugged. "We've had a disagreement or two."

"You know there is this thing called apologizing," Dare pointed out.

"And grovelling," Knox suppled.

"It's not that simple." Drake cracked his neck. "The argument is one that spilled over from my father to his wife."

"In that case, feuds should be buried with their masters," Knox said. "Why drag it down the family line? Just talk with the current duke. He is your half-brother, after all."

"Blood only matters when you acknowledge it," Drake said. "And the man is holed up somewhere in a darkened castle on an unknown moat. I have no way and no time to approach him."

"He sounds like a charming fellow," Dare murmured.

Should he tell his cousin about the meeting he and Leonora

witnessed earlier this morning? No. It didn't seem very likely that it would have anything to do with his cousin's situation. And he'd rather not have Leonora dragged into Drake's matters in any way. The man might look relaxed at the moment, sipping on ale and smelling an unlit cheroot, but he was a ruthless human being. If he thought Leonora could help him get what he wanted, he wouldn't hesitate to use her.

His thoughts trailed back to Leonora and their morning race. What was she up to right this moment? Causing more mischief, perhaps? With whom?

Ah, hell.

Would he run into her if he went riding tomorrow morning as well? Probably not. He'd glimpsed her brother peeking through the window when he passed her house. The man's animosity had practically stabbed through the walls of the townhouse to pierce him. She would have gotten a scolding and likely not be permitted any morning rides anytime soon.

The corner of his mouth pulled upward. Somehow, he couldn't imagine Lady Leonora taking a scolding from her brother without a few choice words of her own.

Drake kicked his chair. "Why the devil are you grinning like a fool? It's a terrifying look on you."

"Nothing you would ever be able to understand."

"Meaning it's about her," Knox said.

Drake laughed, yet his tone mocked, "Could this be the seedling of love? A rake reformed?"

Dare's smile slipped. "What love and what reform? Impossible for a man like me."

"That hardened, are you?"

"That self-aware." He had no illusions about his own character.

Knox nodded. "There is no arguing against that. You must be the most self-aware man I know. But the question needs to be asked. Do you think Lady Leonora is infatuated with you?"

Dare snorted. "Infatuated with me? No. Infatuated with my

reputation? Delightfully so."

Knox chuckled. "A lady living on the edge of danger."

"She delights in the thrill," Drake remarked.

No denying that.

"Don't we all?" Knox said.

Dare pushed at his mug. "I don't."

Both Drake and Knox stared at him. Not a single twitch in their brows.

"Fine, I love the thrill, too." Dare gave them a moody look. "Why are we talking about this anyway?"

"Perhaps because you've been giving the chit more attention than any other," Knox said simply.

"Like when you huddle together in the bushes and whisper in each other's ears."

Dare snapped upright. The rustle he'd heard in the park. His eyes narrowed on his cousin. "You're the mouse."

"What mouse?" Knox asked, confused.

Drake smirked. "Mouse? I don't know about that, but I've been following the widow like a shadow."

"Never mind, I'm sure I don't need to know what you're talking about," Knox muttered.

Dare shook his head. "Lord, you've got more *shadows* than me, Fury."

"Shadows? My reputation has always been shrouded in supreme darkness, not mere shadows, cousin."

Dare snorted. "They are all self-inflicted one way or another."

"Christ, you both are equally morbid." Knox let out a disgusted grunt. "More likely your dark shadows are the result in simple over-indulgence in your vices."

Dare lifted a shoulder in a shrug. Not wrong. Which was probably why he was over the indulgence. If his friends knew how long it had been since he'd bedded a woman, they'd fall on their backs in shock. Even *he* fell on his back each night wondering what the hell was going on.

He just had no . . . *interest.*

He glanced down at his cock. Flaccid traitor. He'd fled the last woman's bedroom, not because her young son had knocked on her bedchamber after hearing her cries, but on account of Little Dare refusing to play. He hadn't bothered since.

What did a man do when even pleasure held no more pleasure?

Not only was it humiliating, it was damn disturbing. How else did a man vent? Drinking? Gambling? Horse racing? Carriage racing? What stimulation was better than a woman's embrace?

He dragged in a deep breath of air and scowled. The stench of this damn place.

Knox whistled. "What's with that sudden troubled look?"

"I am troubled. You—you both—are troubling me."

"Come now, we are merely trying to make sense of this new obsession of yours," Drake drawled.

New obsession? He hadn't been flirting with Lady Leonora for all that long, but he supposed he had been flirting rather obsessively, *exclusively* with her. Was it *her* causing this strange, frustrating dry spell? Was she not only an heiress but a witch as well?

Dear God.

Had she put a spell on him?

Chapter Five

LEONORA SURVEYED THE crowd with sharp eyes. *She* should be attending tonight, shouldn't she? Although the Duchess of Crane still wore black, that hadn't stopped her from attending events, which made her the talk of the *ton*. A mysterious widow shrouded in questions. Questions like was she so in love with the late duke that she would never again wear color? Was she mourning something else? Did she just enjoy the way she looked in black?

Leonora also wondered about this.

Why did the duchess still wear black? Some rumors suggested she'd worn black for some years before the duke's passing, as well. Leonora couldn't fathom wearing the same color over and over, year after year. But then, she didn't know the duchess's past or present. If she was who Leonora expected she was, this woman had also abandoned her as a child.

She absentmindedly plucked the leaf of the potted plant next to her. Leonora honestly didn't know how to feel if this turned out to be the case. She'd long ago come to terms with what her family had done. And they had not abandoned her. No matter in what capacity, they had remained in her life.

The duchess could have a valid reason . . .

But some things were inexcusable. Even so, pure curiosity drove her to discover the layers beneath the carefully guarded and yet so carelessly exposed secret. Though, to be fair, no one had meant to expose anything that day. They had only been unguarded when discussing the matter among themselves, never thinking Leonora could hear them. However, it didn't change the nature of what she faced.

Secrets within a secret.

She wanted to crack open every last one.

Heart would be perfectly happy to help her marry her prince and live a life worthy of a fairy tale. But how could she, in good conscience, drag a prince into their web of secrets? Secrets that might ruin everyone they touched if they were ever exposed. And there was no guarantee that they wouldn't be. Not that she ever planned to expose anything beyond her family, but if Calstone could comment on an uncanny resemblance, others may as well. And one unguarded conversation had already been overheard.

There were no absolutes here.

She could never do that to someone outside the secret. At least not without their knowledge.

"Spying, I see."

Leonora turned to a grinning Dare. Tonight, he wore a blue jacket, made striking because it matched the color of his eyes. It made him look impossibly dashing and utterly sinful. Be it all as it may, flirting and living in the moment were good, too. "I am observing. Spying would imply I'm looking for something particular, and at the moment, I am not."

"Ah, the nuances of small details." He came to stand beside her. "Even I could feel the burn of your gaze, and you're not looking at me."

Was she that obvious? "It's not *that* bad."

He just continued to smile. "She will be arriving soon. The duchess."

Leonora shot him a skeptical glance. "How do you know?"

"I saw her carriage arrive as I entered."

Ah. "Keen eye."

He crossed his arms over his chest. "Spying—observing—

won't help you find the information you seek."

Thank you, Dare. "I'm very aware of that. I'm merely observing for the time being."

"Has your mother returned home yet?"

She shook her head. "No. Apparently, according to a missive she sent Heart, she and my father are still in Wales."

"And the plot thickens again."

"Quite so." She sniffed the air surrounding him, trying to place the scent that had wafted in with him.

"What?" He looked down to sniff his clothes. "Do I smell bad?"

"Not bad, no." Rather rugged and masculine, though, which was different from his usual refined scent. She quite liked this one. It felt more true to the man. "But I sense a bit of smoke, and this is the first time you've ever smelled like that."

"Oh?" His brow took on a smoldering waggle. "And what do I smell like at other times?"

This was why one should never compliment a rake. She shrugged. "Cheap comments."

His brow fell. "Should I be erudite and point out that comments can't smell?"

"Can't they? They are mixed with your breath, are they not?"

"Are you saying my breath smells?" He cupped a hand at his mouth and sniffed. "Lies."

"Well, if nothing else, your breath should smell of smoke, just like you. Assuming it was you smoking, of course."

The brow lifted again. "There is one way for you to find out."

Leonora turned him, meeting his gaze. Lord, her heart. "Are you suggesting what I think you are suggesting?"

He leaned in close. "What do you think I'm suggesting?"

She leaned in a bit farther, too. "Sniffing your mouth."

His chest rumbled with laughter. "That would be a first." He slowly smoothed his thumb over his lower lip, as though he was soothing an itch. Leonora bit down on hers.

Although his smile didn't slip, his gaze suddenly took on a

weight that threatened to drag a person deep into the depths of a world unknown.

A shiver skittered down her spine.

The cry of a bird followed by the flapping of wings startled her from the daze the man had cloaked her in. She glanced in the direction of a huge blue-and-red bird that had invaded the ballroom. It cried out again, this time following its cry with the squawked words, "The earl is an idiot, the earl is an idiot."

"What in the world . . ." All around, people gushed about the new arrival and its tart beak.

"What the devil is that?" Dare asked in wonder.

"A bird . . ." Leonora murmured, watching as it settled on a pillar a short distance away.

"I can see it's a bird. I mean what is it doing in the ballroom?"

"It must have escaped from its cage. I'm envious."

Dare gave her a curious look. "Wishing to break free from a cage, Lady Leonora?"

"Of sorts." It was more like she wished to break free from a family secret and claim her true identity. But Leonora knew she could never do that.

"Is there even a cage that can hold you?" He glanced at the bird, and muttered, "Or that thing, for that matter."

Leonora suddenly sympathized with the big, colorful bird. It had escaped one prison only to fly into another, just a little larger. "The whole world is our cage."

A snort of laughter. "Very dramatic."

The corners of her lips twitched.

"It's some sort of parrot, isn't it?" Dare murmured.

Leonora nodded. "I believe so. Very pretty."

His arm brushed hers, a casual touch that lingered just enough to be noticed. "Not as pretty as you."

Leonora snorted, but her heart couldn't help but give a little dance at the compliment. *You are so easy, Leonora!* One compliment and you are preening like that parrot!

"The earl is an idiot, the earl is an idiot," the parrot cried.

"His beak is not so pretty," Leonora said.

"Agreed." Dare pointed at a plump, mottled-faced man amidst the crowd. The Earl of Plummington, their host.

So then . . . "The earl's pet is calling him an idiot?"

"It seems so." Dare chuckled, and Leonora's gaze followed his to a woman snickering behind a fan. "I would guess the countess had a hand in this."

Oh dear. "How utterly devious. Why would she do some-thing so . . . so . . ."

"Underhanded, not to mention humiliating to her husband?" Dare finished her sentence. "First, you must ask what he has done to her."

"Do you know?" Leonora asked with curiosity.

He shook his head. "But since your friends caused such a scandal by releasing copies of White's betting book, all sorts of odd things have happened all across London."

"Well, good for the countess, then."

Dare grinned, nodding his approval. "Are you joining the festivities at Huntington Manor tomorrow?"

"Oh, you mean the picnic beside their lake? I hadn't planned on going, no."

"Pity. I have it on good authority that the duchess is attend-ing."

"And what good authority is this? Don't tell me you have spies in her household!"

He laughed. "Saints, no. Nothing like that. I overheard some chatter."

"Chatter cannot be considered a good authority."

"If that's not good authority, I don't know what is."

Leonora laughed, her attention once again drawn to the parrot's loud cry. She froze when it seemed to look straight at her.

She grabbed Dare's arm. "Am I mistaken, or is the parrot looking at us?"

"Don't be absurd. How can the bird be . . ." he cocked his

head, "looking at us . . ."

"Perhaps it's attracted to your blue jacket."

Dare glanced down at his clothes. "Well, if it is, it's got fabulous taste."

What a peacock statement!

The bird suddenly launched from the pillar and took a path directly at them.

What on earth!

DARE HAD NEVER been so mortified, petrified, and horrified at the same time in all his life. Of all the heads in the ballroom, why the blazes had the parrot chosen *him*? All he wanted was his nightly dose of sunshine, and this damn bird seemed determined to ruin that for him.

Talons threatened to claw at him, as the flap of the bird's wings sent a gust through his hair.

What is this bird's problem?

He swatted at the thing, dodging its attempt to use him as the sitting post. Why did it have to be so big? And bright. Dare squinted at the loathsome thing. Had Leonora been right? Was the thing attracted to his jacket?

Preposterous.

Dare shooed the bird away when it aimed to land on his shoulder. Or was it his head the thing was after? "Damn it!"

Leonora laughed, stepping away from him with wide eyes. "Just let it land on you!"

"On my dead body, sure," Dare bit out, sidestepping the crazy thing, "but not while I am breathing."

All the fascinated eyes that had followed the bird from the beginning were now fixed on this damn scene. On him. Them.

Another burst of laughter. "What did you do?"

Dare gave another swat. "What do you mean what did I do?"

"I remember reading somewhere that birds remember when

someone has wronged them."

"Hogwash." Dare retreated several steps in hopes the bird would give up on him and choose another target. "I did nothing to this blasted creature."

Dare glared at the temptress standing off to the side, hand covering her mouth as she tried her best *not* to burst into peals of laughter right in his face. This was what a man got for chasing the sun.

The bird loomed over him like a bad omen. The price he paid for being greedy.

"Hand me your fan," Dare demanded.

"My fan? I don't like to carry one. What would you even do with it?" She stepped forward and held out her arm so that the bird could settle there, and to Dare's astonishment, the bird changed course.

His face went blank. This colorful monster would bloody Lady Leonora's milky-pale skin with its claws! Dare sidestepped to block the bird's path to her arm, shoving his shoulder at the thing instead.

There! *If you want to land somewhere, use me.*

The bird accepted his offer and settled on his shoulder. Dare stilled as the bird's feet clenched around his shoulder. It didn't hurt, but he could feel the strength of its talons through his clothes.

Leonora blinked at him with wide eyes.

It was then that Dare realized that he and Lady Leonora were tangled up in each other. Not in an obvious way but, then again, perhaps too obvious in the eyes of their audience if one were to consider it from another perspective. One of her hands had grabbed hold of his when he'd blocked the bird, the other settled on his chest.

Dare stared into sparkling blue eyes, forgetting entirely about the bird. "You're staring, Lady Leonora."

"You're staring too, Lord Dare."

"The earl's an idiot!" the bird cried.

He flinched.

Ah, yes. He was an idiot. Perhaps the biggest idiot in all of London. Because right at this moment, with a damn bird on his shoulder and her so near to him, he didn't want to move. He didn't want her hand to leave him. Not even for the sake of propriety. And that scared the hell out of him.

"Everyone is staring at us." He hadn't looked away from her, but a marble statue would be able to feel all the stares on them.

Regrettably, her hand fell away from his chest, and she took a step back, clearing her throat and patting her cheeks. A horse bursting into the hall right now would be less obvious. Her gaze flicked between him and the bird. "Shall we just blame the parrot?"

"Naturally, it's the parrot's fault. Speaking of which," he deepened his voice and called across the ballroom, "can our hosts please come to collect their bird?"

"The earl is an idiot!"

Dare scowled. "I'm a rake, not an idiot." Should he just shrug this bright mass off his shoulder? Its talons were beginning to bite into his shoulder, and the thing wasn't light. More importantly, its beak was huge. If it decided to nip at him, it was going to hurt. A lot.

Leonora's bubble of laughter finally spilled over. "This is most amusing. You know, most men won't refer to themselves as rakes. They just *are*."

"I'm not most rakes."

She shook her head. "I cannot refute that."

He could feel the creature turn its beady eyes on him. "I'm going to ring this bird's neck if it calls me an idiot one more time."

"Oh, come now. The bird isn't calling you an idiot."

"I'm an earl, and it's on my shoulder. It now *feels* as if I'm the idiot." He was feeling a lot more than an idiot at the moment. He felt hot, too. And it was a heat that spread from his chest in all directions in his body. He hadn't felt this hot in a long, long time.

He couldn't look away from her, the way her face brightened in amusement at his expense, that lovely face making everything in him twist.

"But you are not *the* earl," she reassured even though it didn't sound all that reassuring.

His gaze finally left her and swept their audience in search of their host, who had yet to show his face. "Do you think this will matter to the gossip rags? You should leave before you get dragged into the headlines as well."

"I fear it might be too late for that," she said, amused. "I didn't know you cared about the gossip sheets so much."

"I don't care for myself," Dare said, trying very hard to ignore the parrot shaking out it's feathers on his shoulder. "I care that you might be ridiculed."

She inched closer to him, directing a smile at the parrot before her eyes landed on him. "Ah, my heart just skipped a beat."

This minx. Damn if a beat of his heart didn't skip, too. "Devil take it, what the hell do we do now?" A quick sweep of the room confirmed all the hushed titters had calmed somewhat.

"There is nothing else to do. All we can do is be swept along by whatever gossip erupts until it dies down. Which is quite thrilling. And quite the moment. Dashing off now will only make it worse," Leonora pointed out.

"Only you would call this thrilling." Where the hell were their hosts? His gaze caught on one particular figure staring at them. "And don't look now, but the duchess has arrived and is staring at our debacle."

A sparkle entered her gaze. "She is?"

"Don't look," Dare hissed beneath his teeth when she started to turn her head, "or she will know we are talking about her."

She shot him a sulky glance. "But I want to look."

"Try to hold back the urge," Dare said, swallowing a laugh. "You might benefit from practicing a bit of self-restraint. Unless you *want* her to know?"

Her lips puckered in a brief pout before settling back into

place. "No, you are right. I want to observe for now without raising any suspicion."

Dare watched her fight the desire to blatantly turn her head and search for the woman in question. His amusement at her expression slowly faded his annoyance at continuing to be the center of attention in a ballroom with a parrot on his shoulder.

"Lord, it's hard," she sighed.

"Lord?" a voice boomed, causing them both to flinch. "It's good that you know to pray. You'll need your prayers after tonight, Leonora."

Dare turned to Heart, who had a murderous look on his face. The man also looked tired, Dare noticed, as though he had endured trial after trial—the kind forged in the pits of hell. Dare inwardly sighed but lifted his lips into a smile. "Nothing to see here, Heart. Just a bit of a pickle."

"Says the man with a parrot on his shoulder and bird shite on his back."

Dare's smile slipped. The bird had done what?

He glanced at Lady Leonora who inspected his clothing, gasping when she stepped around him. The titters grew louder.

Bloody wonderful.

"Fiction or fact?" he asked Lady Leonora.

"A big, white, scattered fact."

Dare finally turned his head to glare at the bird. Some things, like this infernal creature, belonged in a cage, or in a damn habitat better suited to its noisy, insufferable existence.

Beady eyes stared back at him.

Calm.

Unruffled.

You damn feathered blackguard. Where, in what life, did a parrot shite on a man in a damn ballroom? Had fate or luck or whatever higher power existed above him finally forsaken him?

"Plummington!" Dare roared. "Come get your damn bird!"

Then the thing opened its beak again. "I'm a rake, not an idiot. I'm a rake, not an idiot."

Bloody hell.

Chapter Six

THE NEWSPAPER SLAMMED onto the dining room table, and a furious finger jabbed at the bold print sprawled over the paper. *"Lady Leonora and the Infamous Earl of Dare Caught in a Bird Scuffle,"* Heart growled with eight parts fury and two parts disgust.

Well . . . Leonora bit her lip to keep amusement from spilling over. She had expected some version of events to make the gossip rags. She should probably be less delighted, but her moment with a rake and a bird was now immortalized in ink. How marvelous.

Another paper slammed over that one.

"Feathered Fiasco: A Lady, a Rake, and a Parrot Pique!"

Dear me.

Another paper slammed down.

"Plumage Pandemonium."

Honestly . . .

Another paper.

"Beak Versus Brocade."

Leonora grimaced as her brother's fury rose with every paper. "I understand, Heart."

"Do you?" Another paper. *"Winged Warfare."*

What could she say? "They are certainly witty with their headlines."

"Witty?" Heart's face had thunder on it. "What about this is witty? It's a damn disaster." He stabbed the latest paper with a finger. "*A Lady and a Rake Embroiled in an Unlikely Avian Affair!*"

Avian affair? She bit back a laugh. "Honestly, Heart, no person in England will take this seriously."

"Do you imagine anyone cares if it's true or not? This will ruin you, Leonora. You are *ruined*."

She scoffed. "Don't be so dramatic. I'm not ruined. I'm fodder for entertainment, that is all."

"How the hell can you say that with a smile?"

She locked eyes with Heart's stony gaze. "Because it's all rather amusing. Besides, I'm only ruined if I *act* ruined. Then people will respond accordingly. If I don't act ruined, I won't be ruined."

"What horrifying logic is that?"

"Weren't you there?" Leonora countered with a smile. "It's not like Dare and I were caught in some indiscreet act. We were in a ballroom crowded with people."

"That doesn't matter. It says you were entangled with each other."

"Now that is utter nonsense. At most, I used the earl as a crutch when I lost my footing." Though in truth, she had never lost any footing. Maybe one or two heartbeats, though. "I suppose we shall see soon enough."

His eyes narrowed. "See how?"

"There is an event at Brimfield Park at the lake. Unless it's raining, it should still be on."

"You cannot be serious," he growled. "You plan to attend this event?"

"Why not? It's the perfect place to act normally."

He shoved the papers to her. "Do you need more reason than these papers? It's a bad plan. I forbid it."

"Your anger is clouding your head, Heart." She picked up a paper. "This is exactly why I should attend. To show the world how unaffected I am."

"Yes, you seem quite so." His eyes bore into her. "*Are* you unaffected?"

Well, if amusement counted as affected, then no. But looking at Heart's red-patched face, it was probably better not to mention that or he truly would bar her from attending. She settled for a question. "What reaction are you looking for, Heart?"

"A normal lady would be in tears."

"What can I say?" She grinned at him. "I am not normal." It was hardly surprising—the whole family was not normal. And honestly, it was hard enough not to burst into peals of giggles just thinking of that parrot and Dare's soiled jacket without having to pretend to be normal on top of it.

"I'd be so much happier if you were."

"Why?" Leonora challenged calmly. "If you focused more on your own life, you wouldn't need to pin your happiness on mine."

"You are my sister."

"I am your *family*," she countered meaningfully. Not that he would ever catch onto the meaning, daft man. "I'm also a woman, which means if I marry, I leave this house. And guess what, Heart, you would still be here—alone with no one to fuss over. Which is rather distressing for a man your age. Hence, you should focus on yourself and pay less attention to me."

"When you marry, I shall too."

And he questioned *her* logic. "Why wait?"

"You need me to answer that?"

She shrugged. "In any event, there are no suitable matches for me at this time."

He crossed his arms over his chest, glaring at her. "What constitutes someone suitable for you?"

"Someone more like me than not."

His gaze turned dull. "What the blazes do you mean by that?"

"You truly are hopeless, Heart," Leonora said exasperatedly. "Should I spell it out? I want a man who is more like me character-wise than he is the exact opposite. I am afraid there are not many prospects this season."

"Because you are being difficult."

She shrugged again. "I am what I am."

"Words no man wants to hear." He gave her a vexed look. "What about Lord Turnberry? He asked you to dance the other evening. A waltz, as well."

She curled her lip in distaste. "He is the exact opposite of me."

"Mandeville?"

"Too opposite."

"I saw you laughing with the Duke of Calstone."

"*Polar* opposites." Well, not exactly, but Heart didn't need to know that.

His look turned sour. "Look inside yourself, Leonora. Do you truly believe there is a man the same as you?"

One did come to mind. A certain earl who was so handsome even the parrots flocked around him. But while it was true they were similar in many ways, he didn't count. Not in terms of marriage—a topic she wanted to nip in the bud. She regarded her brother and smiled sweetly. "Why, yes, dear brother. You."

His face slackened. "What?"

"I wish to marry a man," her smile widened, "*just . . . like . . . you.*"

"No."

No hesitation whatsoever. How intriguing. "No?"

"You can't marry a man like me."

"Why ever not?" She cocked her head to the side. "Is there something wrong with you? Are you not the quintessential man about town? *Normal* lord of the realm? Also, aren't we so alike?"

"No, no, and no. And don't ask questions you are not prepared to hear the answers for."

She propped her chin on her hands. "I am very prepared or I would not have asked. Unless you are the one not prepared to answer."

"Your impudence is not appreciated."

"Well, that is certainly nothing new. It also won't stop me from giving it."

"*Well*, I shall give you something in return: a warning. Stay away from Dare."

"And what if I don't want to?" She definitely didn't.

His jaw clenched, and she swore his eyes turned darker. "Then are you saying *he* is the same as you? Dare? A libertine with a reputation black as night?"

"He wasn't born that way," Leonora pointed out. "But he is closer to being the same as me than Mandeville, Turnberry, or Calstone."

"Horseshit."

"Such foul language." Her gaze lowered to the dark circles beneath Heart's eyes. He didn't seem to be sleeping well these days. And he'd appeared no more well-rested when she'd glimpsed his face last evening as he caught sight of the duchess right before he dragged Leonora from the bird spectacle. She'd also seen the way he did *not* look at the duchess, which had seemed more obvious—at least to Leonora's eyes—than the moment when he had looked at her.

Heart . . .

The duchess . . .

What story was between these two people?

Leonora wanted to question him but refrained. She'd heard the rumors about her brother, noticed the looks some women cast him. Heart had been a rake in the past. She could be wrong, but it could explain his harsh aversion to Dare—he could simply dislike the man as a visible reminder of his own checkered past.

"In any event," she pushed back her chair and rose to her feet, "I must get ready for the park. Harriet will pick me up later. Shall you be joining us?" Heart at a picnic in a park. The idea seemed so wholly out of place it brought a smile to her face. Probably because she'd never witnessed such a thing in all her life.

"Saints, no."

Leonora lifted a brow. "Not even to chaperone me?"

He waved her comment aside. "Go and prove your unaffect-edness to the *ton* with your friends. Send for me when it blows up in your in that pretty face of yours. I shall be waiting on pins and needles."

Leonora chuckled.

The duchess would be there. Another chance to observe her and their supposed mutual likeness. "In any case, I am also attending in hopes of being introduced to someone," she murmured to her brother.

He glanced at her curiously. "Who?"

"Oh, no one you'd know." *According to you.*

"Why am I feeling suspicious all of a sudden?"

"Perhaps your conscience is bothering you."

His eyes narrowed. "My conscience? What the hell would give it cause to, pray tell?"

"I don't know, Heart. Perhaps you can tell me?" *Confess all the secrets you've been keeping from me.*

His gaze narrowed to two slits. "You are hiding something from me, aren't you? What are you up to?"

She had to applaud his sixth sense. "Nothing too nefarious, I assure you. I am merely doing what I do best—enjoying each moment life has to offer. And, in a sense, I am also trying to find my place in this world."

"You already have a place."

Yes, but that place was rather precarious. "I do not expect you to understand."

Heart gave her a flat look. "I might understand more than you can imagine. I also *don't* understand many things. Oh, this is driving me mad. You are doing it on purpose to vex me, are you not?"

She chuckled, observing the fine lines marring his temple. What burdens did those lines carry? She didn't want to add to them, but she continued to find herself more and more curious, especially after Heart's reaction last night. It couldn't be a coincidence that Heart and the marchioness had become so restless so suddenly after the duchess returned to London. Leonora was twenty this year—a good age to be entrusted with the family secrets, no?

"Not on purpose, no," she told him. "And I'm not up to anything much, though I do have a secret," she admitted.

"Is it about a man?"

Both her brows sprung up. "No."

"Well then, I'll pass on whatever little female secret you are harboring."

Honestly! "I wasn't offering to tell you, you beast! I was merely being reassuring."

He gave her a knowing look. "Well, be that as it may, it's fine. We all have things we keep close to our hearts."

"True." She raked a glance over him. "So long as whatever you are keeping so close to your heart doesn't blacken it."

He inclined his head. "Valuable insight."

"In any event, I hope to see you at the picnic." Perhaps she could observe the duchess's reaction to Heart this time.

"Don't count on it."

⤜⤜⤜⟫⟫⟫

"WHO IS HERE?" Dare lifted his gaze from the ledger before him, frowning at his footman. He must not have heard the man right. After that damn parrot had shat all over his jacket last night, he had found it prudent to pour over account ledgers this morning to shake free from the damn horror that had befallen him.

Now, another potential horror awaited him in the form of this unexpected caller.

"The Duchess of Crane, my lord."

Why the devil was *she* here? He glanced at the clock. Did this have something to do with Drake? Did that warrant a visit?

"Where is she now?"

"The receiving room, my lord."

Dare rose from behind his desk and strode from his study. He drew to a halt in the doorway of the receiving room as the duchess entered his line of sight. She wore a day dress of black silk covered by a black coat, and light-blue eyes stared back at him when she turned, a look that very much reminded him of a certain flirt.

He considered the woman.

It wasn't just her eyes. It was the slight arch of her lip, the soft outline of her face. She could have been the very image of Leonora in her youth had her hair been light brown instead of black woven with strands of gray.

This woman . . .

She must be connected to the Hearts.

"My lady," Dare spoke up, striding into the room. "What brings you to the halls of my humble home?"

She rose from the sofa and he motioned for her to sit back down, taking a seat of his own. She inclined her head and settled in again. "Humble? Not notorious?"

Dare half-heartedly hooked up the corner of his lips. "If you are looking for a quick tussle, I'm not in the mood."

Her eyes flashed, unimpressed. "Does common courtesy not mean a thing to you?"

Dare shrugged. "Are you showing me any by calling on me when we've not even been introduced?"

"A fair point," she said, lifting her chin. "I suppose I cannot expect much, given my uninvited presence. So I shall try to match your bluntness."

"Please do." Her presence in his house didn't sit well with him. Any person could draw the wrong conclusion if this visit ever got out.

"Judging from your earlier comment, I presume I'm not the sort of woman you prefer."

Why the hell would she ask that? "It's true, I prefer a woman with a bit more color."

She gave a thoughtful nod. "Like the lady in your scuffle with the bird?"

Mentioning Lady Leonora . . . interesting. "Quite right. She is the colorful type of bird I prefer."

The duchess stared at him. "She is an *innocent* lady."

"I'm sure she will be ecstatic at your concern." Dare cocked his head. "Why *are* you concerned over that lady?"

"My concern is for a young woman who still needs to find a good match, and nothing good will come of Lady Leonora consorting with you."

How damn presumptuous, madam. Interesting, though, that she knew who Lady Leonora was. Just when he thought the plot couldn't thicken any more. "Consorting? We are friends."

A small brow arched. "Friends? You must think I'm a fool."

"You must think I'm a fool as well, calling on me to warn me off a lady I am well aware you have not met."

Her jaw flexed, but she remained silent.

"Is this the *only* reason you are here?"

She lifted her chin. "I believe you are also acquainted with Drake Fury."

Dare crossed one leg over the other. "You already know this."

She stared him down, and he could not begin to fathom what she might be thinking. The only thing she might not be certain about was whether Drake had his backing or not.

"Yes," she finally answered. "He is your cousin."

Dare inclined his head. "Has he done something to offend you?"

"That is between me and him. To put it bluntly, my lord, I'm here to caution you against stepping into my family matters."

"Is that so?" Dare sat back and rested his hands on his legs. Since Drake hadn't informed him of the finer details of his strife with the duchess, and Leonora hadn't informed him of her connection at all, he had only half the knowledge he needed to be carrying on this conversation. It was quite annoying, but he was also intrigued by this visit.

"I trust you understand what I'm asking."

Not a bloody clue. Was she warning him against the deed

Drake wanted or warning him against getting involved with Lady Leonora? "Of course."

The footman appeared by the door. "My lord, you have another caller."

Dare glanced at the man. "Who is it this time, Graves?" The pope? Prinny? At this point nothing would surprise him.

"Lord Heart."

Well, now. He took that back. *This* was interesting. And deuced surprising.

The duchess's head whipped to the door, visibly flustered, and Dare's grin lifted from ear to ear. "Send the good Heart in." He looked at the duchess, arching a brow. "Seems I am to receive an earful of warnings this morning."

The duchess rose to her feet. "I shall take me my leave."

"Why?" Dare asked. "You and the good fellow seem to have something in common—your concern for his sister, Lady Leonora."

Heart strode into the drawing room and jerked to an abrupt halt when his gaze fell on the female occupant. Dare settled back more comfortably, observing the two. "I gather there is no need to introduce you."

Heart's usual scowl didn't form.

"We've met," the duchess said. "A long time ago. Twenty-one years ago, I believe."

Heart said nothing, just stared at her.

"Heart." Dare's gaze drifted to the newspapers in the man's hand. "To what do I owe the pleasure of this visit?"

Heart seemed to break out of his reverie and marched over to slam the papers into the table. "I am here to warn you."

Dare wanted to laugh. "Away from your sister, I presume?"

"Yes," Heart grit out. "Who the hell else?"

"Why? It's not my intention to harm her."

"No? Every word you engage in with her harms her."

His thumbs twitched. "Tell me, Heart. Are you sure you aren't looking at me and seeing everything you loathe in yourself?"

The man's face drained of color before heat rushed back. He hesitated, his gaze flicking between him and the duchess, his jaw clenching hard. "I see your preferences haven't changed over the years."

Dare's eyes grew wide. Was he talking to the duchess?

"How apt of you to notice," she returned, unnaturally calm.

Heart's face darkened before he swung that dark look over to Dare. "Leonora has a bright future ahead. You will do nothing but ruin it for her." His gaze flicked to the duchess again before reverting. "I don't have to spell out the reasons why."

"You don't."

"Good, I'm glad you're not playing the simpleton with me. A man like you should know to stay far away from a girl like her."

It was a good point. A point Dare had been questioning himself on quite a lot lately, but not one he was willing to dissect with her brother and a woman whose identity was shrouded in mystery. Even so, it rather went against his nature to simply agree, didn't it?

"Lady Leonora is no longer a girl." Dare slowly rose to his feet.

"Compared to you, she is." Heart stepped up to him, his face full of contempt, and uncomfortably close. They were about the same height, so they stood eye to eye, nose to nose. "Stay away from Leonora."

Dare flashed him a smile. "Wouldn't it just be easier to demand this from your sister? Tell *her* to stay away from me?"

At Heart's contorted face, Dare's smile turned knowing. "Unless she doesn't want to stay away, does she?"

"You damn blackguard. Don't provoke me" Heart's voice was low, tight with barely controlled rage.

"I'm not doing anything."

"Not doing anything? Is it your intention to ruin my sister?" Heart bit out through clenched teeth.

"That's never been the case." Ever.

"Then what the hell *is* the case?"

Dare shrugged, slow and deliberate, his eyes never leaving Heart's. "Like I said before, her presence brings a bright light to dreary balls. Neither of us has any wish beyond that."

"How can you claim such a thing with a straight face?" Heart jabbed a finger at the newspaper. "Have you *read* those titles?"

"I have not," Dare admitted. Knox, however, had taken much joy in reading them to him first thing this morning.

"Then read them," Heart growled. "And if you don't stay away from my sister, I won't hesitate to step in."

"Like you are stepping in now?"

"Correct, only you won't like what I do next."

A throat cleared, and both men turned to the duchess they had forgotten about. "Violence is rarely the answer. That being said, I shall take my leave."

Heart took a step back and dusted off his jacket. "No. I was the one that interrupted your"—his disapproving gaze flicked over them—"whatever this is. *I* shall take *my* leave."

Dare arched a brow.

"You didn't interrupt anything," the duchess hissed like a cat that had encountered a big, burly dog.

"It's none of my business," Heart said, casting one last warning glance in Dare's direction before striding from the room. The duchess stared after the man, before she too marched from the room without a by your leave.

Dare had only three words for this damn encounter.

What the hell?

Chapter Seven

THE WIND SWEPT through Leonora's hair as she tilted her head back to soak up the soft rays of the sun filtering through the gray clouds overhead. All around the bank of the lake, couples and families had spread blankets and were soaking up the rare rays before the weather turned on them, as it was wont to do this time of the year. A few sweethearts were on boats on the lake.

The duchess sat a few blankets away, one of the reasons why Leonora had gone against her brother's advice to stay away—or should she say orders. The man had returned from a midmorning outing with all the hallmarks an enraged bear, and all of a sudden, she had been commanded to stay home.

Sorry, Heart. It's a sister's duty to rebel against her brother.

The other reason was that she truly did believe that only if she acted ruined, would she actually be ruined.

She'd purposely chosen a spot not so far away from the duchess, and every now and then, she would peek in the woman's direction. She didn't know if she was imagining it, but every so often, it seemed that the duchess would look in her direction, too, but Leonora didn't hold herself in such high esteem to think the duchess was looking at *her*.

She glanced to where Harriet and her husband were strolling near the tree line over yonder. Leonora shook her head. She wouldn't be surprised if they disappeared for an hour or two.

A hulking figure plopped down beside her.

"I didn't think you would join," Leonora murmured with a smile.

"Your ability to be subtle is truly atrocious," Dare said. "You might as well have chosen a spot on her blanket."

Leonora chuckled, shooting him a raised brow. "Yours isn't much better. You did sit on my blanket."

He leaned back against his elbow, a lazy grin tugging his lips. "I prefer to be direct, as you know. Although, after the headlines this morning, I'm surprised you are here at all."

Leonora groaned. "Not you too."

"Ah, your brother has been breathing down your neck about the newspaper articles, too?"

Her eyes widened. "*Too*? Don't tell me he confronted you?"

"He did."

So that was where he'd gone. Leonora turned her body to Dare. "Well, what happened? What did he say?"

Dare's eyes glinted. "He warned me away from you."

That Heart . . . "So, nothing new."

"For most, it would be enough."

Leonora snorted. "Well, we are not most, or we wouldn't be sitting with each other at a picnic in the park after those head-lines."

He chuckled. "Right you are. A bold move, certainly. How-ever, some might say that it's even more concerning."

"For you, perhaps. Not me."

"Why me and not you?"

"*You* are the rake, I am not. Me being here is normal. Don't you rakes only venture out at night?" Plus, the two of them sitting together should prove they had nothing to hide.

He leaned onto his other elbow as well. "I've never met a woman who played the rake thing as thick as you."

"I daresay you did that all by yourself."

He chuckled and rose to shrug out of his jacket, drawing her eyes to his chest. "Can't argue that." He tossed the garment aside and resumed his former position, the picture of a handsome lord relaxing in the sun.

"What are you doing? Undressing in public now?" Leonora's pulse fluttered a tiny bit.

"Shall I scandalize a few mamas?"

"Why not? You are the subject of many a warning to debutantes. I wouldn't be surprised if they study you in finishing school. Perhaps a lecture entitled 'How To Spot a Rogue With One Glance.'"

He laughed. "You might benefit from that teaching. Why aren't you heeding your brother's warning about me?"

"Listen to him? Dear lord, where would the fun be in that?" She might as well retire from society and live an uneventful life.

"It's not all about fun."

"I beg to differ." Very much so.

He looked over to her. "How so?"

"We only ever have the moment we are living in now, don't you agree?" Her gaze turned toward the lake. "Tomorrow, we might have nothing."

"True, but does that mean you must engage with me? Am I that fun?"

She glanced at him. "You don't think so?"

"I have no denial about who and what I am."

Which was why she enjoyed his company so much. "But you do know how to have fun," Leonora said. "That is all that matters."

"You're the first woman who has ever called me fun."

"Then we make quite the pair, for I'm the first woman not seduced by your charms."

"Ah come, now, not even a little bit?" He waggled his brows at her.

Rogue.

"I've thought this for a while," he went on, "but you're quite the outspoken chit. You shouldn't be telling rakes about rake things."

Leonora leaned back on her elbows, too, lifting her face toward the sky. "My brother was one, if the rumors about him are to be believed." She suddenly laughed. "Had I been born a man, I probably would have been one as well." She caught his stare from the corner of her eye. "What? You find that so hard to believe?"

He shook his head. "Just . . . I have no words."

"See. I must have beyond-average charm to leave you without words."

"You aren't wrong about that." He rolled onto his side to study her. "Will you tell me this grand family secret of yours?"

"Now, why would I do that?"

"Because I'm growing more curious by the minute even though I know I shouldn't. And we are friends."

Friends . . . "That still doesn't warrant a tightly kept secret to be revealed."

His eyes probed hers. "Aren't you a bit too cavalier with this family secret? If it were that much of a secret, I shouldn't even know that the secret exists."

She pursed her lips. "That's true."

He fell onto his back, covering one arm over his face. "How bothersome. I never knew curiosity could be this horrible."

Leonora bit her lip to keep from laughing. His tone had taken on an air of complaint, but it still held a smidgeon of amusement. "In any event, I suppose I should thank you. You were right, she is here."

"Of course." He smirked. "I—"

"You are always right?" she finished for him.

"Lord, no. Not always. I have been wrong too many times in my life to claim such a thing."

She eyed him askance. "Well, it's good that you aren't overly confident. What were you going to say then?"

His arm remained in place over his eyes, but a smile played on his lips. "Merely that I have my moments. So, how is your *observation* going?"

"As well as observation can go. I haven't gathered the courage to approach her yet. What would I even say? It's not like I can ask her my questions outright."

He lifted his arm to look at her. "Why not start by asking your family?"

"Heart?" No, she couldn't do that.

"Wouldn't it be easier?"

"You've met Heart, haven't you?"

"I wish I could say that I hadn't."

Leonora flicked her gaze to the boats in the lake. "I'm not always even sure I want to ferret out the truth. It was buried for a reason. Yet I still have this burning curiosity within me that's growing each day."

"Will it make you happy to know the truth?"

She couldn't quite say. Would it? "Perhaps, but it is sure to make others unhappy."

"Don't worry about them. Just worry about you."

"That is more easily said than done." And also, "I'm scared to ruin things."

"That doesn't sound like you." Leonora glanced at him and chuckled at his brow attempting to reach his hairline. "You are the boldest woman I know."

"You know a lot of women. Are you sure *I'm* the boldest?"

"There you are wrong," Dare said slowly. "I don't know a lot of women. Not in a way that would make us friends. When I say you are the boldest woman I know, I do mean every word."

A small shiver went through her at his words. "Well, thank you." But would he still use the term *friends* if he learned her secret? *Dare, the duchess might be my mother. Do you understand what that means?*

And her mother might not even be aware of her.

Leonora blinked.

But shouldn't she be aware, though? The woman had given birth to her, after all. It wasn't as though she couldn't be aware of her existence at all.

But then . . .

It had been twenty years. Leonora didn't know what had happened in the past, so it was best not to jump to conclusions she could not prove. She could only assume the woman thought she was truly Heart's sister. Otherwise . . .

Let's not think about that.

It wasn't like Leonora had grown up without a mother. She'd grown up being loved. Even Heart, that beast, had always been her pillar supporting her. Well, usually.

A shadow fell over her. Looming. "Leonora."

She sighed. Why was it that whenever she thought of the devil, he appeared? Leonora looked up to catch sight of Heart staring at her with a gloomy expression. Beside him was the Duke of Calstone with a foolish grin on his face.

What was *he* smiling about? Whatever the man was thinking was probably grossly exaggerated.

"Heart," Leonora greeted. "I thought you said you weren't attending."

"I thought I told you to stay away from *him*," he shot back.

"Well, it's too late now." Her gaze flicked to the lake, the only escape left to her if she wanted to stay a bit longer. She also felt a bit of a rebellion stirring. "Dare and I planned to go on a boat."

Heart's gaze dragged between the two.

"No."

"Yes."

"No."

"*Yes.*"

"NO."

Dare chuckled beside her, and Leonora rose to her feet. She sent him an imploring look. "Shall we?"

"Where are your friends?" Heart demanded. "I thought you were attending with Leeds and his wife."

She shrugged. "They have gone to take a stroll."

"That's too bad," Calstone, Leeds's closest friend, said. "I had hoped for some much-needed distraction. How can they tell me to meet them here and then run off?"

"Well, I assure you, my brother is a prime conversationalist. I'm sure in his company, you shall never be bored."

"Let's go," Heart said, not giving up.

Dare rose to his feet. "But the lady promised me a ride on the lake."

Leonora sent the man a heartfelt grin and clapped her hands. "Fabulous!"

She wouldn't be hauled off today without a fight.

Fabulous?

Dare's gaze flicked between Lady Leonora, Heart, and Calstone. How the hell had they ended up in the same rowboat? Heart he could understand. But did the duke really have to join them? Could he not have excused himself? Or was he interested in courting Lady Leonora?

Dare didn't think so.

Or perhaps there was a possibility that Calstone, like the duchess staring at them with a burning gaze from her blanket at the edge of the lake, was part of this mystery Lady Leonora was trying to solve.

However, he didn't really think that either.

In which case, it was mostly likely that the man was truly just bored and was now entertaining himself with this drama. But he could have entertained himself from the bank. Dare sent him a sour look. Why cramp himself in this small boat with them?

Time and time again, he found himself entangled in Heart affairs. Part of him couldn't rightly help himself, but the other part, the times-like-this part, he must be bloody insane. He was like a defenseless child in the face of her beseeching looks.

Dare gritted his teeth. His father would roll in his grave if he saw him now. Perhaps that was a good thing. However, every brooding glance from the man across from him was a damn warning. If he weren't more careful, he might end up in a park, pistol in hand, second at his back, defending his honor when he hadn't even seduced the chit!

His eyes met Lady Leonora's, seated next to her brother, and she winked at him. Winked! Daring minx. Her entire demeanor was the exact opposite of her gloomy sibling. She practically brimmed with delight, except for the occasional annoyed glances she directed at their chaperones.

"Well, this certainly is relaxing," Calstone remarked.

Relaxing my arse. This was about as relaxing as falling arse first into a bed of thorns. Although, who needed thorns with Heart's cold, glowing eyes stabbing steel at him? It was all he could do to sit still and not wiggle about in discomfort.

"Was this really necessary?" Lady Leonora asked, mimicking his thoughts with that one question.

"Yes." Heart didn't back down an inch. "I warned you."

"And me," Dare murmured.

"Yes! About that, Heart," Lady Leonora said with a narrowed look to her brother. "How could you confront the earl when he has done nothing wrong?"

"Done *nothing*?"

Dare stared at the man. Boldness certainly ran in the family. Given Lady Leonora's comment earlier, it was plain he hadn't informed his sister about his little visit to Dare's home. Or about his other visitor. Perhaps it was time she found out. "I did do nothing. However, I do applaud the concern of you and your lady friend."

Heart's face fell.

Lady Leonora glanced at him. "Lady friend?"

"It's nothing." Heart sent him a warning look.

Dare smirked. "If you say so. The Duchess of Crane was quite startled when you left so abruptly."

Lady Leonora's eyes stretched wide before they narrowed to slits, unfortunately aimed at him. "The duchess came to see you?"

"Yes."

"*Why?*"

"I'd like to know that as well," Heart muttered.

Lady Leonora's gaze whipped from him to her brother, her eyes taking on a different glow, as though she were a baby shark who had just got her first whiff of blood. "Why would you like to know that as well?"

"I . . ."

She arched a brow.

"That . . ."

It lifted a notch.

"I . . . That . . ."

Dare grimaced. He almost for sorry for the man. He had turned into a tongue-tied boy right before their eyes. Surprising. He'd thought Heart would shut his sister down, not flounder to this extent.

"Well?" Leonora demanded.

"What? Can't a man be curious?" Heart finally tossed back. A glare jabbed his way. "Why are you turning it on me when she called on Dare?"

"Don't get the wrong idea, Heart. Her call was merely a matter of family business, that's all," Dare said. It was the truth, after all.

"What family business could she possibly have with you?" Heart growled.

The scrunch of Lady Leonora's brow deepened. "Heart! That's unforgivably rude."

Calstone picked at his jacket.

Heart had the grace to look sheepish. "He is the unforgivably rude one. Not taking anything I say to heart."

"And why should I?" Dare responded. *I'm not your lapdog.*

"Why don't you keep your mouth shut?" the man snapped back.

"Heart! Why should *he* shut his mouth when you're the one spouting nonsense? He has the right to speak just like you have the right to growl."

"Now, gentlemen," Calstone interjected. His gaze flicked to Lady Leonora. "And lady. Let's not get our feathers into a twist. We are all in the same boat. Quite literally."

"Some of us don't belong here," Heart muttered.

Dare arched a brow. "Agreed."

"I meant you."

"And I meant you." Dare glanced at Calstone. "And him."

"I'm in agreement with Lord Dare." Leonora folded her arms across her chest. "You are the interlopers. My apologies, Duke."

"Oddly, I take no offense at being called an interloper."

That's because you are a deliberate interloper, you dandy.

"The only interloper I see is the one sitting across from me," Heart harped.

"You keep harping and harping on the same thing, Heart." A certain bird came to mind. "Are you Plummington's parrot?" The moment the words left Dare's mouth, he knew it was a mistake. A mistake he couldn't take back.

The man leaped to his feet, fury rolling off him like waves.

"Heart!" Leonora cried out as the boat rocked.

Dare cursed as he reached to grip the edges of the boat before changing his mind and reaching for Lady Leonora, pulling her over to his side. She had been seated opposite him, caged in between Calstone and her brother. Dare didn't know what Heart might do next, but the boat did not have an even distribution of weight as it was. Rocking the boat might land them all in the damn water, and he couldn't let that happen.

Well, he would try his best not to let that happen.

However, Calstone, for all his poise, had lurched to the side when Heart leaped up, tilting the boat even more. It was the final straw for Heart losing his footing, and he tumbled into the lake. A great splash sent water spraying in all directions. Dare shielded Leonora from any stray droplets and kept her anchored as the boat rocked back and forth at the disturbance.

Good. *You deserve it.*

Lady Leonora's hand clasped his leg, craning her neck to stare at the water. "He won't drown, will he?"

In this shallow water? A man could only hope.

The next moment, Heart emerged from the water like a sea creature ready to wreak vengeance on whoever had disturbed him, glowing eyes directed at him.

Dare sighed. He should have stayed in bed today.

"Get your hands off my sister!" the creature roared.

This damn man . . . But they were once more in a bit of a tangle as the boat continued to rock back and forth.

"The boat is still unsteady," Dare defended himself, slowly retracting his arm. She snatched her hand back, too.

"Well, this is certainly something else." Calstone carefully rose to help the man.

"Don't!" Dare called, seeing the man's bootstep skew, and watching in horror as the duke stumbled for his balance. Nothing could have prepared him for what happened from that moment onward.

The boat capsized, and all of them plunged into the lake. Bloody everlasting hell! At some point, his arms circled Lady Leonora, and he did not let go once as cold water seeped through his clothes. He and Lady Leonora came up sputtering at the same time as the duke.

"Dear God!" Calstone exclaimed. "What horror! I must stay away from water and boats for the rest of my lifetime!"

"Are you all right?" Dare asked Lady Leonora, his gaze roaming over her face for any signs otherwise.

She wiped at her face. "As right as I can be."

He looked down but shouldn't have. The water came up to her waist, but the plunge had left her clothes drenched, dripping, and clinging to her like second skin.

Almighty heaven above.

His eyes burned.

I shouldn't have looked. I shouldn't have looked.

Calstone cleared his voice. "There is no back door or servants' entrance, is there? I could use a nice, clean escape right about now."

Dare glanced toward the man, moving to block the duke's line of sight of Leonora. "This isn't a damn house. We are in a lake."

"I thought so, yet I had hoped that I was dreaming."

"Why?" But then he followed the duke's gaze to the shore and promptly cursed.

Every single eye on the embankment was trained at him. Even Heart had gone silent.

Not. Good. Not good at all.

Chapter Eight

IF LEONORA HAD known she'd be soaked in a lake from head to toe, she might have rethought some of her decisions. As moments went, this was not one of the best. Honestly, it was one of those moments that one didn't quite enjoy *in* the moment but might be able to draw a laugh from *after* a good amount of time had passed.

About the only thrilling sequence of this spectacle was Dare, him drawing her to him before the boat capsized and then becoming a bundle in his arms as they did. And the fact that he was at present, like her, soaked to the bone.

A rake falling into a lake.

Very well, there was a bit of enjoyment in that!

The men, however, had gone utterly silent, and on an instinctive level, Leonora understood it was a full ten parts bad. But all she could do in this particular sequence of events was appreciate Dare, hair dripping water onto his face, and the sculpted contours of shoulders through the shirt that stuck to his body.

By Jove!

Such masculine beauty.

She'd been aware of Dare for some time now, of course, but she couldn't say she'd ever thought about how his body might look beneath his impeccable tailoring. Until now.

This was Dare.

She'd always known it, in one sense, yet for the first time, she *felt* it. The true presence of this man had been cloaked, or hidden amongst their banter, their seemingly innocent flirtation. But that was all misdirection. A pretense from both sides. One they happily ignored while they were both having fun. Dare could become a flirt at the drop of a hat, but he was not a man to be trifled with.

Ah, heavens! Leonora wanted to trifle.

She wanted to trifle so much! How might it feel dragging a hand down his back? Would those hard ripples flex beneath her fingers? If he kissed her, would she be able to taste all of his secrets?

Calm down, Leonora!

Had she lost her mind?

Yes, yes she had. And happily at that.

"Leonora," Dare's soft whisper came. There was a slight hesitation in his low, gruff voice, a question mark woven into her name. No more than a few inches separated them, and she could feel the warmth of his body stroking along the ripples of her skin. Her gaze lifted to meet his to find his eyes were burning into hers. "You are staring."

Yes, well, who wouldn't stare? Who wouldn't forget about the water, forget about the discomfort and chill of being soaked in the presence of such a body? She couldn't resist any longer. She poked at his chest, not hard, but not gently either. Her prod was filled with curiosity. He jerked as though an electric spark had arced between them, but he didn't move away from her. His expression remained calm, almost too calm. Except for those stormy blue eyes.

"Isn't that my line?" Leonora murmured back, matching his low voice. "You are staring."

"It can be, just not now." He nodded to the left. She turned her head slowly to blink at the picture of a lakeside crowd gathered on the bank to see what had happened.

Drat.

She'd ogled Dare while all eyes were on them!

Double, triple drat.

Heart, who'd been silent up until now after finding himself tangled up with his own unexpected person—Calstone—found his voice again. "What a damn disaster. I can't imagine tomorrow's headlines. This is all that damn interloper's fault."

Leonora scowled. "Don't be such a blame pusher, Heart. You're the one who jumped to your feet and started this disaster. Lord, one would think the water would have doused your fire. Should *I* do it for you?" Best believe she'd give him a good whack over the head, audience or not.

His fierce scowl turned to her. "Just who do you think you are talking to?"

"I've been wondering that for the better part of six years!"

"That's a damn long time to wonder about something!"

A dramatic sigh came from Calstone. "Let us not start a fuss again."

Leonora ignored her brother and started to wade to the shore. As soon as Heart had opened his mouth, the forgotten chill had started to seep back into her skin and bones.

A hand on her wrist stopped her. "I'll carry you."

She glanced at Dare. "Carry me? That would be rather shocking, wouldn't it?" But not unwelcome.

"True." His gaze dropped to her bosom, and a heat spread across her cheeks. He whispered, "But it would be less shocking than what you are revealing at the moment."

Her gaze tracked over his chest before meeting his gaze again. "That makes two of us. We can always strut out with confidence."

"Or we could scandalize our peers with modesty and help each other cover the most revealing bits?"

"That might work as well."

Before her words had a chance to turn cold, a hand snaked across her back and she was lifted up into his arms. A small gasp flew past her lips as she looped her arms around his neck at the swift lift.

"Dare! You blackguard! Put my sister down."

"And then what?" Dare shot back. "Don't be a fool."

Heart motioned for her to be handed over. "I will carry her."

Leonora snorted. "You will not."

"Ladies, ladies, ladies," Calstone drawled, wading between Heart and Dare. "Have you forgotten so soon that we have an audience? Let us all just get out of the water."

Oh, Lord. Why did that keep slipping her mind? She could only imagine the headlines tomorrow. That parrot would be a distant memory in the face of the lake spectacle. At least it wasn't *just* her and Dare this time. "We shall surely appear in the papers again tomorrow. Should we make haste?"

Dare unhurriedly made his way back to the shore. "It's too late, love. Rush or not, the damage has been done. Just relax and—" Dare slipped and fell back into the water with a splash, Leonora being dunked right along with him.

She let out a short, high-pitched scream before her entire upper body became submerged again. What rotten luck!

"Bloody hell!" Dare cursed, rising with her in his arms.

How strong was this man?

Leonora tried to squirm from his embrace, but his arms held her perfectly—and tightly—against him, so she just gave up. She had wanted to touch him, *feel* him, but she could hardly enjoy the moment now that her awareness had shifted fully to all the people on the embankment. "Let me go if I am too heavy."

"I'm all right, and you're not heavy. My foot slipped on something squishy."

Leonora shuddered. Something squishy? "Hurry! We need to get out now."

"We can't hurry. We might slip again."

Heart's loud snort came from somewhere behind them. "How incompetent. Drop my sister again and I will end you before all these people."

"Ignore him," Leonora tossed loudly over Dare's shoulder,

but she decided it wasn't enough and also cast a glare his way. Her gaze caught on something moving toward them in the distance. Something big. Something long. Something with ridges along its back.

Her heart stuttered in her breast.

No, it couldn't be. They didn't live in England. Except . . .

"Dare."

His gaze met hers. "Yes?"

"Do crocodiles eat humans?"

His hold tightened. "Why? What's wrong?"

"Don't look now," Leonora said slowly, unsure if her eyes were deceiving her or not. "But a crocodile is moving toward us."

His brow rose. "Now is hardly the time to jest."

Time had seemed to slow upon glimpsing the thing, and it suddenly sparked back to life twice as fast. "I'm not jesting! There is a crocodile! Run!" She clutched his neck as though her life depended on it. "Heart! Calstone! Run!"

Two foul curses followed her cry.

Pandemonium broke loose.

Dare didn't even look back, he just cursed and picked up his pace. "If you are jesting, I shall take you over my knee, I swear."

"Why would I jest about my life?"

His grip was firm, his body tensed with the effort of ambling toward the nearest spot on the shore. Fortunately, they weren't that far away. The water around them made it difficult to rush, and with every stumble, every slip, Leonora gripped Dare tighter. She might very well suffocate the poor man by the time they reached solid ground.

That swimming log grew larger and larger as it approached.

Leonora forced her panic down. If she panicked, Dare would panic, too.

The shoreline wasn't kind either. Weeds made it hard to navigate, and sucking, squelching noises alerted Leonora to the mud trying to swallow Dare's boots. But the man never faltered. He was a soldier with a mission. He didn't stop, didn't even pause to catch a breath until they finally reached grass.

Their hosts rushed forward. "It won't bite!" Lord Brimfield cried. "It won't bite!" He almost sounded like that blasted parrot.

"Who the devil keeps a pet crocodile?" Dare demanded.

Well, they could at least be thankful that all eyes had turned to the crocodile. Though Leonora just needed a moment for her heart to catch up before she could appreciate the feeling.

"It's not a crocodile, it's an alligator," Lord Brimfield defended.

"Is there a bloody difference?" Dare snapped.

Good question. Leonora didn't know either.

"Yes, of course," Lord Brimfield said. "An alligator—"

"Forget the bloody difference," Heart growled, having caught up to them. "Is it legal?"

Silence followed. Another good question.

"Brimfield," Calstone said, loosening his wet cravat, "I don't have to tell you the dangers of having such a creature in the water while you have guests on your property! Where did you even acquire such a thing?"

By this time, Leonora was no longer listening to the chatter. Her pulse had settled some, her body felt exhausted, but a calm had also settled over her.

"Are you cold?" Dare asked her softly. "Just hold on for a moment longer."

Take all the moments you need.

Her eyes drifted over the scene surrounding her. From a turn about the lake in a boat to dashing from an alligator.

At least they weren't ruined.

But they were a spectacle.

DARE DIDN'T WANT to let go.

He was wet, utterly bedraggled, and he was doing something scandalous in full public view under the guise of being a concerned and honorable gentleman, but he didn't want to let go. The sensation of her body against his felt as natural as breathing. It made his pulse quicken in a way he couldn't—wouldn't—explain.

Damn Heart. This was all his damn fault.

What the devil was wrong with the man? Dare understood Heart didn't want him near his sister, but shouldn't he show a bit of decorum instead of lashing out like a bumbling bear? Dare at least had the wherewithal to behave to some degree. Of all that happened between him and Leonora up until this point, everything headline-worthy hadn't been deliberate.

Calstone suddenly cursed. "It's still bloody following us!"

"He won't attack!" Brimfield cried.

Dare cursed and clutched Leonora tighter to him, moving farther away. How the hell was an alligator in this lake? Brimfield should be taken to task for this.

Cries erupted from the audience.

That was the sound of an alligator coming onto shore.

"Oh, dear," Leonora murmured, her neck craning over his shoulder. Her breath warmed his skin, and a sweet scent tickled his nose, a sweetness not even the lake water could wash away.

Yes. Oh, dear indeed.

He swept a quick gaze over the situation. All eyes were on the reptile, and the gazes that were occasionally still cast to them couldn't help but quickly return to the toothy danger that threatened the merriment.

More cries and gasps filled the air.

For a moment, Dare didn't know if he should curse the alligator or praise its existence. He didn't want to become the creature's lunch, but for the most part, it diverted everyone's attention away from the catastrophe that was the four of them.

A fool's thought.

That alligator was *part* of the deuced catastrophe.

A hand patted his shoulder. "Put me down."

Dare glanced down at Leonora, her soft-blue eyes on him.

"Are you sure? Your dress must be heavy." He was having trouble walking himself. And this sponginess of each step was detestable. Also, if he could hold her just one moment longer . . . "We also have an alligator on our tail." The last was meant to tease.

She peered over his shoulder. "My brother is big and slow. And he has more meat. If the creature is going to eat anyone, it is him."

"How savage."

Dare slowed his pace and glanced back. All the other couples on the lake had rowed to the furthest part of the shore to clear the water and give a wide berth to the alligator who lay on the embankment, unmoving.

To the side, their hosts were explaining that the thing was harmless and that no one was in danger.

Unbelievable.

"The thing is a *pet*? Who keeps such a pet?"

"I have to agree. What do they feed him?"

"I'd rather not know."

They reached their former spot on the blanket, and Dare reluctantly set Leonora back on her feet but stayed close at her side, ready to snatch her back up and run should danger once more present itself. She instantly removed her slippers and tossed them aside while Dare reached for his discarded jacket, but before he could drape it over her shoulders, a soft voice intercepted.

"Here take this."

He turned, only to encounter the Duchess of Crane offering Leonora a shawl to cover herself. His gaze flicked to Leonora, who stared at the woman unblinkingly.

So conspicuous. She'd have made the worst spy.

He draped the jacket over Leonora's shoulder. "No need. My jacket is thicker."

The duchess turned her attention to him, slowly withdrawing her hand. He didn't miss the ever-so-fleeting flash of annoyance. "That's true."

Dare almost thought she would say something about having

called on him earlier that morning. Warn him away. But her gaze returned to Leonora.

"Would you like for me to escort you home?"

Dare should his head. "No need. I shall take care of Lady Leonora." The little temptress still stood in a daze, and he didn't know why, but he felt that she wasn't quite ready to be in a confined space with this woman.

"You are both soaked. It's better for you to return straight home, Lord Dare, don't you think?"

Leonora's brows furrowed slightly.

"It's on my way," Dare objected. "No trouble for me at all."

"*I'll* take her home."

Heart.

He was looking straight at Leonora, this heated gaze not once touching Dare or the duchess. Dare secured his jacket more tightly around her shoulders, effectively yanking her from her daze.

"Oh, right, thank you for the jacket."

No need to thank me, love. But before anything could be said further, their hosts arrived at their spot. "Lady Leonora," Lady Brimfield remarked. "I hope Basil didn't give you too much of fright!"

Basil? Who named a damn alligator Basil?

Lord Brimfield nodded. "Look, he returned to the water. He is harmless, I assure you."

"I'm quite all right," Lady Leonora murmured, clutching the lapels of his jacket with both hands. Why did that simple action make his heart skip a beat?

"Brimfield," Heart reprimanded, "like I said earlier, that thing is not a pet!"

"I disagree," the man said. "Any animal tamed could be considered a pet."

"A wild animal is still a wild animal!" Heart disagreed.

"Leonora?" Harriet's voice was worried as she and Leeds strode over, sweeping over the excited crowd. Leeds crowded close to his wife. Almost as close as Dare was with Leonora. Dare scrunched his brows together but couldn't find it in himself to step away even though he knew he ought to. "We saw what happened in the distance. Are you sure you are all right?"

"I'm fine," Leonora reassured her friend. She did seem to have recovered. Thank God. Her eyes found him. "What about you?"

"I'm fine, too."

Her voice softened with concern. "You slipped and fell."

Don't remind me of that humiliating horror, please. "The water broke our fall."

Her lips quirked. "You also carried me. I'm not light."

He flashed her a row of teeth. "And I'm strong."

All eyes turned to them.

Right. Not the time or the place.

"My apologies," the duchess said to the group. From the corner of his eye, Dare saw Heart flinch. "I have not been properly introduced to any of you, so forgive my interference. I'm Cassandra Faiththorne, the Duchess of Crane."

"It's a pleasure to meet you, Your Grace," Lady Leeds said with a smile. "I'm Lady Leeds, and this is my husband, the Marquess of Leeds."

"A pleasure meeting you." Her gaze turned to Leonora.

Dare sighed. Could it be any more awkward? How had the witty temptress suddenly lost her speech again? "Well, no introduction is needed for me."

"Dare," Heart growled.

He grinned at the man. "And since Lady Leonora and I are soaking wet—you as well—before we all catch a cold, I suggest we retire home." Like Calstone, who had disappeared. Smart man.

"No!" Lady Brimfield cried. "First, you must change here. I've already instructed a servant to retrieve a few sets of clothing. I cannot allow my guests to leave all wet and bedraggled."

Bedraggled. *Why thank you very much.* It was rather pitiful when someone else pointed it out, wasn't it?

"No need. I shall take my leave." Dare glanced to Leonora while the woman continued prattling on at Heart. He dropped his voice to a whisper. "Shall you be all right?"

She nodded, and Dare frowned at her rather subdued presence. This was not at all like the Leonora he knew. It was as though the sparkling woman had retreated into a shell.

"Are you sure?" he pressed.

"Dare," she whispered, her hand snaking out to grip his wrist.

"What is it? What's wrong?"

"Can you carry me again?"

Worry instantly sprang forth, his eyes tracking over her with a sharp gleam. "What's wrong? Are you hurt anywhere?"

She shook her head. "No, it's just . . . my legs feel awfully shaky."

Dare didn't hesitate. He lifted her into his arms and strode straight to the house. Behind them, Heart cursed and demanded something, but he didn't bellow or roar. A bloody miracle. Perhaps their current misfortune had finally infiltrated his senses.

Another miracle would be escaping the affair unscathed, but Dare didn't think they would be that lucky. One miracle a lifetime was already many.

Two?

Impossible.

Chapter Nine

"*THIS IS PREPOSTEROUS!*"

Was what her brother should have been shouting, but his lips didn't so much as move an inch as they entered their home. Usually, it wouldn't even have mattered if they had company. Today was a prime example of that. If Heart had something to say, he would say it. Or to put it more accurately, Leonora thought, if Heart had somebody to scold, he would scold.

Yet even with only Harriet here—and she'd been present for many other scolds—Heart had remained uncharacteristically silent. Luckily, the strength in Leonora's legs had returned the moment they left Brimfield house. Even more fortunately, Harriet had followed her and Dare and decided to return with her.

The moment Leonora shed her wet clothes and changed into a simple dress of white, she fell back onto her bed next to her friend, uncaring whether her hair was still damp. If she had to fight with it, it would be tomorrow's problem.

Her gaze fell on Dare's jacket, draped over her chair.

Her heart tickled.

"Are you sure you are all right?" Harriet asked. "You look a bit pale."

"That's because I just had the fright of my life."

"Well, I'll admit, that alligator startled even me, and I wasn't even in the fray," Harriet said with a furrowed brow. "Even so, if something is amiss, you can tell me, you know."

Leonora nodded. But she didn't want to burden her newly wed friend with her shocking secrets. The last thing she wanted was for Harriet to worry about her. A woman in young love should enjoy the delight while still fresh.

Besides, she didn't relish the idea of reliving any of this afternoon yet. She still couldn't quite believe she had clamped up to the degree she had when the duchess offered her . . . what had she offered her again? Ah, it didn't matter. Thank all the holy saints for Dare's sharp eyes! He alone had noticed how thrown she'd been by the encounter.

"Nothing is amiss," she reassured her friend. Nothing she couldn't handle. "The past two days have been a lot. Today especially."

Harriet snatched up a pillow to hug. "Who can blame you? The papers today were mocking enough. I am afraid to see what they shall say tomorrow."

Leonora groaned. "No, I don't want to think about it. All I want to do is forget."

Harriet chuckled. "Dare seems quite taken with you, which surprised me. I don't think he's ever been so concerned over a woman before."

Leonora glanced at her friend. "Ah, well, haven't you heard? We've been bonded by a parrot."

"You cannot deny that bird was quite determined to steal your rake."

Leonora grabbed a pillow and hit her friend. "Don't talk nonsense!"

Harriet laughed and suggested, "Why don't we go shopping for hats? It might bring the color back to your skin. Oh, right, you don't like hats, do you? We can always try to empty Heart's coffers on the latest fashion plates."

Leonora shook her head. Honestly, the events of the day had

exhausted her. "You should go. Leeds must be waiting for you."

"Leeds will keep your brother company for a while, don't worry. Your bath should be ready soon as well. Then we can go shopping."

"I beg of you, don't drag me to the shops. My legs might fail me again."

Harriet's expression returned to that of concern. "Now I know something is wrong. Bond Street is your second home. Are you sure it's just fright from the alligator?"

"No, it's the fright from everything. Heart. Dare. *Calstone*. I still don't understand why *he* was in the boat."

Harriet laughed. "Oh, do not fret about him. If that man even catches a whiff of drama—which is to say *entertainment*—he would jump into the Thames to swim after it."

Leonora had to agree, given what she'd seen of him so far. Not that she *really* cared. But the duke seemed to be a safe, effortless topic for the moment. "Which then makes *him* the entertainment." He would love the irony of that, she was sure.

"How right you are! As for your brother, it's only natural he'd be concerned after the bird fiasco."

"I wouldn't call it a fiasco." Call it a masterpiece.

"No? Well, I suppose it was just another pet gone wild," Harriet suggested. "However, the papers turned it into one with their headlines. Any family would be concerned."

Family . . .

Leonora rubbed her eyes as an older, still delicate face swam within the edges of her memories. Big blue eyes. A slender, heart-shaped face. A look of uncertainty that reached straight into her heart like a vise and *gripped*.

Who was that woman to her?

Her real mother?

Someone else?

Leonora didn't have enough of the scattered pieces to make a confident assumption, but judging from Heart's reaction, the duchess was most certainly something. At least to him, if not

Leonora.

As if Harriet could read her thoughts, she suddenly exclaimed, "Oh! And why didn't you tell me you knew *the* duchess?"

Leonora blinked. "That's because I don't. You heard her; she hadn't been introduced to anyone."

"Then why was she staring at you all concerned?"

"Because I am a fellow lady who got tossed in the lake?"

Harriet arched a brow that seemed to say: *Are you sure?*

"Honestly," Leonora said, infusing meaning into her tone. "Today was the first time I met her. And why are you so intrigued by *the* duchess?"

Harriet leaned back onto her elbow. "Well, I heard the duke was a nasty man. Everyone is talking about it."

"The late duke?"

Harriet nodded. "He had scores of mistresses and bastard children scattered all over England. I feel so sorry for those poor children. And all the women of course."

Leonora grimaced. "How unfortunate." Though not unheard of. She couldn't imagine still wearing black if she had a husband such as that. "Tell me, Harriet, would you feel sorry for me if I were a bastard child?"

"What are you talking about?" Harriet said, her brows drawing together. "I suppose I would. Then again, you are so strong, you wouldn't need my pity."

"I wouldn't be so sure," Leonora drawled playfully. "I wouldn't be a true lady."

Harriet snorted. "So? There are several times a day I'm not either."

Leonora grinned at that. "I would be of *questionable* birth."

Harriet gave her a flat look. "The way the *ton* tiptoes around the delicate topic of pregnancy, all births should be considered questionable."

Leonora laughed. "I'd still be a pariah."

"Well, at least you would be an authentic one."

"Authentic . . . not a word I've ever given much thought to. Would it still be authentic if someone is hiding from the world?"

"It's authentic if you are not allowing it to hold you back." Harriet glanced at her. "You know, there is a world outside of the *ton*. I've thought about this a lot."

That surprised Leonora. "Why?"

Harriet shrugged. "Curiosity, I suppose. Some other things."

"Did you wish to explore the world?" Leonora asked. If she were honest, she hadn't really thought about the world beyond theirs. She'd been living as though it could be taken away from her at any moment, but not envisioned what could come next. Yet the thought of there being a whole other world beyond the *ton* gave her a measure of comfort.

"Of course, though to be honest, Leeds and I have created our own world, and I am more than happy to reside there all of my life."

"Ah, yes, the delightful bubble of love."

"It's more than just a bubble; it's more than just love. It's family. It's a life that exists beyond society. Yes, we are still within its realm, but it's rather freeing."

Leonora enjoyed that sentiment. "You mean you get away with more when you are married."

"Exactly."

"So, I should marry."

"Oh, Lord, please don't marry just for the sake of marriage. If you find the right man, then yes."

Leonora laughed. "Do not fret, my dear friend, I shan't marry for the sake of marriage. But I'm still looking for my moments." Her moment to rule all moments, to be exact.

"Of course, of course." Harriet nudged her with a leg. "Just don't get so caught up in all the smaller moments that you miss the big one. And for the love of everything, find a man worthy of you."

"And what if I am the one not worthy?" Leonora asked lightly.

"However can that be?" Harriet exclaimed. "That alligator must have scattered your wits today!"

Leonora shrugged. "It's not the alligator. I just feel a tiny bit unworthy at times," she admitted. "Not much, but like an imposter in someone else's world."

A moment of silence. "That's not much?" A short laugh. "However, I do understand."

Leonora slanted a glance at her friend. "You do?"

Harriet nodded. "I'm not sure why *you* feel this way, but I know that worthiness comes from a place in your heart, nowhere else. I've learned this since I married Leeds." Her friend gave her a wistful smile. "Trust me, Leonora. If we look anywhere else to find our worthiness, we will get lost. I do not wish that for you."

"Well, do not worry on that score, at least. I am very good with directions."

"I do not doubt that."

Leonora glanced back at the ceiling of her room, her gaze trailing over the patterns strewn overhead. Worthiness from within. She quite liked that. Titles, at the end of the day, could never compare to what was in the heart.

Perhaps one day she would feel it and believe it at the same time.

"It's been a long time."

Dare lifted a lazy gaze to the woman approaching him where he reclined on a sofa of the library. The widowed Marchioness of Pilkington, otherwise known as the queen of the demimonde. He didn't bother to stand, and she didn't bother to sit. In fact, he wagered she enjoyed looking down on her prey.

"I've been busy."

"Too busy to visit my chamber?" the lady purred.

Dare bemoaned his luck. "Yes."

She laughed. "But you are here now."

Her suggestive tone brought the start of a throb to his temples. "Not for you." The only reason he'd entered this house of depravity, which he usually had no qualms about, was because he had been invited here of all places.

He hadn't objected, since he thought he might also be able to relieve some pressure that a certain temptress evoked with her sweet scent, the memory of her . . . in a dress that clung to her body like a goddess . . . her body pressed against him . . .

But the moment he'd walked through those doors, whatever remained of that mood—which wasn't much to begin with—had disappeared.

"If not me, then who?" Lady Pilkington did not give up.

He didn't think it was possible, but his mood sank into even darker depths. He'd forgotten about this trait of hers. "A friend." More precisely, his cousin, Drake.

It seemed ridiculous now that he'd thought coming here might relieve his tension. Aye, he had an itch, but neither the marchioness nor any other woman here sauntering about this estate would even begin to scratch it. None of them could take *her* place, which was quite a troubling predicament for a man like him. It left him with nothing but provoking memories and a hard cock.

I need a drink.

If only he enjoyed drinking beyond the occasional ale or glass of port. He loathed the lack of control inebriation brought. A man who lost control over his body and senses made for a rather pitiful image. Just look at his father in his last years.

"I see—"

"Dare," Drake's low voice drawled, cutting off whatever Lady Pilkington was about to say. "Aren't you a sight for the eyes?"

Dare glanced over to Drake striding toward him with a lazy gait. His gaze drifted over the scar that started at the edge of his hairline, drawing over his eyebrow, jumping the eye socket, and continuing its path to stop at his jawline. The scar that usually looked frightening in stark daylight seemed more subdued in the low lighting of this drawing room.

"You're late," Dare said.

The scarred brow rose. "I thought I'd have to wait for you to finish a romp."

"As you can see," he sent a pointed look at Lady Pilkington, "I'm not romping today."

She pivoted on her heel and sauntered away on a huff.

"What was that about?" Drake asked, staring after the woman.

"Small annoyances."

Drake lowered to seat himself comfortably in a chair. "Is she why you're in a brood? The lady not up to standard?"

"Probably." Not quite, be he didn't want to explain. He could not make heads or tails of his standards anymore. "How are things in Brighton?" They never talked about Brighton in front of others. Not even Knox.

"Same as always. Just about the same as my progress with the deed."

Ah yes. "I saw the duchess at Brimfield Park today."

"Did you, now?"

Dare crossed his arms over his chest. "Saw her before that, too."

"The lovely widow called on you then?"

So he knew. "Is that why I received a rare invite from my dear, old cousin?"

"I'm curious what the widow had to say," Drake admitted, wasting no words.

"Well then, she didn't say all that much. Something about staying out of her family matters."

"Admitting she knows I'm family? Interesting."

Dare shrugged. "She might know, but what she doesn't know is whether you have my support."

"Luckily, I don't need your support."

"Such gracious words, cousin." Not that Dare minded. He'd rather not play nursemaid to adult men.

"What about you?" Drake asked. "You're working on seducing a little bird, I hear."

A little bird? Leonora? "She is just a friend."

"Just a friend?" Drake's low laughter prickled the lines between Dare's brows.

"What? Can't I have a friend?"

Drake said nothing, though his glowing eyes held a whole conversation in them. Damn man. Time to change the topic. "Just what is it about this property that has you crawling out of your darkened hole? Why do you want it so badly?"

Drake shrugged. "The property was left to my mother by hers."

Ah, his mother, one of the duke's many mistresses. "Why does the duke have the deed?"

Drake clenched his jaw. "Why else? To use the money made from the land to pay for his indulgent lifestyle."

Interesting. "What did your mother get in return?"

"Me."

Dare grimaced. He shouldn't have asked. Everyone knew the late duke had a way of getting what he wanted, and once he had it secured, he'd toss away any excesses he didn't want. In this case, that had been his aunt and his cousin. He attempted to lighten the mood. "Don't sell yourself short, you are worth a lot."

He let out a bitter laugh. "Land aside, it's my mother's ancestral home. I want to get it back for her. She's suffered enough."

Worthy goal. "Why not explain this to the widow Crane?" She seemed like a reasonable sort. Maybe.

"The widow and I are at a deadlock."

"Of course, the deadlock you will not tell me about."

"It's best if you don't know."

"I shall take your word for it," Dare said. He had no desire to press. "What of your half-brother? The current duke."

"Crane loathes our existence. Would you entertain the bastard son of your father's mistress?"

He supposed not.

But then, one of those bastard sons was *his* family. So, maybe he would? It was a rather difficult situation. It's hard to say how anyone might react. "The woman is still in black," Dare commented. "Perhaps give her more time."

"If she is wearing the black for him, I can't understand how she could love such a monster." He removed two cheroots from his inner pocket and inhaled the scent. He handed the other over to Dare.

"Much obliged." He bit it between his teeth but didn't light it. "In any event, I think many things are not as they seem." He didn't believe things were ever just black or just white. And then there was Leonora's curiosity about the duchess. "Have you ever met Lady Leonora Heart?" Dare asked, watching his cousin's expression closely.

"No," Drake said. His gaze met his. "Why would I meet anyone that innocent?"

It was a good point. "What about her brother? Heir to the Marquess of Heartly?"

Drake shrugged. "Can't say that I have. The only nobles I rub shoulders with are you and Knox."

Dare nodded his head thoughtfully. So whatever Leonora's curiosity about the duchess, it was likely unconnected to Drake's affairs. A comforting thought.

Drake eyed him. "Should I have met them?"

Dare shook his head. "He and the duchess seem to be acquainted with one another."

"Is that so odd? She hails from your world."

Yes, but the undercurrent between the two sizzled with tension. And that was with a mere look. Dare had been in the game long enough to recognize the signs of entanglements, even if he avoided them at all costs.

"Do me a favor," Dare said. "See what you can find out about Heart, will you?"

"Aren't you a bit too curious about your little bird's family?"

Dare narrowed his gaze. "You say it as though she is a nuisance."

"Aren't all little birds?"

"Still so damn jaded. And stop calling Lady Leonora a little bird."

"Says one jade to the other."

"You do know there is a difference between the two words, don't you?"

Drake shrugged.

Dare leaned forward, elbows resting on his knees. "Does your mother know that you are trying to retrieve the deed for her?"

"No. She wouldn't encourage it. But the duke is dead, and I'll be damned if my mother will be robbed any longer. I'll get that property back, even if it kills me."

"It could be with a solicitor and you're wasting your time with the duchess."

The veins in Drake's jaw jumped. "I know for a fact that the duchess has the deed in her possession."

Dare didn't ask how he knew. He sat back in his seat. "Very well. I'm sure you'll do as you see fit. How are the other Furys?"

For the first time that evening, the corner of Drake's lips lifted. "Causing mayhem as usual."

Dare nodded. Drake had seven half-brothers, six of them by-blows like him. They had started a family of their own, and they all lived in Brighton. They *ruled* Brighton to be more exact.

And they loathed the upper class.

It must be hell for Drake to approach him in London, his discomfort evident by the fact that he'd set himself up in the rookeries rather than a more favorable part of London, which he could very well afford.

"Well." Drake rose to his feet. "I'll be off. The perfume of this place is making my stomach churn."

Dare scowled. "It was your idea to come here."

"It was yours first. I merely went along with your previous

indulgences."

"Well, stop, or next time I'll challenge you to a fight."

Drake grinned at that. "Can you still throw a punch in your old age?"

Dare glared at the man. "I'm not that old."

"Fine, but for a man who doesn't like pain, you shouldn't toss out challenges."

Dare didn't deny it. He was made for love, not fighting. Pain wasn't really his thing. He certainly didn't like feeling it. Chaos seemed to be more his thing lately. Specifically, the chaos that was her.

And he was consumed.

Chapter Ten

LEONORA BLINKED AT the sight of the man standing before her. Normally, she would smile whenever she saw him. Today, she couldn't find the motivation. Also, the sight him in her drawing room . . . utterly disturbing!

And a touch thrilling.

It had been three days since she'd left her house. Three days since she attended any event. And five days since she'd last sunk beneath the river in the arms of this man. She hadn't set out to avoid him or any of the balls and musicales she'd been invited to, it was just that Harriet's talk of worthiness had bound her to her room in reflection.

Something Leonora had never done before.

She'd been reflecting on her position, on worthiness, and it was a topic not for the faint-hearted, since no matter how she looked at it, worthiness was something she came up short on every single time she considered it.

Harriet advised that she find a man worthy of her, but her friend didn't understand Leonora's position. If anyone should be weighed against that word—*bastard*—it should be her. Her friend might accept her if the truth became known. But would anyone else?

The truth . . . if she was right about her birth, she was a by-blow.

I, Leonora Heart, am a by-blow. There she'd admitted it.

She'd never done so before, even in her own mind. After she'd gained the knowledge as a child, she'd been careful not to allow that word into her head even as she'd decided that since *it* was the case, she would enjoy all the moments she could.

Well, *it* had a name now.

By-blow.

A word meaning the very opposite of worthiness.

She stared at the man before her, impeccably attired in the latest fashion. He'd chosen the color blue for his waistcoat this time, the same color as his eyes, and when he turned to meet her gaze, the smile that stretched his lips took her breath away.

Worthiness . . .

Even a rake, she couldn't match on that score. Rake, libertine, wastrel—they were just monikers assigned to the man based on his infamous reputation. At his core, he was still Rake Sloane, the Earl of Dare, born within the scope of worthiness along with wealth and privilege. No man or woman or king or queen could dispute this. The only way this man could ever become unworthy was if he did some dastardly deed and never atoned for his sins.

Unlike her.

Yes, Leonora was born into wealth and privilege as well. The only thing that really separated them was the circumstance of their births.

Such a small thing.

Such a big thing.

She glanced around the room. Was this a mistake? Had he accidentally wandered into her home? Ridiculous, Leonora! She could do nothing but ask, "What are you doing here, Dare?"

"Am I not allowed to call on you?"

"I . . . no . . ." She gave him a helpless look. "But you've never called on me before."

"I never missed your face before."

"Well, at least you are honest." She sank into the chair. "Is that the only reason, though? I suspect not many ladies enjoy the honor of being called upon by the infamous Lord Dare."

His brows gathered into a storm. "What's wrong?"

Could he tell? "Nothing."

He simply regarded her. "Then why the glum face?"

"Well, have you seen the papers?" There was no way she could have a conversation about worthiness with this man. It would reveal far too much. And she wouldn't need to when she had such an easy excuse for low spirits at hand.

"That is what your absence is about? Where is the woman who boldly attended a picnic after the avian debacle?"

"She was caught in an alligator scuffle."

He snorted. "Nonsense."

"Well, I'm feeling quite fragile at the moment."

He sent his hallmark brow lift. "Oh, come now, don't look so sad."

She averted her gaze with a small—very small—tilt of her lips. "You should stay away from me, Dare."

"Because of some headlines?"

"Because I shall reduce your infamous reputation to that of a spectacle. Every eye in London will be trained on us after this."

He took a seat next to her. "It seems a bit more than that is behind your absence. I know I might not look it, but I have been known to have an excellent ear. You can tell me anything. I'm also good at keeping secrets."

"Of that, I have no doubt."

That ever-present smile of his broadened, drawing another beat of her heart into disarray, and lifted the corners of her own lips just a bit. What was it about Dare that made Leonora want to prod and tease? Want to throw caution to the southwest wind?

"I have something that might make you feel better."

"Oh?" How intriguing.

He leaned closer, so close that Leonora was afraid that he might hear the skip of her heartbeat. "It's not something I can tell you."

"Then what?" Leonora didn't have to ask, but the question

left her lips anyway.

"I shall have to show you."

"Well, are you going to keep me in suspense? If it's something you have to ask permission for—" His lips cut her off mid-sentence.

Leonora froze as his mouth brushed over hers provocatively. She stared at him, blinking when his eyes opened to stare back.

"Close your eyes," he murmured against her.

"Should I?" Oh, Lord, her heart.

"That's how you kiss. With eyes closed."

Her lashes fluttered. "But then I can't see you."

"Do you want to see me or do you want to feel me?"

Feel. "See." Both.

His lips stretched into a grin, and Leonora's mouth followed as if feeling him smiling against her lips was the most contagious thing in the world.

"Fine, I'll close my eyes."

"And open your mouth."

She laughed, but complied, since a kiss with Dare . . . she hadn't realized how much she wanted it before this very moment.

When the kiss came, it wasn't anything that Leonora had ever expected. She felt every brush, every stroke of his tongue. She didn't know how to kiss a man back—she'd never been kissed. But Dare had been right about closing her eyes. And about opening her mouth. But if Dare was a good instructor, he was an even better kisser.

He effortlessly guided her into a foreign dance.

And she felt everything.

Not just the kiss, but every little hair that rose across her skin as well as the shiver that skittered down her spine and raced straight to the tips of her fingers and down to her toes.

There was nothing she could do but feel.

One arm snaked around her and brought her up close to his chest. This wasn't the first time she'd been *this* close to him. But it was the first time she *felt* close to him. The man's presence, usually calm and flirtatious, turned to an air of subtle command and enveloped her with a confidence many men seemed to lack.

So this was the true power of Dare's charm. Unleashed, it was quite terrifying.

His tongue retreated to trace the seam of her lower lip before he nipped it with his teeth.

He'd been right. Her mood had turned for the better. Well, perhaps hotter. Her whole body seemed flushed with heat.

"You can open your eyes now."

"Why?" she breathed. "Is it over?"

"It doesn't have to be if you don't want it to be, but we are still in your drawing room."

She raised her eyes to meet the hawkish gaze focused solely on her. The powerful, commanding presence had vanished again, and his place the flirtatious rake reigned supreme once more.

"Do you feel better?" he asked hoarsely.

"I cannot say." She aimed to tease, since any other answer might come out wholly inappropriate. Like *kiss me again*. A rake kissed a lady. This was certainly one of her top moments.

"But you're not sad anymore."

"I was never sad," Leonora murmured. "Just caught up in my own thoughts for a while."

"Moody, then."

"Call it what you will, I certainly don't feel the same as I did when I walked in on you standing all roguish in my drawing room." She eyed him askance. "Speaking of which, aren't you afraid Heart will have a fit of rage when he sees you?"

"He is at the House of Lords."

"Shouldn't you be as well?"

"Are you chasing me away?"

"Never." Merely still wondering what on earth had just happened and how she would ever recover from that kiss. And whether she even wanted to recover . . .

She wiggled her toes and pumped her fingers. She wanted to

experience that feeling again. Because she'd felt more than just the kiss and her body's reaction to the man. She'd felt *precious*.

Worthy.

But that wasn't entirely the truth, was it? She enjoyed Dare because he was confident in who he was as a man. He didn't shy away from the truth of his reputation. Dare was a rake. He had built an infamous reputation on his charm.

She fell back onto the sofa.

And Leonora knew better than to fall for the charms of a rake.

DARE ROSE TO his feet and held out his hand. "Let's go." He couldn't stay here any longer or he might kiss her again. And he really wanted to kiss her again. The curve of those soft lips—

"Let's go where?"

He forced his mind out of his trousers. "Anywhere other than this dreary drawing room."

"You don't like my drawing room?" She accepted his hand and rose.

"I don't care for drawing rooms in general." He also didn't kiss innocent ladies in said drawing rooms in general, which was probably why he felt so restless all of a sudden. He needed to move, but he also wanted to stay with Leonora a bit more. Which meant they needed to move together. "You know, you're the first woman I've ever called upon."

"I feel flattered."

"You should." He clasped his fingers with hers. "Are you in the mood for a bit of adventure?"

She grinned at him. "That depends on where we are going. If it's to a ball with a parrot or a lake with an oversized reptile, I shall pass."

"How about a boxing match?"

Her eyes widened, and she took an eager step forward. "Let's go."

Dare laughed "So enthusiastic." This was what he had missed the past three days. Missed it so much it had felt as though the sun had set on his daily life.

"I've never been to a boxing match before, so who am I to deny myself the opportunity when the moment presents itself?"

Dare nodded. "Then let's go."

He didn't think much as he led Leonora to his carriage and set out to Drake's fight. She'd whispered a few words to the butler, and they had set off. He hadn't intended to go but then decided for it. It was the only place he could think of to take her since she never wanted to do things ordinary ladies wanted to do. Perhaps this was what they both required.

The kiss . . .

That had been a mistake.

He'd known it the moment his lips brushed against hers. But Dare wasn't a gentleman. He could admit he'd made a mistake, but he wouldn't regret it. Regret held no place in his life. Regret ruined. Regret killed. And he might just die from all the fire such a tiny kiss had provoked, but he wouldn't regret it.

So long as it didn't happen again, and again, and again. He should be fine.

"Do you like boxing?" Leonora asked as she settled in the carriage across from him, immediately pulling pins from her hair.

His gaze spun to hers, brows gathering. "What are you doing?"

She looked at him. "What do you mean?"

"With your hair?" She was going to send his thoughts straight back to his trousers.

"Oh, well, I can't very well look like a lady attending a boxing match, can I?"

"I don't think it's something you can *not* look like, Lady Leonora," Dare said slowly, watching as she removed each pin until all her tendrils of hair cascaded down her shoulders and back.

He adjusted his cravat. Bloody hell.

Dare loved hair.

He loved long hair.

She pointed at his jacket, and he glanced down at the black he wore today, a question quirking his brow.

"Hand me your jacket."

His head reeled back. "What? You want this?" He tugged on it for good measure.

She wriggled a finger. "Yes. Your jacket. Hand it over."

Dare sighed, but didn't argue. He shrugged out of his jacket with a mutter, and it was snatched from his fingers before he could hand it over. "Are you planning to wear it or do something else with it?"

Her answer was to put her arms through the sleeves. "What?" She smiled. "You still have your shirt and waistcoat."

"Do you believe that will make you look less like a lady? And this is the second jacket of mine in your possession." Another out-of-character thing for him. He preferred his clothes to be attached to him when he left a woman.

"I believe dressing even the slightest bit down is better than arriving dressed as I was, yes. And I shall be sure to return both jackets."

He ignored the last. He quite liked the idea of his clothing being in her possession. "Shall you slouch as you walk as well?"

She rolled her eyes, a gesture that would normally have annoyed him had it been any other woman. However, she made it look rather endearing. Rather adorable.

Ah, confound it. There was something very wrong with him.

And no, it hadn't started with the kiss. That much ought to be noted—as well as this burning pulse in his chest. To begin with, it wasn't something that *started*. It was something that had developed with time. With every shared smile, every inappropriate flirtatious comment, every dance with stolen touches.

It should have surprised the hell out of him that she hadn't run for the hills, but this, this was his little bold temptress. Then again, it was also a wonder he hadn't succumbed to kissing her sooner. Only in as much that kissing was a line neither of them had ever crossed until today.

And Dare knew all about crossing the lines.

The first time was the most thrilling. Sometimes the hardest. Sometimes the most anxious. But once crossed, every single time after that it became a little easier and a little easier. Until there were no more lines to cross, and black and white blurred into shades of gray.

"What's with that look?" she suddenly asked. "Is it your turn to feel sour? It's just a jacket." She smoothed her hands over the black material. "It's pretty and feels nice." So long as she liked it. "I already feel tons better."

He smiled at that. "Well then, whenever you feel moody or sad, whichever, you can just think about my kiss."

"Are you saying I should think about you forever? Why Dare, what a scoundrel you are."

Forever? Wouldn't *that* feel pretty and nice? "Did I not do you a service today by cheering you up?"

"Then I should thank you for this service?"

No. "How about doing me a service? Something I can draw from whenever I feel restless. Then I shall forever think about you, too."

Intrigue lit her gaze. "And what would this service entail? Shall it be a kiss, too? One of a different kind, perhaps? Or shall a compliment do?"

A kiss of a different kind. Little Dare twitched. "Please don't compliment me." She arched a brow. What could he say? "I've heard them all before."

"Is that the arrogance or confidence of a rake?"

"A mere observation."

A light snort. "Red and blue feathers suit you."

Dare cocked his head. "Thank . . . you?" *Wait a minute . . .* "A bird joke? Truly? Is that even a compliment?" His eyes narrowed. "It sounds more like you're calling me a peacock."

"Peacocks don't have red feathers." She lowered her head until her nose touched his jacket and inhaled deeply. "You smell nice."

Lord, what was *that*? Had his jaded heart just stuttered?

He cleared his throat. "What else?"

"You want more?" She laughed and traced a finger over his jacket. Saucy temptress. "Your chest feels hard and nice."

Other parts of his body were becoming hard. Dare swallowed. How could such a simple compliment cause such a big reaction? If he weren't careful, he'd want to hunt down these compliments from her every day.

"Another."

She smiled, and that finger that was tracing his jacket lifted to trail over her lower lip. "Your kisses are nice, too."

Christ Almighty. "More."

She lifted her chin. "No."

Dare blinked, his whole body flaring in denial. "No?"

"Your turn. Compliment me."

He didn't hesitate. "Your compliments are dangerous."

"That's your compliment?" She stared at him, then laughed. "Yours are the worst." She suddenly lifted herself slightly and leaned close, bringing her face up to his.

Dare froze. In anticipation. In terror. In both.

"I shall give you one more." And then her soft lips collided with his cheek in a small peck. "Smooth."

Dare was dead.

Dead.

Dead and gone.

Any moment now he would slump on the seat and never wake up again. Would anyone be able to revive him after this?

No.

If anyone could, it would be her.

And only her.

God, I'm in trouble.

Chapter Eleven

THE WAREHOUSE WAS thick with swirling tendrils of gray smoke, hanging heavy like a dense fog that softened the harsh lines over the scene ahead. Leonora usually didn't mind the smell, or men enjoying a cheroot, but the fumes of burning tobacco and stale ale fused with the sounds of loud laughter, creating a rather stuffy atmosphere.

Yet the excitement was palpable. And intoxicating.

Thankfully, she'd adjusted her attire a bit. No lady would be found *here*. She still didn't quite fit in. It was evident in the quality of her clothes measured against her fellow female attendants' attire. She didn't want to stand out either.

Leonora observed in fascination as her fellow sex cheered and—saints preserve her!—*swore* just as loudly as the men in the room, sights and sounds she'd never experienced before.

"Stay close." Dare's shoulder brushed hers, and she caught the two heated pools of his eyes on her. "Close."

"Close," she mimicked. Her shoulder nudged him back. "Close."

He scoffed, but the corner of his lips inched upward.

Leonora's attention shifted to where their shoulders just touched and held back a retort, heart beating furiously. "I thought there would be more people."

"It's a private match." He paused. "More private than most."

Dare led her through the raucous crowd, keeping very close, protecting her against any jostling, eventually coming to a stop at the fringes of a circle formed around the boxers by the people gathered. In the center, one man was dancing from foot to foot while the other lazily stretched out his arms.

Leonora blinked. "I somehow pictured this all differently in my mind."

"This is not your normal match."

"So, I gathered." However, that was not what she meant. She somehow thought it would be more official. Though why she thought that, she couldn't say.

Suddenly, the man who'd been stretching out his muscles glanced their way. His gaze flicked over Dare before he looked straight at her, dark eyes burning into her. Leonora swallowed back a gasp.

Lord, oh Lord, oh Lord.

A deep scar ran down the length of his face. It gave the man an intimidating and rather menacing appearance. Did he get the scar from boxing? Surely not. Only a dagger or sword could inflict such damage. Which made him seem all the *more* intriguing.

Her lips stretched up in a grin.

She couldn't help it. He was looking at her as though he couldn't quite fathom her presence, so quite naturally the urge to tease, even provoke, bubbled to the surface.

"What are you doing?" Dare demanded from beside her.

"Mmm?" Leonora hummed without taking her eyes off the boxer.

"Stop grinning at him like that."

The man's eyes turned to Dare again before narrowing. Interesting. Her gaze tilted up to him as well. "Do you know him? He looked at me as if he knows who I am."

"If he knows who you are it's because he knows who I am, and I've spoken of you."

He did know the man? Wait—"You spoke about me to him?"

Dare nodded.

That set her heart into another furious flutter. He'd talked about her. To someone else. "Then are you friends?"

"You could say he is family."

You could say? "What sort of answer is that? Either he is family or he is not."

"He's my cousin, Drake Fury."

Her jaw went slack, before glancing back at the behemoth readying himself for a match. Dare had such a scary yet dangerously handsome cousin? Who would have known?

She tracked over that bold scar again. "You look nothing alike."

"Your mouth is hanging open." A big, gloved hand obscured her view. "I'm quite embarrassed for you."

"Whose mouth is hanging open?" She swatted his hand away. "I'm merely amazed you have such a handsome cousin."

"Handsome? There must be something wrong with your eyesight." A grumble. "He is not handsome."

She shot a glance back at the scarred man, who'd now turned his attention to his opponent. "Handsome."

The hand returned. "He doesn't like people looking at him."

Leonora turned to Dare with an I-can't-believe-you-just-said-that look. "Then he shouldn't be boxing in front of a crowd, should he?"

"He doesn't like pretty women staring at him."

She snatched his hand and yanked down. "Now you're just spouting nonsense."

He grinned at her, although his grin only lasted until both men discarded their shirts, putting their bare, hulking chests on full display.

Leonora's eyes widened in delight. *Such a treat!*

Beside her, Dare cursed.

The match started and Leonora had to admit, every punch—whether it missed or connected with flesh—brought a shock to her heartbeat. Cheers and cries filled the spacious room, and foul curses whipped through the air every time Dare's cousin effectively blocked his opponent. It seemed he wasn't the favorite today.

She clutched at her chest, watching in fascination as the two men sparred.

They danced on the balls of their feet with mesmerizing lightness, yet when an arm snaked out, the punches that landed were hard and heavy. Then the scarred man landed a blow to the other man's head, and he hit the ground almost instantly. Blood trickled down the side of his face.

Her hand flew to her mouth. This was . . . Just as quickly, the man leaped back to his feet and the match continued with a roar of cheers. She didn't know where to focus. The bloody punches, the dancing feet, the rippling muscles.

"No wonder these matches are frowned upon."

"Why is that?" Dare's breath tickled against her ear.

Her spine exploded with a sharp, electric jolt. "With one look you can tell these men are dangerous." The way they moved, it was like watching predators. Strengh combined with grace. The tension, the raw power, it could rob a lady of her breath!

Beside her, Dare shifted closer. "Not for you."

"For any woman, I'd imagine."

His eyes burned into her. Leonora pretended not to notice but she couldn't help the corner of her mouth inching upward. Was Dare jealous? It couldn't be. Yet she could practically taste the sourness exuding from the man.

"Jealousy doesn't become you, Lord Dare."

His stormy blue gaze burrowed deeper into her. "I'm not jealous."

Leonora shrugged. "Believe what you will."

"Believe what *you* will."

Was the man a child? Goodness. His petulance didn't feel all that bad, though. However, Leonora ignored his "what *you* will" and directed her focus and keeping her mouth in place when all it wanted to do was split into a huge grin. "Then I will believe it to be true."

Another grueling punch made her attention jerk back to the reality of the match where her gaze was immediately arrested again by the expanse of rippling muscles.

Just enjoy the sight.

There was something primal about two men, shirtless, fighting with bare knuckles, and blood dripping from their wounds. And there was probably something wrong with her for enjoying it this much!

Too soon, the match ended with the scarred man—Drake Fury—standing over his opponent. The winner.

"What a fight," Leonora murmured. So, so, *so* handsome.

A loud, exaggerated snort. "Hold this."

Leonora blinked and looked down at the cravat and waistcoat that had suddenly appeared in her hand. She blinked again before her gaze slowly turned to Dare. When had he removed these items? "What are you doing?"

"Boxing."

Her lips parted and shut. Well, this certainly was a different dance to a different tune!

And then he pulled his shirt over his head and tossed it into her arms and walked out into the arena.

Leonora's jaw dropped.

Her eyes raked over the muscles that rippled across his chest with each step.

Holy heaven.

She would never have imagined that such a body hid beneath his fine gentleman's clothes. Her imagination hadn't even come close to matching the sight! But she couldn't admire him for long. Her gaze caught on someone in the crowd just beyond him.

Her.

The Duchess of Crane.

DARE STRODE UP to his cousin, rolling his shoulders and flexing the muscles in his arms. Though his body wasn't as imposing as Drake's, he wasn't without his own strength. He could hold his own. Boxing was all about footwork, after all, and that was where he excelled. While his cousin had the raw power and brute force, he possessed a level of elegance in his stance that his cousin lacked.

He could match Drake step for step.

It was the question of why he thought to do so that he'd rather not dwell on. If he pulled on that thread, it might unravel his confidence stepping into this spontaneous fight.

"What are you doing?" Drake asked, sizing him up from head to toe.

Dare flashed him a smile. Good question. "A friendly sparring match."

"Stop standing about and fight!" Someone shouted from the crowd, the echo bouncing off the walls of the warehouse. A chorus of agreement followed.

"What's the matter, Drake," another man shouted. "Scared? Just knock him out already. One punch is all it'll take!"

Laughter erupted from all sides, followed by a few whistles. A voice in the back shouted, "Come on, show 'im, Drake!" another added, "Give 'im a good thrashing!"

His cousin grinned. "Does this look or sound friendly to you?"

Dare cracked his neck left to right. "It sounds like your arse is getting a whipping," he said tauntingly, dancing lightly from one foot to the other.

Laughter erupted, some men cheering so wildly it bordered on madness. A man from the back bellowed, "Bet you a guinea on Drake. I've seen him knock out men bigger than a mountain!"

Dare sneered. A mountain, heh? He continued to roll his shoulders, unbothered by the taunts, and certainly not dwelling overmuch on his own madness. He still couldn't think what had possessed him to enter the ring without even warming up his muscles properly—whereas Drake was on fire.

Or maybe he did know what sparked it, though he refused admit it to himself. He couldn't fault Leonora for ogling his cousin, but damn, he didn't like it. And he'd never lost to Drake yet. Nor had Drake lost to him, for that matter. They'd been equally matched in the past, and Dare was exceedingly good at avoiding his cousin's punches—and avoiding throwing any punches that would scar his hands. But he wasn't fond of pain, so they didn't spar much.

You've lost your mind, Dare.

No doubt, no doubt.

"Sounds like you're about to humiliate yourself in front of your little bird, cousin. Brazen of you to bring her to such a bloody event."

"Why? I'm here. It's just a spot of fun," Dare responded lightly. And Lady Leonora was anything but a fragile flower. In fact, she might be the exact opposite of one.

Drake's eyes gleamed with something almost too sharp. "You know it's more than that."

"Not willing to spar with me?" Dare challenged, choosing to ignore the meaning beneath that suggestive statement.

Drake rolled back and forth on the balls of his feet, taking his stance. "This is extremely unlike you, cousin, but I can't say I hate it."

"It's extremely unlike you to care, anyway."

"You're right. I don't care." A foxlike smile formed on his face. "Much."

Dare chuckled. "I'm astonished by the warmth of your heart."

"As am I by yours." His eyes flicked beyond him and back. "Exceedingly so." Drake's smile turned even more crooked, tapping his knuckles together. "I've looked into the connection like you asked."

Dare faltered, stopping himself from glancing at Leonora—though he could feel her gaze on them. "I don't think now is the time to discuss such matters."

A smirk. "Not curious?"

"Not enough, you arse." Was he curious? Yes. Could he do without the information, especially just now? Also yes. But when it came to that little temptress, he couldn't help himself most of the time. Very well, all of the time. He was like a bookworm starved for knowledge—always wanting more.

Drake motioned for him to come at him. "So fickle."

"One of the benefits of breeding."

Drake rolled his eyes. "Are we sparring or not?"

Bloody hell, yes.

They circled each other until the crowd grew impatient with their dancing. The spectators wanted blood. But Drake wasn't the sort of boxer who wasted a punch, and Dare was vigilant when it came to his cousin's fists. This was probably why they were always equally matched and rarely ever challenged each other, even to a friendly match. Every movement was calculated, every step precise, every muscle in Dare's body tense and ready to defend against his opponent.

The air crackled with anticipation.

"The devoted followers are growing restless," Dare taunted.

"They are not my problem," Drake shot back. But he didn't disappoint. In a blur of movement, a fist flew out with lightning speed.

Dare dodged but not fast enough. Just half a second too slow. Pain exploded at the side of his head. Another half second later, before he could recover, his arse hit the floor. A curse flew off his tongue at the same time as the impact.

A deafening roar of cheers filled the warehouse.

Damn it. That hurt like the devil.

More curses sprang into his mind. One damn second. One damn second was all it took the destroy the fantasy that he and Drake were always equally matched.

Drake smirked. "Are you getting up or are we done with our little sparring match?"

Only to be knocked down again? No, thank you. Once was

humiliating enough. "You could have at least saved me some damn face."

"Not in my nature, cousin. Do you need help up or do you plan to marry the floor?"

Dare leaped to his feet and dusted off his hands.

Hell and damnation. He must look like a fool to Leonora. A flush of heat rushed to his cheeks, the blaze bleeding into his neckline. He'd never felt this embarrassed in front of a woman a woman he liked.

Because you've never liked a . . . The thought trailed off into a devastating, deep chasm that formed in his mind. Dear God. Did he like Lady Leonora Heart?

That could not be.

Oh, he fancied flirting with the little temptress. Laughing with her. Being in her company. But that . . .

That didn't . . .

An even fouler curse rolled off his tongue. He liked Lady Leonora Heart. But what exactly did that mean? Like. Such an innocuous little word, one easy tossed about by fools and fops. But for him? It was a dangerous thing to feel.

He wanted to look over at her, but he also didn't dare. Would she be laughing at his misfortune? Would she be shocked? Would she have even the tiniest smidgeon of pity for him?

You are a mess, Dare.

"Don't worry," Drake said. "I did you a favor."

How the hell was that a favor? "What are you talking about?"

"Your little bird didn't see your fall, and I figured it would be a good time to end the match for you."

Dare sneered at him. Bloody arrogant ars—

"Her eyes weren't on you," Drake explained, interrupting the curse in his head.

Dare scowled. Her eyes weren't on him? Then where were they? On Drake? The thought brought a deeper furrow between his brows.

"They also weren't on me, either, if that is what you are

thinking."

"Then explain, why don't you?" The fact that the man could see right through him annoyed the hell out of Dare.

His cousin shrugged and nodded to a spot beyond him. "Your little bird is leaving."

Dare's head finally snapped to where Leonora had been standing, only to find her gone from the spot.

Lady Leonora Heart!

He had brought her here. She was under *his* protection. Where the devil had she gone? Would she truly leave? His gaze moved in the direction his cousin had nodded, toward the doors of the warehouse, and he caught the back of her long hair flowing down his jacket just as she slipped through.

Dare snatched up an unattended shirt and took off at a run.

Chapter Twelve

LEONORA'S HEART LODGED in her throat as she followed the duchess from a distance, hoping she was being stealthy enough. Only, she didn't feel stealthy at all. Oh, no. It felt as if a magnifying glass were trained on her every movement. At any moment, she half-expected the duchess to turn and wink in her direction as if to say, *"Oh, yes, I see you there, darling. Sleuthing is not in your blood."*

She pushed those thoughts away, forcing herself to focus.

Had the duchess seen her at the fight?

She didn't think so. The woman had been staring at the match before she'd turned on her heel and made for the exit. Leonora hadn't paused to think—she'd simply followed. Too many questions whirred in her head. What was the duchess doing here? Alone? What could her motives possibly be? Had she come with someone like Leonora had? And was she truly who Leonora suspected her of being?

She wanted answers.

Needed answers.

Too many threads fluttering loosely in the wind—the secret meeting in the park, the duchess calling on Dare, her offer at the lake. Leonora squared her shoulders with determination. She might feel like a criminal creeping along the street, but she would follow the duchess, and hopefully, today would bring some of the answers she sought.

Leonora's footsteps quickened as she padded after her. She was just about to turn into a street the duchess had already disappeared down, her gaze fixed ahead, and—*crash!*—she collided with something—some*one*—solid.

Lord!

The sudden impact jolted her a step backward, and she gasped, trying to regain her balance as the world seemed to spin for a moment. Firm hands gripped her arms as she wobbled, steadying her.

Oh, dear. This is what happens when you creep about!

She took a step back, lifting her head to apologize, ready to offer thanks for the man's quick intervention, when her eyes locked with his. A cold chill ran down her spine, and for a breathless moment, time seemed to stretch, her heart nearly stopping in her chest.

No.

This was in no way a good moment. What were the horrifying chances? What were the impossible odds of such an encounter?

Heart?

I was careless.

"Careless?" His eyes darkened as his face twisted into fury.

Had she spoken out loud?

"You are right about being careless, Leonora," he growled. "In fact, careless doesn't even begin to describe it! Reckless is more like it!"

Her brain went blank. "What are you doing here? Were you at the fight, too?"

"You are asking *me* that? What the devil are *you* doing here?" He swept the area with a cold look. "Why are dressed like that? Are you here with someone? Whose jacket is that? *Wait*—what fight?"

Leonora struggled to keep up with his flurry of questions, but the last one hit her like a blow. Drat. Why had she asked him that? She'd outed herself without meaning to! And she had no good reason for being here.

"Heart?" A voice came from beyond her brother. His back shot straight, his eyes opening wide.

The duchess.

Leonora instinctively took two steps back while Heart stood at the corner of the two streets, blocking the view between her and the woman. Had the duchess passed her brother and retraced her steps? For now, at least, Leonora was hidden, obscured partly by Heart and partly by the building, keeping her out of the duchess's line of sight.

"Heart? That is you, isn't it?" the duchess pressed. "Are you just going to ignore me? I thought someone was following me, but I never expected to be you."

Leonora stared at Heart.

So many emotions flashed across his face, emotions Leonora had never glimpsed on him before while he kept eye contact with her. The Duchess of Crane meant something to him. Or at least, she had meant something to him at one time in the past. That much was as clear as the sky above them.

He turned to the woman in question.

Leonora stared silently at Heart's side profile, her mind still rather blank. She didn't know how many seconds passed when a hand clamped around her wrist, yanking her back. She stumbled a few steps, and before she could process what was happening, a hand covered her mouth, muffling any protest. Blast it! She was pulled into the shadows of a nearby wagon—one she hadn't even noticed until this very moment—her body pressed against the rough wood.

Leonora blinked as her eyes came level with a half-buttoned shirt, revealing a strong set of chest muscles.

Dare.

Wasn't he fighting?

However, a great sense of relief washed over her. "What are you doing here?" Leonora asked in a hushed voice.

"Chasing after you. Why did you leave like that?"

Her eyes widened as she remembered her purpose. "Oh, that. I'm sorry. The duchess was at the fight, but she left, so I followed her."

"The duchess was at the fight?" He turned thoughtful. "I suppose that makes sense. It's about the only thing that could make you tear your eyes away from me."

Leonora punched him in the arm but couldn't help a hushed laugh of exasperation from following. "How can you jest about such things? My brother caught us."

"He caught you, not me."

A minor detail. "He saw your jacket."

"But he cannot know for sure that it's mine."

"Oh, he knows," Leonora said, somewhat flustered. She wiggled from his embrace and peered around the wagon. "I want to listen."

"Very well but don't lean over so far," he advised, his hands lingering on her arms once more. Had he always touched her like this? Small, seemingly innocent gestures. Or was it that she was only becoming aware of them now?

She glanced back at his face, his exposed chest, and averted her gaze again. Her pulse stirred. Noticing was dangerous. Noticing made her want to notice more.

"What is happening over there?" he asked, hunching beside her but not peeking like she was.

You are happening.

Whatever that even meant. Lord, the man was so . . . so . . . *distracting.* It seemed almost unfathomable that they had now found themselves in this position. This situation, that Leonora herself couldn't clearly define.

She placed a finger on her lips and strained to listen. They had missed the first part of the conversation, but not, it seemed, anything of real significance.

Heart's voice, unmistakable in its exasperation, rang out. "Devil take it, *Your Grace,* how many times must I tell you I'm not following you? Shall I scale the walls of this building and shout it from the deuced rooftop so that all of London might hear? Will you believe me then?"

Leonora arched a brow.

"Forgive me if I find your word hard to trust," the duchess said.

"Believe what you will. You always do."

"Well." A new voice entered the conversation. "This is an unexpected surprise. I thought I saw you at the fight, Duchess."

Leonora recognized that voice, didn't she? Hadn't she just heard it casting taunts at opponents? She glanced at Dare, raising a brow. *Your cousin?*

Those dark-blue eyes settled back on her and nodded. Then he flashed her a roguish grin. Infuriating man. Why was he smiling at her like that? Was he flirting? At a moment like this?

He's always smiling, Leonora.

True. But tell that to the pulse in her wrist!

"Who the hell are you?" Heart demanded. "What is this damn fight?"

"He is my son," the duchess voice came, "and a participant in a private boxing match nearby. I was curious."

Son?

Leonora's breath caught in her throat. A wealth of implications were hinted at in that one word, but she couldn't begin to decipher the true meanings. She shot a look at Dare over her shoulder. If Drake was the duchess's son and Dare was his cousin . . . Did that make them all family? Had she been flirting with her own family? Surely not. Dare and she . . . Her brain refused to process the information.

Even Heart was silent at that, apparently unable to think of a response.

The grip on her wrist tightened, and only then did she realize she'd tried to snatch her hand free from Dare's grasp.

Calm down, Leonora. Dare didn't know her secret, so he wouldn't imagine anything wrong.

"Since when have I been your son?" Drake snapped, drawing Leonora's attention back to the conversation. "We share no blood."

Leonora let out a sigh of relief, not listening anymore. Suddenly nothing else mattered except she hadn't been teasing—*kissing*—family! However, her curiosity sparked again. Even at that, she knew her luck was running out.

We should leave. And soon—before the three dispersed and Heart set his nose back on her trail. She'd rather face him back home than here, so she sank back, surveying their surroundings for a route of escape. As it was, her heart already threatened to burst through her chest. She could only imagine what it would do if they were discovered together, huddling behind a wagon.

Dare caught on. "The alley . . ." he whispered close, sensing her desire to flee the scene while they were still able.

DARE BROUGHT THEM to a halt only when they arrived back in the vicinity of the warehouse. They hadn't wandered off too far, and his carriage should be just around the bend. Dare turned to Leonora. Her breathing was ragged, akin to that of a woman who had just run ten miles without pause, and she bent over, clutching her belly. The day had certainly taken an unexpected turn—more than one, truth be told.

"Leonora . . ." He hesitated. "Are you all right?"

She held up her hand. "Give me a moment."

Her complexion had paled slightly, and the smile that usually played at the corner of her lips—or the very least, sparkled in her bright eyes—had vanished. It was as though the farther they retreated from the wagon, the more her spirits waned. Had she heard something troubling? He hadn't been listening closely, only observing her. And the streets. Guarding.

"Yes, why wouldn't I be?" she answered quickly. Too quickly.

Dare narrowed his eyes on her. He didn't believe her, but he also couldn't drag her troubles from her lips. If she didn't want to confide in him, he couldn't force her. But he could be a rock she might lean on.

He caught a silky tendril of her hair between his fingers. "Perhaps because you look as though a ghost has chased you to death's door and back."

"Don't say silly things."

"You think I'm being silly?" *Should I retrieve a mirror for you?* He'd known enough women in his life to leave the last part unsaid, but he wanted to see the teasing glint return to her eyes.

"Aren't you?" She drew in a deep breath. "I'll be fine in a moment."

He glanced around. There wasn't even water to offer her.

She straightened and attempted a smile. "There. See? I'm all better."

He didn't believe her for a second. Something had unsettled her. Had she feared being caught with him? Granted, it was a frightening prospect, but it also didn't ring true.

"Leonora, the duchess and your brother . . ." His voice trailed off as those blue eyes fixed on him. A flicker of something— something that put her on instant alert—flashed in their depths.

"What about them?" She sent him a pointed look. "Also, shouldn't you first tell me about this cousin of yours? The duchess called him her son, but they don't seem to be blood."

Ah, yes. He'd heard the comment but hadn't thought much about it. Had Leonora thought it true? He supposed she might have. "Drake isn't her son. He's a by-blow of the late duke. She must have been indulging in a bit of sarcasm."

"I see. So, your cousin is illegitimate, then."

Dare heard the note of relief, which further spurred the niggle growing inside him. His brows drew together as Heart's face popped into his head like a sore tooth. He'd glimpsed the man's profile before they'd dashed into the alley. Some feeling about the look on his face, even just from the side, niggled at Dare.

What was going on?

Who was the duchess to the Heart family?

"He is, yes. He has also never been recognized by his father. Not even as he lay dying." It probably wouldn't have mattered even if the duke had recognized any of his sons. The man possessed a cruel nature. His cousin and his brothers were better off this way.

"I'm sorry to hear that," Leonora said softly.

"Shocked?" Dare asked with a faint smile. "Does it bother you? His mother is my mother's sister. She fell from grace after her affair with the duke became public."

"Only slightly shocked. And completely unbothered. Your cousin is fortunate to have you as family."

Her earlier question resurfaced, prompting him to ask, "Would it have mattered if he were her real son?"

"Of course it would." Her eyes widened before she said hastily, "I mean, of course, it would not have. Why would it have mattered?"

Why indeed.

But Dare didn't want to add to her troubles. He wanted to add to her smiles, her brightness, so he simply said, "You do not have to tell me if you don't want to."

"It's not that, it's just—" She paused, drawing in another deep breath. "It's almost impossible to say."

"Then don't say it." He wanted to know, was so damn curious the words nearly stuck in his throat, but he didn't need to know. The latter was better in any case. Knowledge led to entanglements.

Those were never good.

He ignored the voice laughing inside his head, mocking his attempts to stay free from entanglements.

But what could be so devastatingly hard to speak aloud? What family secret could be so impossible to voice? Given Heart's history, and that that it involved the duchess, as well as Leonora's mother and her question about Drake . . .

Dare's gaze fell on Leonora's pinched lips. Her eyes were cast downward, her heart-shaped face so much like. . .

Almighty heaven.

Could it be?

Was *this* the secret?

The duchess had left London twenty odd years ago and never returned until now. Apparently always wearing black. Mourning . . . who exactly? And then there was Leonora's curiosity about the woman.

Did the duchess have a daughter?

Leonora?

Christ in Heaven. Her visit to him took on a whole new meaning, and he suddenly wished he could pluck the forming bud of suspicion from his mind. Leonora's family secrets had nothing to do with him. He didn't want to know them. He didn't want to know any secrets, for that matter. He just wanted to live his life without it intertwining with anyone else's in away way that it could never again *untwine*.

As if sensing his regard, she suddenly looked over, and their gazes locked. Usually, a smile or a question mark would enter at this point, but they remained cautious.

Assessing.

An odd sense of pain swelled inside him. He'd always felt Lady Leonora to be like the sun in the sky—beautiful, bright, and wholly out of reach. Too warm for a man like him to touch. He could only ever bask in the scant she rays allowed. To him, she was as unattainable as that fiery globe, offering a measure of light to men like him prone to walk in darkness.

Without her light . . .

He would stand in nothing but shadow. Who would have thought the sun had such a heavy burden to carry? A burden Dare wished to hell he could bear for her. A burden that could at any time cause this sun to lose its glow.

This secret she carried—he knew at once she carried it alone. Not because no one else in the family was privy, but because they wouldn't have included her in the secret. If his suspicions were correct, he could understand why. But this clever temptress had discovered the truth anyway, and it had taken on a new form of burden. It was one he could never carry for her, but he longed to take it on if it meant she would smile again. Even just once.

No, he couldn't carry her burden, but perhaps he could lighten its weight.

Entanglements, Dare. You'll never be able to take this back.

Then so be it. For the only thing he wanted back this instant was her spark of light, the slight corner of her lips tilting up. Even the slightest measure of warmth would do. He would take any stray ray at this point. Not for him, but for her.

"The duchess," he paused when her gaze returned to him, but only for a moment. "You have an uncanny resemblance."

Her brows furrowed. "I . . . we do?"

"Yes," Dare said. "The shape of your jaw is similar." Though she had the same eyes as Heart, which had made the family's ruse so believable all these years.

"Oh?" She looked uncomfortable. "I hadn't noticed."

Little liar. Little burden-keeper. This was indeed a secret that could shock the proverbial trousers off London. But most importantly, most frighteningly, it was a secret that could render her instantly and forever ruined. Was this why she was so bold in seizing moments? So brazen and fearless in her approach to life, in her flirtations with him?

It made sense.

"She is your mother."

Chapter Thirteen

*S*HE IS YOUR *mother.*

No.

She is your mother.

No.

She is your mother.

I don't know.

Leonora thought she might be sick. All her life, or at least, since the age of fourteen, she'd known her life could change instantly if someone ever discovered those four words. Not the words themselves, exactly, but what they implied.

But no secret was eternal in this world. The time she'd had up to now, she'd hidden the truth behind layers upon layers of moments that no one could ever take from her.

What happened now?

There was never a time when Leonora believed she could hide it forever. Her family couldn't hide it forever. They already hadn't. She had learned the secret, after all.

That was how precarious a position a secret held. One person knowing could topple the whole thing.

You are illegitimate.

She'd understood all these years that she was an imposter. She didn't belong with the title she had. But she hadn't allowed it to bother her. She'd decided, no matter who she was or who she was not, she would live her life to the fullest while fully knowing at any moment any and all privilege could be taken away from her in a matter of a heartbeat.

That heartbeat had arrived with Dare's words.

She stared at him. A droplet of rain fell on her cheek. The coolness of it startled her, but the sudden downpour of emotions was what made her shiver. She turned on her heel and strode in the direction of Mayfair. Her mind had drawn another blank. She wouldn't deny it, even though she didn't know the full truth of the matter yet. Whether the duchess was her real mother or not, she was still illegitimate.

And that *was* the truth.

"Leonora. Where are you going?"

"Home."

"Are you going to walk there alone? The skies have turned. There will be a downpour soon."

Drat it. Soon? It had already started. One drop turned to two turned to three turned to a soft pelting of rain. She wanted to run, wanted to seek shelter, but that would mean stopping. And waiting.

"Leonora, wait." Footsteps followed her down the street.

"No." She wanted to escape. To escape him most especially. She'd flirted with him boldly. Unashamedly. She'd loved it. But that was before he knew the truth.

Now. . .

Leonora had never realized how inferior she would feel once the truth became known. Known to *him*. Whether he would keep her secret or not didn't even enter her mind. The idea that he might look at her differently—that alone was enough to cause a throb in her breast.

Was she still the same person to him?

A hand clamped around her wrist and pulled her to a stop. "Leonora, do you think I care about such matters?"

She whirled on him. "Why wouldn't you? Or do you not understand what the weight of what your words imply?"

"I understand." His eyes burned into hers as though they wanted to impart a weight of their own. "But I don't care."

Impossible. "Why not?"

A gush of impatience blew from him. "I. Don't. Care. You can just deny my words, you know. Tell me I'm wrong."

No. "Why would I do that?"

He stepped up close to her, his gaze burning even hotter. "For your peace of mind."

Her peace of mind? If he knew in what blank state of chaos her mind spun at the moment, he wouldn't say such a thing. Acceptance, perhaps, but never peace. True peace. "This secret has never brought me that."

"Peace, mayhem, you don't have to hide it from me." The sincerity in his eyes, his voice, wouldn't be denied. "So she is your mother? The duchess. That is why you are so interested in her."

Leonora averted her gaze. "I don't know."

He planted his face before hers, drawing her eyes to him. "But you suspect, don't you?"

She gave a reluctant nod.

"Then Heart . . ."

Leonora suddenly laughed. Ah, yes. Heart. Her father. "Can you even say it out loud?"

A low chuckle followed the wake of her words. "I can't."

He stepped closer and pulled her into his arms. Leonora's brows furrowed as her cheek rested on a hard, partially wet shirt. Around them, rain pattered, but she didn't care. Her arms circled his waist. Time felt momentarily paused even though everything around them was still moving. The rain. The world. The beat of her heart.

A moment later her chin was lifted and soft lips claimed hers. Arms banded around her like steel as his tongue swept into her mouth, clasping her against his chest. Her body stirred at the contact, a comforting heat blooming within as the chill that had gripped her before began to fade.

The picture of his rippling muscle as he walked into the ring blasted any other thoughts from her mind, reminding her to live. Now. In this moment.

This was all she had.

And that drove her to spear her fingers through the silky strands of his wet hair, leaning into him more. Demanding *more*.

Dare didn't disappoint.

The kiss took on a new depth as he gave his interpretation of *more*. Leonora had always loved flirting with rakes, and she loved flirting with Dare the most, but she had never kissed any of the other men she'd flirted with. So it would be too presumptuous to say that he was the best of the best when it came to kissing.

However, she'd wager that he was.

Her entire being was covered with gooseflesh. And she was free. Free from the hidden title she carried, her history, her birth. She was simply herself with him. And that was enough. All ill thoughts disappeared. He had brought back her perspective of her situation that she'd almost forgotten. Her family, at least the ones in her life, had no ill intent. What they'd done, they'd done for her. It didn't matter whether her place in society was fragile. What mattered was the people who stood by her side no matter what.

And in this moment with Dare, she felt something was different. A foundation beneath her feet. Not something brittle, but something that might hold up in the face of a storm. Perhaps she didn't have to carve out a more permanent place for herself, something unshakable. Perhaps she'd had it all along.

She didn't need to find a rock to lean on. She could just be the rock.

She also realized she liked this kiss.

A lot.

He drew unhurriedly away from her mouth, releasing her lips to look at her. A finger traced down her cheek. She blinked through the drops of rain.

"That's better."

Her brows furrowed. "What's better?"

"The look on your face right now."

Leonora didn't even want to imagine how flushed her face was or what look had entered her eyes. All she knew was a soft warmth had spread through her entire body.

"How can you say such a thing to a woman you just kissed?"

"Quite easily, I assure you." He grinned down at her. "If it's you."

If it's you.

"Even knowing what you now know about me?"

"What is it that I know about you? That the circumstances of your birth are different from mine? Lord knows, half the *ton* are illegitimate if you ask me. That doesn't define your character unless you allow it."

"Fine words, Dare."

"You sound surprised," he said with another little smile.

She returned his grin. "I always am when it comes to you."

He chuckled, glancing up at the pouring sky. "Shall we find shelter, or do you wish to become as bedraggled as you were that day in the lake?"

Honestly, at this point, she didn't care. She scarcely felt the rain or the chill. But they couldn't stand here all day. "Let's find shelter."

Dare snatched her hand and pulled her under the overhang of a low sagging roof of an old, forgotten building. She could scarcely believe that he had come to terms with her secret so quickly. So smoothly.

Did he truly not think differently of her?

Was it because he was a rake?

She eyed him skeptically. "You're not going to tell anyone about my secret?"

His affronted gaze snapped to hers. It was the first time she had seen such a look appear on his face. It was almost funny. "I would never do such a thing."

She nodded. "Good."

He leaned in close. "I never kiss and tell."

HOW MANY TIMES could a heart beat in a minute? Dare had never felt anything as fast as the racing of his heart in that moment as he stared into her eyes, lips hovering over hers. He started counting each beat while his body calmed down. *He* calmed down.

Ah, entanglements.

"I don't kiss and tell, either."

Christ, no words a rake ever wants to hear.

Dare straightened and dragged a hand through his hair, the same path she'd used, his scalp still alive with prickles. The drizzling rain created a cloak of privacy around them, setting them in a world of two. A world of their own. A dangerous world, one where he could feel her presence as clear as the sun in the summer sky.

But he had no business lingering in it.

His eyes tracked the streets, everywhere but her, his brain racing.

Escort her back.

Get a grip on his wits.

Continue on.

But it was in that *continue on* that his befuddlement lay. Continue on *how*? Flirting? As they had been? Dare had never kissed a woman and continued on. He got the urge to kiss a woman, to seduce a woman, he succeeded, and he never looked back. He didn't do entanglements.

Leonora was an entanglement.

A big, bright one.

She was such an entanglement she might as well sprout tentacles and latch on to him. He could *feel* those invisible tentacles lacing around his limbs.

They threatened to choke him to death.

He let out a low chuckle, but it came out rougher than he intended. "Good, then we kiss and never, ever tell."

She stared at him, bemused.

Dare cursed. That didn't sound right either.

Fortunately, she nodded and said, "Heart must be looking for me."

He stole a glance before looking away. Color once again infused her cheeks, and the sparkle that had left her eyes had once again returned. A relief.

Her situation . . .

He still couldn't fathom how she could call Heart her brother in such a manner with a straight face knowing the truth. It might have reduced a lesser woman to a puddle of tears and hysteria. Not Leonora.

How admirable.

Ah, hell. Another tentacle.

She was dangerous to him in a way no other woman had ever been. Which, in hindsight, didn't come as any surprise. The surprise was the depth of danger. That, he had never fully grasped.

Dare cleared his throat. "He should suspect that *you* suspect the truth by now, should he not?"

A small sigh. "I'm not sure. He can be quite dense at times. Though I have no doubt he will interrogate me once I return home."

Of course he would. The man seemed to act first, his head trailing behind. Leonora certainly didn't inherit her intelligence from him. "Interrogate him back."

She tipped her chin, her gaze meeting his. "Interrogate him back?"

"Why not? He caught you red-handed in a place you're not ought to be with a person you're not to be with. You did the same." Dare impressed even himself with his reasoning. And Leonora could best Heart in any argument, he was sure.

Her eyes lit up. "That is true." Her lips pursed. "It's about time I questioned Heart over his actions and got to the bottom of some of the truth."

"Only some?"

"Whatever his reasons, I know he didn't want me to get hurt."

Dare had to agree. That man was protective and yet at the same time appeared to be at a loss. He couldn't say he would have done anything differently had he been in his exact position. If an infant were dropped at his door? He shuddered. No, he couldn't even imagine such a thing or what he would have done.

Do not *get involved.*

That he needed constant reminders spoke volumes. There was also the matter of Drake and situation with the duchess. His cousin wouldn't say anything about what had happened between the two of them, but he couldn't imagine that Lady Leonora would be embroiled in their affairs. Neither had anything to do with Dare, and he was glad he hadn't made a decision to help Drake.

You are on your own, cousin.

He dragged hand through his hair again. He wouldn't pry, no matter his curiosity. But they did need to get home and out of this rain before the wind picked up.

He took her arm. "Shall we make a dash for it? The carriage should be around the bend ahead of us."

She nodded. "Let's go."

"Wait." He tucked a wet, matted strand of hair behind her ear. "Do you want to cover your head with my jacket?" His gaze dropped to his jacket that she still wore. That still clung to her body. Not like second skin, but like his skin.

All this, Christ, and Heaven. *Where are your thoughts going, man?*

Not in any good damn direction.

"No need." She patted her head. "My hair is already wet, and I don't mind it. It's rather refreshing."

Dare didn't question her. He nodded. "Very well, let's go."

He took her hand and they dashed through the rain to the carriage, each step feeling more like they were running through mud. The shallow puddles of water were quickly being replaced with rivers running down the narrow street.

"Heavens! Where did all this rain suddenly come from?"

"The sky."

She shot him a filthy look, and Dare laughed, the tentacles that seemed to squeeze around his neck loosening.

Yes, that was right. He was Dare and she was Leonora. There was comfort in that, comfort in who they were: an heiress who had no intention of reforming a rake and a rake who could never be reformed.

The tentacles disappeared.

However, he could be imagining this, but something lingered in their stead. A shadow of their presence. A whisper of something unexplainable, curling at the edges of his senses. A slither of a touch that should not exist. Because the air had shifted. The silence had a pulse. And whatever had been there . . . was not entirely gone.

He cursed.

It would vanish eventually.

They had just reached the carriage when a shout echoed off the buildings lining the street. Leonora skidded to a halt and glanced over her shoulder.

"Heart?" he asked.

She nodded. "Sounds like him."

"A furious him." Dare yanked open the carriage door, nodding at the driver. "Let's go before we are beheaded today."

A light, amused chuckle. "How dramatic, even for you."

Dare began to follow her into the carriage, but a chill skittered down his spine. Nothing good would happen if Heart caught them together. His foot halted midrise before he lowered it back to the ground.

Her eyes cut to him. "What are you doing?"

Dare nodded at the driver. "Take her home."

"Dare? Aren't you coming?"

He shook his head. "I can't."

"Heart . . ."

"Don't worry. I still have something to discuss with my cousin, and it's best for you if your brother doesn't catch us together. You have enough to worry about as it is."

"What about you?"

Him? What about him? He had things he worried about as well. All of which had to do with what had happened here, and none of which he wanted to dwell on, which left him in a hell of a predicament.

"What if I want you to come?" she said. "What if I want to escort *you* home to today?"

"No need."

They stared at each other. Another face overlapped with Leonora's, an older face. His mother's bright and smiling eyes had once glistened like hers. But it hadn't lasted. It never lasted.

He was his father's son.

Never forget that.

Dare quirked his lips into a smile that felt all too familiar, all too natural. A mask he'd trained his face to bear well. "I'll be fine." He shut the door and took a step back.

And he would be fine.

After all, he always had been.

Chapter Fourteen

LEONORA'S DAZE HAD yet to leave her as she fell back on the bed still soaked from head to toe.

The truth was out. For Dare, anyway.

And if she'd learned anything in her life, it was that the moment the stem of a flower was cut, it could never be reattached. Courtesy of her adventures in the garden as a child, she was also well aware that neither would the stem ever grow back. When it was cut, it was cut. All you could do was display the flower until it inevitably wilted.

Lord, she was growing morbid.

But how should she feel about Dare finding out? She didn't know. Perhaps there was no right way to feel.

And what about that kiss? And that look on his face before he closed the carriage door?

"Arg!" She covered her face with her hands. "What am I going to do?"

What could she do? Nothing, that's what! The thing to do would have been to deny his guess, for it had been a guess.

"Why didn't I do that?" Why, why, why?

You know why.

The thought lodged itself in her mind, even as the next crept in: *Do I really?*

The truth of the matter was, she didn't want to carry this

secret alone anymore. Her family knew, but she wasn't supposed to, leaving her isolated in her own knowledge. She could confess what she knew to Heart, but she didn't have the heart. Ironic, that.

Dare putting the pieces together may have taken the burden of solitary knowledge from her shoulders, but it only added another. Another she hadn't fully thought through.

Himself.

In the distance, a door slammed, and she sighed.

Here we go.

She didn't have to wait long before heavy strides thundered down the hallway, followed by her door slamming open. *Poor door* was all she managed to conjure by way of thought as her gaze fell on Heart. The oak seemed to take a beating in her place.

"Well, I am glad to see you home," the raging beast said in a tone dripping with resentment.

"Where else would I be?"

"Stow the sarcasm, Leonora. You know exactly what you have done today."

She should hope so, or she might be better suited for Bedlam. She considered sitting up to face her brother fully but couldn't muster the strength. "Is it better or worse than what you have done?"

"What the devil do you mean by that?"

Leonora sighed, her gaze drifting over the bird-like patterns of the wallpaper before moving to the pretty pattern of the wooden moldings across the ceiling. "If you don't know, then I suppose you've done nothing."

Nothing.

That little vexing word again. Nothing was the problem. Nothing ever changed. Same tune, same lyrics, same dance. Over and over.

Heart cursed. "I warned you away from that man, Leonora. I'm not bloody jesting here. He is not the sort of man befitting for you."

She turned her gaze to him again. "And what sort of man is he?"

"A rake. A libertine. A wastrel."

Like you? The question hovered on the tip of her tongue, but it couldn't pass her lips. It could never pass. No question about his past ever could. Or about her own past. Or about anything to do with this family secret they had all tried so hard to keep from her yet, in the end, failed to do so.

It wasn't their fault. If she hadn't been a curious child, she might never have discovered the truth.

"Are you not listening to me?" Heart demanded, repeating. "A rake. A libertine. A wastrel."

Maddening man. "I'm listening, Heart. I heard you the first time."

"Then why aren't you saying anything? You are never to see him again, do you understand? Don't push me on this. Not anymore."

"I understand your concern, Heart, but you shall have to be more specific than that." She propped herself up. "Just so I'm not mistaken in the identity of *that man*." It was a blatant taunt. She might not ask the questions she wanted to ask, but she still wasn't feeling all that accommodating at the moment. A chill had settled into her body yet again, and she didn't know if it was from the damn clothes or their infuriating conversation.

"Dare," Heart spit out the name as if it were a foul curse. "If I ever see you with him again, I will marry you off to the first man who asks for your hand!"

How laughable! Marry her off to the first man who asked for her hand? One word from her and that would never happen. "What if it's Dare?"

"Leonora!"

"I suppose that is a definite no."

His eyes flashed. "Yes!"

"Oh, it's a yes?"

A filthy glare fell on her. "I'll say it again: Stay away from him. Today was the last day I tolerate this."

She straightened herself, adjusting her posture, reaching to hug a pillow. "How can you accuse a man when you didn't even see him today?"

"Are you going to deny you were with him? Whose jacket are you wearing?"

Leonora glanced down at Dare's coat. She'd all but ripped it from his body with her demand for it. She resisted the urge to duck her head and sniff, but without even having to go that far, the undertone of his scent still surrounded her. Deep. Intoxicating. And utterly wild.

"He will be the ruin of you."

Yes. He just might.

But she was already ruined. A ruined woman in disguise as an innocent lady.

The memories of today flashed through her mind again, and an indiscernible feeling sparked in her chest. She still couldn't shake his expression right before he'd shut the carriage door. What had that been about? It was almost as though he was telling her something without telling her anything. Much like Heart over here.

She shook her head. She couldn't think about Dare now. She had her *brother* to deal with. One rogue at a time.

And then she remembered that *he* had been caught, too. Dare's advice.

She flung the pillow aside and crossed her arms. "What about you, Heart? Who did *you* meet after running into me?"

He blinked, the fierceness of his countenance softening. "Me? Oh, an old friend."

Leonora narrowed her eyes for good measure. "A female friend?"

"You already know."

"Yes, but I'm just wondering how you could meet an old female friend in such a questionable environment?"

He stiffened, his lips pulling up in a sneer. "It wasn't a meeting as you very well know. We simply . . . met."

She tapped her chin in thought. "She sounded awfully familiar. Like I've heard her voice before."

"You won't know who she is even if I tell you."

A blatant lie. Who was the one denying the truth now, heh, Heart?

"You cannot know that," Leonora murmured, watching him closely.

Blue eyes, the same color as hers, held her gaze in unflinchingly—indeed, he didn't move a muscle. There was no doubt the two of them were family. The Hearts inherited their distinctive blue eyes from a long line of ancestors. And yet, that was where the resemblance stopped. Period.

"Why are you so interested in whom I meet?"

"Can I not be interested in what female friend my brother met in such a place?" Or why that female friend had called on Dare? Or why she'd offered to escort Leonora home on the day they fell into the lake? But Leonora couldn't ask those questions. As with so many others, they wouldn't form on her tongue.

"You've never shown any interest in my acquaintances before."

"We don't have to speak about today's incident if you don't want to. But speaking of acquaintances, it seems as though you know the Duchess of Crane. She's on everyone's lips these days."

His face went blank before he said, "We were introduced years ago, that's all."

"So, she could be considered an old acquaintance, then. She is very beautiful. Did you ever court her?" His face lost most of its color. There could be no doubt. They both knew it—that was clear—but she wanted him to admit it. She wanted to hear the truth, some blasted measure of the truth, from his lips.

"No, I've never courted her." He suddenly scowled. "How the hell has this been turned onto me? None of this matters. This is about you, not me. Heed my warning this time, Leonora," he finished firmly, turning on his heel and striding from her chamber. He'd been rattled. She'd never seen him so rattled before. He also hadn't lied—at least about courting the duchess. If he had, things might have ended so different for all of them. It didn't matter, he'd said.

Oh, but, Heart, it does matter.

It matters a lot.

Father.

DARE DIDN'T KNOW why the hell he stepped into the ballroom when he knew he should be staying as far away from polite social events as possible. He hadn't run into Heart yesterday when he'd seen Leonora off, but the man must have been livid to find his sister, his *family*, in a less-than-savory part of London with a less-than-savory man.

Was she all right?

Had they fought?

Did Heart know she knew?

Curiosity burned in his chest. As did concern. And that concern all but replaced any curiosity as the evening went on and she remained absent. Was Heart keeping her prisoner? Could he do that? Probably.

He hated how his mind spun, like a damn fool, wondering what she was doing, how she was feeling, and what she was wishing would happen. He hated not knowing. Hated not being able to help her. All these questions were driving him mad. If Leonora had at least been here, he'd have a damn sight less to worry over.

"Are you lost?"

Dare looked over to Knox approaching with a long-stemmed glass of champagne in his hand, painting the lie of a refined lord dripping with elegance.

In truth, he was a bare-knuckle fighting ruffian.

"Lost?"

"Yes," Knox said before taking a sip of his champagne. "You have the look of a boy who has stumbled into a place he shouldn't have. You seem distracted."

"I am." Why bother lying? He could even argue that he had stumbled into a place he shouldn't have simply because she wasn't here.

"Drake told me that you came to his boxing match with your lady love." Eyes that saw way too much studied him.

"She's not my lady love."

"Yet she is the source of your distraction, is she not?"

"What about you? You spoke with Drake. What else did he say?"

"Not much, honestly. He is impatient to return home."

Dare snorted. What was going between him and the duchess? She'd shown up at the warehouse to watch him box, for Christ's sake. A damn strange occurrence. There seemed to be a deep conflict between the two. Also, not many knew this, but the duchess had played the biggest part in his mother's fall from grace—she'd revealed her pregnancy to the family causing Drake's mother to be expelled from her family home, and society at large, leaving her and Drake on the streets. The only family member who had shown any pity was her sister, Dare's mother. She'd used her own funds to help them settle in Brighton and visited them from time to time.

A nasty affair.

"If he is that impatient, he should up the ante or make amends." The latter he'd never do.

"True."

Dare certainly didn't want to be dragged into a feud of any sort. He thought of Leonora, her family secret. The same fate awaited her should the secret ever come to light—at least where society was concerned. She'd be cast out. Ostracized. Fortunately, Heart would never abandon his family. Just look at the lengths the man had gone to in order to protect her. Drake's mother hadn't been that fortunate.

But even if the worst somehow happened, *he* also wouldn't allow Leonora to be entirely abandoned. She possessed too much light for Dare to ever allow that.

And he appeared to be a moth.

Ugly little things, unable to help being drawn to a flicker of light and a bit of warmth. But they could only ever flit around it, never entirely obtain it.

He sighed.

"Well, I'll be damned," Knox said, amused.

"What?" Dare swept the room to map out the best exit for a hasty departure. No use standing about in boredom. He couldn't even muster up the spirit to pretend to enjoy himself. He should just go to bed.

Knox studied him with a keen gaze. "I've never heard you sigh like that before."

"Like what? A sigh is a sigh."

"Not *that* sigh. That sigh is laced with the ache of longing."

"Don't be ridiculous." He would never, ever sigh with an ache of longing. How did that even happen? What did that even *sound* like?

"Am I really the ridiculous one?"

"Well, you'd have to be. How else would you know what a sigh of longing sounds like? You could only know it if you have experience with it yourself, old chap."

Knox pulled a face.

That's better. "Why are you even here?" Dare continued, changing the subject. "Don't you have a gambling hell to run?"

"I own it," his friend corrected. "Which means I just pore over the accounts. I have a manager who takes care of the rest."

"That still doesn't explain why you are here." Dare sent him an annoyed look. "Drake sent me a message, didn't he? Why else would you bother coming if not to hunt me down?"

Knox chuckled. "Quite right."

"You could have led with that instead of spouting nonsense."

"But that would be no fun."

Dare scoffed. "Couldn't he have sent a note?"

Knox shrugged. "He said to tell you the duchess warned him not to bring in the Hearts into family matters."

"Warned *him*? Why would she do just a foolish thing?" She must have caught sight of him with Leonora at the boxing match. And seeing as he hadn't heeded her warning when she'd visited, she'd turned to his cousin.

What a damn joke. The Hearts *were* family, were they not? And didn't she think he and Drake would find her words suspicious? Just who was dragging in whom? It was like waving a flag at a bull to point him in the direction he should go.

"Can't say why the duchess does what the duchess does," Knox said with a shrug. "Only that she does."

"If she has anything to say to me, she can say it to my face. Drake, too, for that damn matter."

"You know he won't venture into our parts of town."

Dare didn't answer. He spotted Lady Leeds and her husband stepping off the dance floor and made his way toward them, leaving Knox behind. Drake didn't venture into their parts of town, yet they all had no qualms stepping into his territory. Could there be anything more ridiculous than that?

Damn it.

He wanted to help his aunt get something back from the disaster her life had become, but the situation had become more complicated than it had first appeared, more tangled.

"Leeds," he greeted as he approached the couple. "Lady Leeds."

Leeds gave a curt nod. "Lord Dare. How are you this evening?"

Adrift. "As well as ever. Can you point me in the direction of Lady Leonora? I have something I wish to discuss with her."

"Lady Leonora? Oh, you don't know?" Dare's back went stiff as Lady Leeds addressed him. "She is ill and won't be attending tonight."

Ill?

The ballroom and everyone in it vanished, swallowed by that one, terrifying word. It echoed in a loud wail, bouncing back and forth between all corners of his mind. *Ill* . . . It could mean so many things. In some cases, people who fell *ill* never recovered. The very word was like a disease itself, injecting a chill into his blood and pumping with each beat through his veins.

"Harriet," Leeds suddenly spoke up. "Perhaps you should clarify."

Her gaze darted between Dare and her husband, her eyes suddenly widening. "Oh! It's nothing serious. She picked up a bit of a sniffle, I believe," she explained. "Or so her missive to me claimed."

Dare stared at Lady Leeds, processing the information she'd imparted. Leonora. Ill. A sniffle. How? Why? What exactly was the matter with her? How serious was this sniffle? And why did his chest feel so tight?

Lost.

Knox had been right. He felt the loss of Leonora's presence. He could even admit there was a small ache. He felt out of place without Leonora here. As though he no longer belonged. When had this started? Since when had he become a lost little boy whenever she was not around?

This was a problem.

This was no ordinary "like." This was something else entirely. A madness of sorts. An internal bell that signaled he'd ventured into a dangerous place.

Ill . . .

"I see," Dare murmured and nodded his thanks.

"Are you all right?" Lady Leeds asked.

"I'm fine, thank you. Please excuse me."

With one last nod, Dare strode from the ballroom.

Chapter Fifteen

LEONORA'S EYES FLUTTERED open. Around her, the chamber was dark, except for the small sparks of embers still alight in the hearth in her chamber. How many hours had it been? How many days? She couldn't say. Her mind was still much too fuzzy.

She shouldn't have been so stubborn. She should have changed into warm clothes the moment she'd arrived home after their little adventure in the rain. Then she wouldn't have felt so miserable.

She struggled up to her elbows, her limbs sluggish. Blinking against the haze, she turned, searching for the water Heart had placed beside her bed.

"Leonora."

The voice—deep, unmistakable—cut through the fog in her mind.

A yelp tore from her throat, her heart lurching as she whipped to the other side of the bed, clutching her nightgown as if it could serve as armor. Her gaze instantly locked on a man who most certainly should not be in her chamber! Certainly not in her bed! Yet here he was, lounging on top of the covers, fully dressed, save for his shoes, as if he had every right to be there. He was propped up on one elbow. Watching her.

Her pulse pounded. "Dare? What on you doing here? Wait, no, *how* are you here?"

"Are you thirsty?" He rolled off the bed and padded over to the decanter, filling a glass with water and handing it over. Her eyes followed his every movement.

"Thank you." She took the glass and soothed her parched throat with big gulps of water. Satisfied, she placed it back on the table.

He sat down on the bed beside her, reaching out to place the back of his hand against her forehead. "Still warm."

Leonora stared at him, all sorts of foreign sensations flitting in her body. "How did you get into my room?"

"The balcony," he said softly.

She glanced at the double doors. She could have sworn she'd locked them. Her gaze swung back to him. "Are you Romeo?"

His lips quirked, but the smile didn't reach his eyes. "Impossible."

"Why?"

"That would mean that you are Juliet, and she has much too tragic an ending."

"Him too."

"He is not the one who matters in the story."

She shuffled back against the pillows, trying to ignore the warmth creeping up her neck. "Oh? Well, you still have something in common, don't you? Climbing up into bedchambers."

"This is my first time."

"I don't know if I believe you."

Something unreadable flashed in his gaze. "You should. This is the first time I've ever snuck into a woman's chamber. However, I'll admit," he chuckled, "I have a skill for sneaking out."

He dipped a cloth in the washstand and cleansed the sweat from her face. The coolness was a blessed relief against her overheated skin. His touch was gentle, unhurried. Leonora wanted to ask what he was doing—or why he was doing it—but she was afraid if she did, he would stop, so instead, she asked, "How did you know I wasn't feeling well?"

A dark look crossed his face. "Lady Leeds said you had the sniffles. This is not the sniffles. You were almost on fire when I arrived."

"So you've been keeping vigil over me?" A rake caring for a lady. This certainly was moment for her diary.

"Someone had to." He set the cloth aside. "Someone did."

She settled deeper into the pillows. "I dismissed my maid earlier. It was just a small fever."

"Small is not what I would have called it."

Leonora studied the man. His usually finely styled hair stuck out in every direction. She also couldn't quite pick up on his mood. He seemed tired, brooding even, yet he could still manage to smile. "You've taken quite the risk. If my brother finds you here, I cannot save your life."

"Speaking of him, did you confront him? I thought for a moment he'd locked you up."

"I meant to, but I couldn't." She let out a small breath. "I might not be locked up, but the words are—forever locked in a breath that refuses to pass my lips. I keep swallowing them back."

His eyes roamed over her face. "Then you can do nothing but wait until they are ready to pass."

Leonora sighed. "I suppose. I did ask him about his history with the duchess. He lied right to my face."

"He claimed no connection?"

She nodded.

They were both quiet for a moment.

"Could it be that she is not your mother?" he asked.

"How can that be?" Leonora said. "Even you have commented on our likeness."

"Yes, well, there is no denying that there's a definite likeness. However, a lot of people look alike. Not all of them are related."

She should thank him for attempting to reassure her. But, "She called on you . . . spoke about me. No, I won't be so easily thrown off course by Heart. However, I'm a terrible sleuth."

He chuckled. "We have that in common."

Leonora nudged him with a leg. "What about you? Are you any closer to finding what you are looking for?"

He shook his head. "It appears that in both our cases, unless we, or rather my cousin, boldly confront the parties for what we want, we will get little in the way of answers."

"What a predicament."

He exhaled a long breath. "Indeed. So it's best you focus on your health. How are you feeling?"

"Better."

"You should rest, then." He rose to his feet. "I will take my leave."

"Are you leaving? So soon?" If asking boldly was the only way to get the answers she sought, she might as well start with him. "Why did you come in the first place?"

"I don't know." He dragged a hand over his face and laughed. "I left the ball tonight with every intention of going home, but before I knew it, I ended up here."

"Were you worried about me?"

"Yes" His gaze met hers. "Don't ask me why, but I was."

Leonora grinned at the man. He looked so put out that she wanted to laugh, but she refrained, allowing him to save face— just a bit. "I won't ask, don't worry. Thank you for coming, though. I must admit, it's quite thrilling to wake up with a rake in my bed."

"You are impossible, do you know that?"

"I might claim the same about you." She paused for a small moment. "When we last parted . . ."

He shifted restlessly. "What about it?"

"What were you thinking right before you closed the carriage door?"

His brows furrowed. "What was I thinking?"

She nodded. "I've been racking my mind trying to decipher the look on your face, yet I am still at a loss."

"I cannot say I remember my exact thoughts."

"They don't have to be exact. Do you remember even the

smallest bit?" She would have trouble forgetting that look until she had an inkling of what had been behind it.

He was quiet for a moment, then answered, "I believe I was thinking it was best to put distance between us."

Distance? "Why? Because of Heart?"

He nodded. "I didn't want him to catch us."

She sensed the truth in his words, but she also sensed he wasn't telling her everything. Leonora decided to let it go—she preferred not to dwell on one thing for too long. If Dare said that was what he had thought, she would believe him.

"Well, at least you need not worry that he would ever force you to marry me. You would be the last man on earth he'd try to force to marry me."

"He said that?"

"Oh, yes." Leonora smiled faintly. "He cried about his usual warnings to staying away from you and all that."

"Perhaps you should listen to him."

"I could, but I can't help it when you show up in my chamber, now can I? This goes beyond flirting to something more clandestine, don't you think?" Leonora chuckled, exhaustion tugging at her eyelids, yet she fought them like a cat refusing to walk away from a drip of milk. She wanted that last lick. She couldn't resist.

He reached out to tuck a curl behind her ear. "I suppose that's befitting a notorious rake."

"It never gets old hearing you call yourself a rake."

"It never gets old hearing *you* call me a rake and *still* flirting with me."

"There is not much I can lose, you know." She meant it as a jest, nothing more, but his expression still darkened.

"That's not true, Leonora. You have everything to lose."

She placed her hand over her mouth and yawned. "I still can't base my entire future on the hope that a secret never gets revealed. But I can seize all the thrills."

"I'll help you keep your secret." His eyes softened. "And

where I can, I'll help you seize those thrills."

"I'll hound you if you break that promise, Dare." She'd probably hound him even if he didn't.

HOW MUCH DO words cost?

This was the thought that raced through Dare's mind as he made the first promise he'd ever made to a woman other than his mother. And the cost of this promise . . .

It couldn't be calculated.

He never made promises to anyone that he couldn't keep, and he never knew that he could keep any promise, so he simply didn't make them.

But he'd just made one tonight. Mainly because he understood something about the fear of being discovered. He never fought the title of rake. It was a moniker assigned to men like his father, and Dare never denied that part of himself. However, the title also served as a convenient mask, hiding the shadows of him he didn't want to be revealed to the world.

Shadows that could devour anyone if they came too close.

The same shadows that haunted his father.

He swept a hand through his hair, glancing to the balcony.

"It looks as though you bit into a sour grape. What are you thinking about now?" Leonora asked softly, her voice still a bit husky.

He chuckled. "Promises."

"A man like you, I see how that can put you out of sorts." She clucked her tongue. "Making them or breaking them?"

He met her gaze. "Both."

"Do not tell me you are worried you that you cannot keep mine?"

"I'll take yours to my grave." Of that he had no doubt. "It's just . . . I've never made a promise to a woman before."

A smile, so soft, so understanding formed on her face, Dare wondered if he was even awake and not in a dream. "So I'm your first promise? How frightening." Yes. How frightening. "And how exciting."

Exciting? This woman was truly one of a damn kind. "What's so exciting about stealing my first promise?"

She gave a small, short, laugh. "I cannot pin the exact thing, but I shall tell you when I do. That is *my* promise."

"Then I shall hold you to that promise."

"Just so you know," she said slowly, her voice turning solemn, "if the truth of my birth ever comes out, it won't be your fault unless it came directly from you."

"It will never come from me," Dare vowed. He would take that secret not only to his grave, but into the afterlife as well, and even then, he would never spill it.

"Then it will never be your fault. So it's not a promise that you can break."

Her eyes glowed at him, like twin suns. Dare almost felt blinded by that look. Saints, how could such a woman exist in the world? How could she put so much trust in him. It was addicting. "You're tired. Get some more rest." He glanced at the balcony again. "I should go."

"I'm not tired," she protested.

"You can barely keep your eyes open, yet you are not tired?" He arched a brow, amused by her stubbornness.

"I'm not *that* tired yet." Leonora snatched the sleeve of his arm. "Don't go."

Dare paused. "I can't stay."

"Why not? You stayed before." She patted the spot beside her. "You were lying on my bed right here."

That had been . . . a sort of madness he couldn't explain. "You were asleep. I could ignore my conscience."

Her lips parted before she demanded, "How could you ignore your conscience then and not now?"

"Simple. You're awake now, along with those teasing lips. I'd be tempting fate." Not just fate—every damn thing he could tempt, whether it be wrath, seduction, or ruin itself.

"You cannot tempt fate, for fate cannot be tempted."

He almost laughed. "What an audacious thing to say."

"If it's you, I don't mind saying it."

If it's you . . .

Those words alone were enough to tempt a jaded man like himself. Did she have any idea how easily he could become consumed by them? Did she have any understanding of how dangerous those simple words could be? No. She didn't. She couldn't. She was much too innocent. Or she wouldn't be saying such things to him.

"I thought you might have been lying when you said you didn't care about my family secret," she continued quietly, her tone heavy with sleep.

His brows furrowed. "I don't."

"Prove it," she challenged, squirming into a comfortable position for sleep.

Dare had the sense if he didn't, this little temptress would fight sleep all night. "How?" Dare asked, even though he suspected the answer would be just as dangerous as the woman.

"Stay."

He was right. And she had won.

Without a word, he moved to the bed, lying down once more, this time flat on his back, above the linens, his gaze fixed on the shifting shadows the embers in the hearth cast upon the ceiling.

Those were safe. Not tempting. Just shadows.

He adjusted his thoughts. "I know you don't want to hurt Heart, but have you ever thought that he might not be hurt but rather relieved?" he asked finally.

"I haven't thought of it like that," her soft voice came. "I suppose I am afraid to add to the burden. And also of how the balance of our entire family would change. I must be a painful reminder of Heart's past."

He turned his head to look at her. "No, not painful."

Her gaze locked with his. "How do you know?"

"For the most part, people avoid what's painful and stay close to what brings them joy. Heart has never avoided you. He's always kept you close. That alone is an answer."

Her lips curved in a smile, reaching all the way to her eyes. "Thank you. What a nice thing to say."

"Don't doubt Heart too much," Dare said, holding himself back from inching closer.

"His heart would be warm if he heard how you defended him, I'm sure."

"I'm not defending him," Dare muttered in denial. Heavy denial. "I'm reassuring you. *Your* heart should be the one warmed."

"It's warm," she whispered, her tone so soft he almost didn't catch it. "Perhaps a touch too much."

"Well, we cannot have that," Dare said, and then teased, "A heated heart could lead to a Shakespearian-like tragedy."

"Or comedy, depending on the way you look at it."

"Just so long as we're the ones laughing and not crying." Tears . . . he shuddered.

"That is such a male thing to say," she said on a chuckle. "I do enjoy sheading a tear over a good play."

"Remind me never to escort you to the theatre, then."

"Why ever not?"

He slung an arm over his eyes. "I don't think I could survive your tears." And that was the God's honest truth. Leonora crying . . . Just imagining it made his chest constrict.

"Well," her voice danced with a playful edge, "mostly they were tears of laughter."

That, Dare could very well also imagine. To laugh until he cried, heh? "I've never experienced something that funny before." A sudden memory filled his head. "Oh, wait. When Knox fell down the stairs one day, I believe I laughed my arse off, then. There might have been tears."

She chuckled, the sound soft and almost strained, as though the effort of it cost her more than the chuckle itself. She'd be asleep soon. "I wish I could have seen that."

"Him falling down the stairs?"

"No, you laughing your arse off. I imagine it would be quite the sight."

He should have known. "I don't think it was."

"Hopefully, in the future, I can be the judge of that."

Hopefully . . . in the future . . . "We shall see."

"You know, this is the first time I have brought a man to my bed."

Dare nearly choked. "What an unladylike," and damn unexpected, "thing to say."

"I live to shock you." Another slow chuckle. "Perhaps one day I shall even shock you into tears."

"Please don't." Heat spread through his chest and filled his body. When had he ever just laid next to a woman before? Just . . . talking. This was a first for him. Something he thought he would never experience.

"Goodnight, Dare."

His eyes fell on her. She'd drifted off into a slumber, her cheeks still rosy with a bit flush. So damn beautiful. "Good night, temptress."

Could he ever afford the cost of all the things he had said tonight?

Chapter Sixteen

Three days later, the March Ball

THINGS WERE CHANGING.

Leonora could feel it in her bones.

Heart hadn't been home since the day of the boxing match. That was to say, he came to shoot glares at her every evening, but for the most part, he'd been absent.

Which was very suspect.

Especially since Harriet had confirmed that the duchess hadn't attended any events since then either. Leonora pursed her lips in thought. It should bother her more, yet remarkably, she felt rather unbothered by it all.

Heart was her father. The duchess, she was pretty certain, was her mother. And she had no doubt that those two had matters they needed to hash out, hurts they had to forgive. Perhaps that was what they were both up to. And then there was Leonora herself. She wondered how they would approach the topic of her. Would they divulge their past to her? Would they attempt to keep their secret?

She gave a light snort, stuffing another lemon cake in her mouth.

With Dare unraveling her secret, and the night she'd spent with him talking until her eyelids could no longer win the battle, one thing had become clear—she didn't want to be ruined by a secret she'd had no hand in creating. She had spent too many years living from moment to moment, each one precious, knowing it could all be taken from her at any time. Tonight, though, she wanted to seize one more moment for herself—a moment where she could start a secret of her own creation. One away from the shadows of the one she had inherited.

She wanted to seize Dare.

And she wanted to seize him tonight.

If she didn't do it tonight, Leonora had a feeling that the chance might slip away forever. She wanted that chance. She wanted it like nothing she had ever wanted in her life.

I won't let you go tonight, Dare.

She scanned the room, looking for her quarry. If Dare saw her now, he would probably tease her that she was searching for the duchess, never dreaming that tonight her target was him.

There. She spotted him across the ballroom, her face splitting into a grin as their eyes met. The possibility existed that he would refuse the moment she wanted from him, but Leonora didn't dwell on the answer she might not receive from him. The best she could do was try.

And she was looking forward to trying.

Very much.

She winked at him and turned on her heel, striding from the ballroom. She knew Lord and Lady March's residence like the palm of her hand, having visited with her parents as a young girl enough times to have discovered every nook and cranny.

Her goal: the library.

Whether Dare would follow or not remained to be seen. She slipped from the room quite effortlessly. She quickly padded to the library on light feet. She had attended tonight with Harriet, but she'd told her friend not to worry about her, for she had some mischief up her sleeve.

Poking her head through the door, she breathed a sigh of relief when nobody was present. She glanced back down the hall and flashed a smile at a familiar person's urgent approach. She slipped into the room with a chuckle.

Books filled the space from the floor right up to the ceiling in a magnificent display of knowledge and imagination.

"Leonora." His voice was low, hesitant.

She turned, a slow smile curving her lips. The suspicion in his gaze only made her laugh softly. "You came."

"What are you up to now?"

She stepped deeper into the library. "Close the door."

His brows furrowed. "Why?"

"Because I am tempting you."

"You do that every damn day," he muttered under his breath but still closed the door. "And should you really be doing that? Purposely tempting me?"

"Yes, I think I should." And so much more. "Why, don't you think so?"

He leaned back against the door, staring at her. "I can list out reasons upon reasons why it's wrong."

She laughed. "Please don't. I'm sure I wouldn't enjoy them."

"They're not meant to be enjoyed. They are meant to inform."

"I don't want to be informed." She wandered over to a shelf and trailed a finger over the spine of a book, keeping her eyes locked on him. "I want to tempt. Will you allow yourself to be tempted?"

His eyes burned into hers. "I don't think you know who you are tempting."

A thrill shot through Leonora. Didn't she? She begged to differ. "Rake Sloane, infamous rake, also the Earl of Dare."

He pushed off from the door, a slight chuckle escaping him. "Hearing it like that is quite disconcerting. It's as if my parents wanted me to be immoral."

"It is a rather ironic coincidence, don't you think?" She cocked her head to the side, biting her lips before saying, "My point is, Dare, I know exactly who you are. I know your reputation."

He stopped before her, those blue pools almost brooding as

they studied her. "Yes. I do have a dark reputation, but you do not."

"I don't care about that," Leonora said boldly. He couldn't scare her no matter what he said. "I'm here to create a secret moment of my own."

One brow arched, the air between them thickening. "Is that why you want this? Because of your family secret?"

"If I'm going to be ruined, I shall not be ruined by a family secret."

He reached out to grasp her chin. "Then by what will you be ruined?"

"You."

The word hung between them like a challenge. A promise.

"A dangerous statement, Lady Leonora."

"It shall be a secret." She stepped into him, her chin lifting to hold his gaze. "Our secret."

"And what will your future husband think about this secret of ours?"

"Probably the same thing he would think if he discovered the other secret." Her fingers caught his. "I have thought about nothing but this for three long days. I don't want to live with regret. I might not know what the future holds, but I do know that tonight shall hold. Us. Fused together."

"Christ, Leonora . . ." His voice cracked on her name. She heard what he didn't say. *I can't be reformed.*

But she didn't want his reformation.

She just wanted him.

She laughed and turned to saunter over to the shelf on her left, shooting a sidelong glance at him. "What if I told you in order to help me keep my secret, you *must* ruin me. Would you help me then?"

"I'd tell you it was the most ridiculous line a woman has ever tossed at me."

"What if I told you I will be ruined tonight, even if you walk out that door?"

His face lost all expression. "Don't tempt a rake, Leonora." His voice turned thick. "My self-control isn't as strong as you might imagine. And I am no gentleman."

"You keep calling yourself a rake, but I have yet to see the proof." She lifted a taunting brow. "Or is the title nothing but a mask you wear?"

His gaze grew hot. "Even if I were to ravage you to ruin, I wouldn't do it here where anyone could walk in on us."

Leonora grinned. "You wouldn't be doing it here." She reached out to a book and tilted it down, the shelf before her creaking as it slowly swung open.

His eyes widened in disbelief. "A secret room."

"A secret *reading* room to be exact."

He strode over, peering inside. "How do you know about this place?"

Leonora flashed a proud smile. She'd caught his interest. "I know a thing or two as well."

Dark, turbulent blue eyes met hers. "You did think this through."

"I didn't decide the terms of my birth, Dare. No infant can. But I can decide my own source of ruination, and I refuse to let it be my birth. I don't expect you to understand, but I'm a walking ruin already. I'm just asking you to do what rakes do best— ravage. Do you dare, Lord Dare?"

His reply came instant, "God, yes." Then he cursed. "I've never seduced an innocent before. I don't know if I can be gentle. I don't know if I can be whatever you need me to be."

A thrill shot up her spine. "I don't need you to be gentle. I just need you to be you."

"Now you are only provoking me." He suddenly reached over to pick her up and toss her over his shoulder.

A gasp flew from her lips. "Dare! What are you doing?"

"Ravaging an innocent." He stepped into the room, which was a smaller version of the library, only it had no windows. Rows of books lined the walls, and plush carpets adorned the floor. In the corner stood a desk with candles and a tinderbox.

He set her down. "This is pure madness, you know this."

"Then let's be mad together."

He tucked a curl behind her ear. "I shall light some candles. By the time the last one is lit, if you are still here, there will be no going back."

Oh, Leonora didn't plan to go back.

Only forward.

Leonora pressed the door shut with a *click*, sealing them inside. Her pulse thrummed. No escape. No second thought. Only ruin.

COULD A MAN die if his heart raced too quickly?

If that were possible, Dare was in trouble. Deep trouble. And yet, even though he knew he shouldn't be doing this, he had still picked her up and walked into this secret room.

He was not strong enough to walk away.

He was not *that* good.

His temptress wanted him to ruin her, and he would oblige. Only, he couldn't rid himself of the sense that he was the one about to be ruined tonight. She would ruin him. Not in any obvious way. No, what Leonora threatened was something far more dangerous. She would unravel him. Make him forget every carefully placed wall, every vow to keep his heart unattached. His life untangled.

Once he touched her, there would be no undoing it. No forgetting the way she looked at him now—like he was something more than a rake, more than a man who played at seduction but never truly surrendered to it. She was toying with disaster, but so was he. And Dare had the terrible feeling that when the dust settled, he would be the one left in wreckage.

But only if he didn't keep his wits about him.

He was still a rake.

Hardened.

Flickering light illuminated the room in a soft orange glow. Illuminating *her* in a soft orange glow.

"I want to kiss you." Christ, he was holding on by a thread, but he also didn't want to make any sudden moves.

She laughed, and a slender arm reached out to him. "So kiss me."

He placed his hand in hers, jolting when a sizzling spark exploded between them. His calm shattered. His lips found hers right about the moment his chest burst into a flurry of wild, unforgivable beats—half panic and half daze.

His tongue coaxed hers while his mind and his heart battled each other.

Dear God, had he developed feelings for her? Feelings that poets would start with a *L* and end with an *E*?

No, Dare couldn't accept such a thing. And yet he couldn't stop wanting her. She called forth emotions inside him he had believed long dead.

It was intoxicating.

He pulled away from her, breaking their kiss, searching her face. His whole body erupted in flames at her unfocused countenance. They had no future. A man like him . . . He could not give her what a woman like her deserved—happiness. For life. Even if he could give her all of it, all of himself, it would be a broken fragment, the last shard left of a long line of broken Dare men. Nothing in him was whole. Nothing in him deserved her.

He didn't deserve her.

If he had any moral scruples left in him, he would walk away. Walk away and never turn his head to her again. But even while he didn't deserve her, neither could he resist her.

Hell and damnation.

What should he do?

Ravage her without regret. And whatever flutters pushed against his chest, he would keep to himself. He had no qualms about asking his heart to suffer in silence. He was used to it. Yearning, longing for something he didn't understand—it was second nature.

"Dare?"

Yes. "Call me Rake."

She hesitated only a fraction of a second before she murmured, smiling, "Rake."

His name on her lips. God save him, there lay the trouble. The simple sound of it—his name, from her—had the power to undo everything he was trying to keep together. His lips found hers again, pouring into the kiss all the things he would never, ever speak out loud.

He loved her.

Dear God, he loved her.

He loved her so damn much. But being the man that he was, his moral compass about good and bad was skewed at best. Even if she pleaded for his affection, begged for his responsibility, noble sacrifice was not within his scope of being.

He was no hero.

Would never be.

Her hands found his face. Dare almost growled when she pulled back and breathed, "Your turn."

His turn?

She grinned at him, planting a soft kiss on his lips before drawing back again. "Say my name."

"Leonora." Her name left his lips before he could stop himself. "Leonora."

Damn near a plea.

Her hands circled his neck. "My arms just broke out in goose-flesh."

"Christ, Leonora. Are we really doing this?" Was *he* really doing this? This was about the only resistance Dare could manage. The only words he could utter to appease the conflicting desires within him. He wanted her. Badly. He also didn't want to taint her with his shadows.

"A rake is this hesitant? Should I beg?" She chuckled. "Beg a rake?"

"I'm also still just a man." *Who doesn't want to hurt you yet cannot let you go.*

"And I am also just a woman."

"An innocent one. A *smart* one."

"Well, then, since I'm so clever," she pressed her bosom against his chest, "you cannot question my choices."

He should have seen that coming. Ah, this woman. "I don't want to hurt you."

"Who are you hurting?" Her grin turned suggestive. "Surely not me?"

Ah yes. He couldn't hurt her because she didn't feel the same way for him . . .

He leaned close to inhale the scent of her skin. "I promised myself, when it came to you, that I wouldn't do anything I'd regret." *Anything I'd need forgiveness for.*

"How funny, Dare." Her hands framed his face. "So just don't regret." One of her hands dropped to trail a finger over his jaw. "I certainly won't regret anything that happens in this room, trust me."

He captured her wrist, searching her gaze. She didn't move, merely stared at him with bright eyes, allowing him to see all the truth reflected there.

That small hint of encouragement was enough for any last resistance to crumble. He loved her. He loved her in a way that defied reason. He loved her in a way he had never loved any woman in all his life. And he couldn't give her forever, but he could give her tonight.

He brought her wrist up to his lips, brushing a gentle kiss against her hand, a silent promise. "No regrets, then."

Her smile took on a new light, a sultry one. "No regrets," she agreed.

"You will be the end of me, you know?"

"I know." She leaned into him, saying like a true seductress,

"That has never been my intention, but it might just become it."

"What *has* been your intention?"

"With you?" Her tongue darted out to lick her lips, sending a shiver to the base of his spine. "I don't rightly know."

He chuckled. "Now, that, little temptress, I do believe. I also don't know what I'm doing half the time either, especially where you are involved."

"Then let's not know together."

But I do know more than you, temptress. "But—"

She cut him off with a finger over his lips, both teasing and commanding at the same time. "That word, or similar, is not allowed in this space."

He kissed her finger. "I was merely going to say that I do know something. You shall now be thoroughly ravaged."

"Finally." Her arms circled his body, squeezing. "For this night," she said, "you are mine."

Christ. "Leonora . . ."

"You don't like me saying it."

"I bloody love it." He lowered his head until his lips touched her ear. "There are many types of love I can give you," he whispered. "But true love . . ."

No hesitance. "I'm not asking for true love. I'm just asking for your love, for one night, this night."

Ah, hellfire.

Never in his wildest, most erotic musings had he imagined that Leonora would ever offer him such a gift. The gift to taste her. To love her. To pleasure her. It had always just been a distant whisper, and unspoken desire.

They were never supposed to become friends.

They weren't supposed to become lovers.

But for this night, she was his. He would love her. For this night only. As for the rest . . .

That was for tomorrow to decide.

Chapter Seventeen

A MOMENT TO rule all moments.

This was what she'd wanted from the very start. And if ever there were a moment to rule all moments, bringing this man to a trembling mess was it.

If I rule this moment, then I rule him. Not in the way of chains or commands, but in the way that left him breathless beneath her touch, that made him look at her as though she were both his temptation and his undoing. His doom and deliverance.

He, who commanded the gaze of countless women with a mere smile. Who had no intention of ever being shackled. He was here, unguarded in ways that had nothing to do with flesh—exposed in a manner she had never seen before. It was in the way his breath trembled slightly whenever he spoke, in the fleeting spark that danced in his eyes. Even in the way his fingers lingered on her skin, hesitant yet bold.

And she had done that.

The knowledge sent a thrill through her, a heady rush that ignited her blood. To bring him—this unrepentant rake—to such a state was intoxicating. To see him as he truly was. Stripped bare of his defenses, he was no longer the Earl of Dare, the infamous rake, but simply a man.

And tonight, he was her man.

Yes, this moment was hers to rule.

Her breath caught when Dare stepped back, shrugging off his jacket and tossing it over the chair at the desk. His hands moved to the buttons of his waistcoat, and in one swift motion, it joined the jacket—and was seconds later followed by his shirt.

The man didn't play about.

He grinned at her. "Are you enjoying the view?"

Lord, yes. No mental pictures could compete with *this*. This was . . . not quite perfection, but not quite *not* perfection. She had seen a muscled chest before—but never like this. Never with all that strength, all that power, directed at conquering, directed at *her*.

She nodded, and he chuckled.

His body was no overly chiseled sculpture, but it was a body that might have inspired one. A masterpiece in its own right.

It inspired her—to take action.

She reached back to tug at the laces of her gown, then slowly pulled the sleeves from her shoulders. She'd dressed smartly for tonight. No complicated dress with complicated strappings.

Instead, a gown to aid in her ruin.

She must have done right, for his eyes shot flames across her skin. She grinned and tugged the sleeves lower.

"What are you doing?" he asked, tone raw.

She smile widened. "Oh, my apologies. Did *you* want to do the undressing?"

He cursed but didn't move an inch. "Have you always been such a tease?"

"You know I have been." Her gaze tracked over his muscles to his trousers. "You should remove them, too."

"So demanding."

"I already saw your upper body at the boxing, now I want to see the rest."

"You saw? I thought you left?"

"I saw enough to make me *not* want to leave." However, some things took precedence over male chests. "Are you removing your trousers or not?"

"Of course." Both hands moved to the buttons of his trousers. "As the lady wishes."

Leonora watched with suspended breath as he undid those buttons achingly slowly before pushing his trousers down his legs.

Lord above.

She swallowed at the magnificent sight.

"Should I remove them completely?"

"As you like," she just about managed not to choke out.

His grin turned wolfish. "What about my boots?"

"Whatever is fastest." She stepped up to him and pushed her hands up his chest. A sigh escaped her at the hard planes beneath her fingertips. "However, we cannot undress as though we have the whole night at our disposal." Secret room or not, the danger of being caught vibrated along her flesh in ripples. Forget the night, an urgency sparked the air that couldn't help but catch Leonora's breath as she drew in that magnificent body of his.

He loomed over her half-naked, hand closing around his cock, eyes boring into hers.

She inhaled sharply.

Where on earth should she look? That erotic sight of his chest or his face? Was there a right way to stare or a wrong way? Leonora opted to spend a few seconds on each delightful region.

He suddenly chuckled. "This is a first."

"What is?" Leonora stilled, slowly moving her gaze from a certain provocative image back to his eyes.

"Staring at me so blatantly like I am dessert."

"A lemon cake, my favorite."

He chuckled, retreating until the back of his legs met a sofa. With a swift tug, he pulled her down with him, on top of him. Leonora gasped as he shifted, one hand slipping behind her back, the other guiding her legs around his waist. "This is sweet?" His fingers traced up her thigh, dragging d her skirts along with them.

Sweet, yes.

"You're so bloody beautiful."

"You're not too bad—"

He captured her lips in his, his tongue swallowing the last of her words. "More touching and less talking."

Leonora obliged his request and dragged her hands down warm hard muscle. "As my rake demands."

His lips were on her again, dragging, sucking, tongue plundering. She couldn't get enough of this man. Enough of this moment. Enough of his touch. He was stealing the very breath from her lungs, this kiss a claim, a demand, a surrender all at once.

His hand skimmed down her back, mapping her with possessive strokes, fingers pressing into her waist as though committing every one of her curves to memory. Heat pooled low in her belly, a delicious ache curling around her spine as she arched closer, seeking more—more of him, more of this fire, more of everything he had to give.

Everything that happened in this hidden library . . .

So good.

She had chosen this. Dare had accepted. Therefore any consequence was of no consequence. They were two people who had made a choice.

"Bloody hell," he breathed against her lips. "I can't hold back."

The urgency in his voice made her smile. "No one is asking you to hold back."

He cursed. "Christ, Leonora, you cannot say that to a man."

"Why not?" She pressed into him provocatively. "I can't hold back either. Or do you want me to hold back?

"Hell no." He let out a shaky breath. "Don't you dare do that."

She kissed him on the mouth. "I won't, but you must not either."

And then his fingers were *there*. Circling. Entering. Leonora moaned into his mouth. Thank heaven she'd dressed with temptation in mind, and it was paying off. No frills, no fuss—just easy access to ruin.

"I wish I could undo your hair."

She shut her eyes and drew in all the sensations of his touch, his whispers, the sensation of his fingers. "Not tonight." His teeth grazed her chin, a sharp, fleeting nip that caused goose flesh to erupt all over her body.

Not tonight?

What did she even mean with that? The thought barely had time to settle before he stole it away, replacing it with the slow, maddening stroke of his fingers teasing another moan from her lips. Then—oh. Something else. Something bigger. Nudging.

Oh, God.

It was happening.

His nose buried in the curve of her neck, and that wild, intoxicating scent of his enveloping her. His tongue followed, sweeping over her skin, tasting her. Then his teeth—with just enough pressure to make her breath catch—dragged over her collarbone.

And then he was inside her.

Leonora gasped at the fullness.

In all the time she'd spent imagining tonight, she never once truly grasped how *it* would feel. Straddling him, her knees pushing into the pillows on either side of his hips, him *inside* her, hidden away in a secret room . . . In her wildest dreams she could never have envisioned this. It was more. More consuming, more intoxicating. And yet there was something else, something she hadn't expected.

Power.

A whisper of it slid through her, faint but undeniable.

His breath fanned over her jaw as he dragged his mouth to her lips. "How do you feel?"

"Ruined."

He chuckled. "Does ruined feel good?" He gave a light thrust, and she gasped.

"Supremely satisfying." *Thrilling.* So many choices meant

nothing. So many choices could be glossed over with a smile. Others, like seducing Dare, didn't mean *nothing* and could never be glossed over. This would stay with her all her life. It might even govern the rest of her days. The thought should have terrified her. Instead, it settled deep, like him—a truth she had no desire to fight.

She pressed her thighs snug against his hips, anchoring herself to him.

I do not care.

She clutched his shoulders, using them as leverage as she rolled her hips in time with his thrusts, claiming him as much as he claimed her. His pace quickened, and Leonora found herself on the edge of splendor. His hand reached between their bodies, teasing over sensitive flesh, pleasure racing through her—sharp, uncontainable, and all-consuming. She rocked against him, not quite able to describe the feeling building inside her. A part of that pleasure was him—his body, his hands, his mouth dragging all over hers. It was everything all at once. Could she stay here forever, suspended in this exquisite torment, this unbearable bliss?

"Christ," he growled. Then, with a low, hoarse voice, he called her name—almost like a prayer.

It left her shattering in his arms.

And she cried out his name in return.

HE DIDN'T DIE.

Dear God, he didn't die. His heart was still racing as though the devil were on his heels, but he was still alive. That was something, at least. More than something was the woman in his arms. In all his rakish life, he had never let a woman take the top position, and yet it came so naturally with Leonora. The way she moved with such seductive confidence, it was as if she had always meant to be there.

He gathered her close but was unwilling to dwell too much

on that thought. Even so, he didn't want to let go, hated that their time here would end soon, and that this might be all there would ever be between them. Yet Dare couldn't say he felt any regret. He didn't like to entertain that emotion, anyway, and they had promised not to. But something, call it a feeling, some foreign sort of nagging, or perhaps something in between, tugged at him relentlessly.

He decided not to dwell on that either.

Leonora wiggled against him, snuggling closer. "Shall we just stay here forever?"

"Of course." He'd just find a way to bolt the door shut.

A chuckle was her only answer.

His fingers itched to undo her hair.

"Have I ruined you according to your wishes?" He promptly grimaced. What a thing to ask a woman. To ask *her*, an innocent. No. Not an innocent any longer.

"Oh, yes," she said, her voice soft with satisfaction. "You've exceeded my expectations."

Dear Christ, Dare.

Did you truly take a woman's innocence? He stared at Leonora, who nestled in her arms.

Yes. He had.

And he would ravage her all night long if they weren't in a secret space in someone else's house. It struck him then—it was the first time in his life he hadn't left the minute after his pleasure had been taken. There was no rush to leave. Instead, a strange sense of contentment, unfamiliar yet indisputable, settled within him. It was a refreshing change, to say the least.

"They couldn't have been that high, then," Dare said after a moment.

She laughed. "Are you fishing for a compliment?"

He trailed a finger over her jaw. Such a beautiful face. Such sparkling eyes. "Only if you are the fish."

"You know, I do feel like a fish at the moment, a lazy fish." She settled deeper, nudging against him with a playful shift of her hips.

"Don't get too comfortable." His hands gripped her hips to keep her steady. Christ, she *did* want to kill him, didn't she?

She wiggled again, a teasing smirk curling on her lips. "Says the man who got comfortable."

"Don't move," Dare groaned, his grip tightening. "Or we won't leave tonight."

"Is that a threat?" she teased, her voice a breathy challenge.

No. Minx. "A promise."

She reared back to look at him, the sudden shift in her posture leaving him both aching with loss and in torment down below. "Tell me, have I reformed you?"

"God, no." She'd corrupted him. "Do you wish to?"

She shook her head. "Such ghastly business."

He laughed. "Seduction is ghastly business?"

"Are you saying I can reform you with seduction? How cheap you are."

"Well, if such a thing could be done, it would be you who could do it." He leaned up just enough to kiss the curve of her neck lightly, his lips trailing over her skin. Bloody heaven.

"Your faith in me is remarkable."

He chuckled softly, her fingers brushing over his chest, also reluctant. "We should go. We've been gone too long. Heart must be looking for you."

Her smile turned sweeter. "Heart is not here."

"He's not here?" This surprised him. No wonder Leonora had come prepared. He damn well hadn't stood a chance. "Strange for him. Then your friend, Lady Leeds?"

"She knows not to look for me."

"Lady Leonora," he claimed a quick kiss, "how dangerous of you."

"Well, I won't go so far as to say that." Her eyes narrowed, a lovely sight made even more striking by the flush on her cheeks. "Are you going to stop flirting with me after this?"

A feeling of protest burst open immediately in his chest. "Do you want me to stop?"

"Are you jesting?" She gave him a saucy look. "Who would I flirt with if not you? The Duke of Calstone?"

"I shouldn't feel this relieved," he said with a grin.

She kissed his chin. "You're that attached to our sparring matches?"

Sparring matches? Heh. They could probably be considered as such. "I suppose I have become a bit attached."

She chuckled. "Now it's my turn to say I shouldn't feel this relieved."

His finger caught a stray lock of hair and twirled it around his finger. "Hearing you repeat my words is quite frightening."

"Because I am a woman?"

"Ye—" Blue eyes met his, and he swallowed the *s*. "I take that back. It's a refreshing change." Like so many things about her. Truthfully, nothing Leonora could say would ever be disturbing to him. Not really. The only disturbing thing was that she could make him question his own damn words. His body. His mind.

Leonora pinched his side, causing him to jerk. "You know what your problem is?"

Of course. "Tell me."

"You are too straightlaced and uptight for a rake."

"Is that my problem?"

"Yes. You don't know how to let your laces loose."

Dare couldn't help but laugh. "Then I shall work on this problem, I give you my word I shall let loosen my laces more often."

"Please call me over for the show."

"You are a damn witch." Bewitching him with her smiles, her touches, her light.

She cocked her head. "Do you always swear like this?"

"Only when I'm bewitched. Only with you."

She laughed. "Don't jest."

He wasn't jesting. He felt bewitched. In the past, he had found himself in many awkward and questionable situations, but this one . . . He couldn't quite wrap his mind beyond this one.

Leonora.

The witch.

The temptress witch.

How long would this spell last? A throb bloomed in the center of his chest at the unbidden question which had no business in his head. Because the answer came to him even more unbidden. The right course of action would be to stop here, to have no regrets, and to never tease and flirt with her again. If he didn't . . .

"You know, my brother threatened to marry me off if I didn't stay away from you."

Dare stilled. Beg pardon? "He said as much?"

"He made a threat."

"Is that what tonight's is all about?"

She shook her head. "Nine parts no, one part yes. I don't care to be threatened into anything. I shall ruin myself before I allow it."

"Well, you are ruined now, little temptress."

Her arms wound around his neck, her eyes sparkling down at him. "I was ruined the moment I was born unprotected by the parasol of the sanctity of marriage."

So admirable, this woman.

Ah hell, damnation, and everything in between.

It was one of *those* nights. The kind where Dare felt in his bones sleep would not be his friend. How many times had these nights occurred? How many of them had he spent alone?

The number seemed to be infinite.

Of course, it would help if he had company, but he never wanted to stay longer with a woman than was necessary. Until this moment, when he didn't want to leave. For the first time, he was tempted to spend the whole night with a woman. But his temptress wouldn't have that, would she?

"Then my only question is this," Dare drawled against her skin, so damn reluctant to end the moment he wanted to howl. "Was one moment of ruination enough or do you require another?"

Chapter Eighteen

"WELL, THIS IS surely a sight I never thought I'd see."

Leonora jerked, her body tensing in surprise. For a moment . . . for a moment, she thought she was still naked in bed, a warm body pressing up tightly against her. The wild, intoxicating scent of him lingering. Mad whispers of all the ways it was bad to meet her in her chamber following her ruination . . .

But no. She was at the dining room table, toast in hand, staring out into the distance, which appeared to be a wall.

Dazed.

She looked to Heart and blinked again. The man looked no better than she had this morning when she'd woken up, limbs still entangled with a certain lord. "You can use this tone looking like you just crawled out of the gutter?"

He dusted off his coat before straightening his sleeves. "I was caught in a scuffle."

"With whom?"

He stepped up and pulled a chair from the table, reaching for a piece of bread as he lowered down. "You don't need to know."

But I can suspect.

"I heard you attended the March ball last night. Alone."

Instant, vivid memories of her indiscretion in the secret library flashed in her mind. She fought every single one back into the far corners of her thoughts to keep a heated flush from spreading across her face, all the while losing the battle to the heat clenching deep in her belly.

"And where did you hear that?"

Brooding eyes lifted to meet hers. "It would be quicker to tell you where I hadn't heard it."

Would it? "I did attend for a short while."

"Did you see *him*?"

"Your spies didn't tell you that much?" Leonora took a lazy sip of tea. "If you must know, I did see him." And so much more. She wished she could have had even more, but when she'd woken again, he'd been gone.

"Then you are determined not to listen to a word I say?"

Very determined. "What is your problem with Dare anyhow? So he is a rake according to the gossip sheets, but that is not a reason to shun a man like this."

"I'm not shunning him," Heart denied. "I am keeping you away from him. Men such as Dare cannot change, Leonora. What are you even hoping for? Do you wish to marry him? Is that what you are hoping for from him?"

She almost choked on a sip of tea. "Who said anything about marriage?"

"Libertines such as him have no concept of loyalty."

And other men do? Leonora was not so innocent that she did not understand what the terms *mistress* and *affair* meant. Both were the consequences of loveless marriages and the duty to produce heirs without any connection or attraction to one's partner.

No, what Heart was truly concerned about was her birth, which made her all the more curious. Just what had happened all those years ago? Why had her real mother left? Why this ruse?

An affair?

A guilty conscience?

She still couldn't bring herself to ask. Opening old wounds were not moments she wished to seize. All she could do was avert the topic to a point of curiosity. "When are Mama and Papa returning?" Grandmama and Grandpapa. She didn't know how to refer to her family anymore! She supposed there was a certain humor in that as well.

"I'm not sure. I haven't heard anything from them yet."

How convenient.

"Also, we are attending a play tonight," Heart suddenly announced.

"A play?" Why? The last time she had attended a play with Heart had been . . . *Never*. Her instincts bristled with unease.

"I can't remember the name, but it's one of your favorites."

"Must I really go?" She was in no mood to attend the theatre. Her body tingled in places that sent goosebumps skittering across her flesh.

The theatre? She'd rather stay in *bed* and comb through the archive of her memories.

Ah, stop already!

"Yes, you're attending with me. It will be fun," Heart said with that face that always made her relent to anything. Though he seemed unusually calm given she'd attended a ball without him. She'd expected more of a scolding, but not even a veiled threat seemed to be forthcoming.

Suspicious.

"Why the theatre all of a sudden?" Leonora asked, bringing her cup to her lips and taking a small sip. Of all the events in all of London, why choose this?

"I thought a bit of bonding time between us would be enjoyable."

Indeed, it would be enjoyable. She couldn't argue that. When was the last time she'd spent time alone with Heart, other than short moments like these? It seemed ages ago. If fact, she couldn't rightly recall, which was rather frightening. It must have been years ago. Somewhere in the country. A village ball or some such.

"Do you remember when you were eleven years old?" Heart suddenly asked. "You asked me why the night sky was filled with light."

Leonora smiled over the rim of her cup. She could vaguely recall, yes. "I couldn't understand why there was still light when it was supposed to be time to sleep."

"Do you remember what I said?"

Leonora thought a bit. It had been years. She couldn't remember all the details but, "Something about how the moon and stars were there so that if anything happened at night, and I got scared, I would be able to find you."

A curt nod. "Some people have no stars in their life and because of that, they can never find their way back out of the darkness."

Honestly. "What a tragic thing to say, Heart." Was she speaking of himself or Dare? It couldn't be about anything else.

"But true."

Leonora studied Heart, her brows furrowing. Today, there was an air to him she couldn't quite identify. An air of sadness? Sorrow? Longing? The best way she could describe it was an air of supreme calmness, as though he had come to some sort of decision, some sort of acceptance.

All in all, it felt like he needed her.

And if Heart ever needed her, she would be there for him, no matter what went on in her own life.

She placed her cup aside, buttered a slice of toast, and placed it on his plate. When he glanced at her, she said, "If there are no stars in your sky, it's only because it's a bit cloudy, don't you agree? It can't stay cloudy forever. And honestly, Heart, this forlorn look doesn't suit you."

"I'm just tired," he said gruffly. "No need to worry."

She nodded and rose to her feet. "Perhaps it's time you looked for a wife."

His head bounced up. "What the devil? I thought we put that to rest. Why should you say such a thing now?"

She gave a light scoff, teasing, "Aren't you the oldest bachelor in London at the moment?"

"Forty is not old, and I don't think I am *the* oldest. I still have a full head of hair."

"Forty is ancient. At this rate, if you do not marry, I will be obliged to procure you some cats."

"Don't you dare do that," he half growled.

"Then brighten up, Heart." Leonora grinned at him. "Life is full of moments to seize."

"What has you in such a good mood?" he grumbled, suspicion twisting his features.

"Stars in the sky, Heart." She strode from the room before casting one last teasing look over her shoulder, "And moments seized."

She laughed at his darkened expression, quickly rushing out before he could draw her back and badger her with questions, her heart racing in her chest like a beating drum. That last had seemed almost like a confession! It *had* been a confession.

Just a very, very vague one!

She sighed. What had gotten into Heart? He'd nearly doused her thrilling memories of last night with his mood. And he was worrying her. Did this have anything to do with the duchess? He seemed a bit at a loss.

But she couldn't seize his moments for him just like he couldn't seize hers for her. Though for tonight at least, they could seize some together.

WHAT THE ACTUAL bloody hell?

"What are you doing here?" Dare asked as he entered his study. Drake reclined in his chair with his feet on Dare's desk while Knox sat across from him. They saluted.

"We've been here all day," Knox said. "Where have *you* been?"

"Sleeping."

Knox arched a brow. "All day?"

"Yes, all day." Dare glanced at his cousin. "I thought you

didn't venture into this part of town."

"I've got news."

Dare plopped down into a chair, crossing his legs as he settled in. He'd had a rare day of laziness, or call it sleepiness. He hadn't had such a day since he was a boy, so he decided to embrace his body's call and stay in bed all day.

"Oh? And what news might this be."

Dark, almost black, eyes studied his. "The duchess has a daughter."

Knox's eyes widened. "I didn't know that."

What was this? Dare scowled. "That's because it has nothing to do with you."

Drake cocked his head. "Did *you* know?"

Dare tugged at his sleeves. "Why would I?"

"Yes," Knox said. "It's none of our business."

Dare stared at Drake with a nasty look. Why did he get a feeling that the peaceful day he'd been having was about to come to an abrupt end? Could he go back to heaven instead? Back to the other bed he hadn't wanted to leave this morning?

What a first. So, that was how it felt like to wake up with a woman in his arms, limbs entangled.

He could get addicted.

Could.

But wouldn't.

"We can use the daughter." Drake stared at him.

No. "We?" Dare snorted. "You are on your own, *mate.*"

Drake's lips curled knowingly. "Why can't we? She is the perfect leverage. We just need to acquire her name."

Dare scowled. "There's no *we.*" He would be damned if he allowed—let alone helped—Leonora become cannon fodder between Drake and the duchess. "Don't cross lines you cannot return from, Drake. Destroying a family so that you can get what you want is not the way to solve this."

"My family was destroyed."

"Your mother made a choice back then, Drake, and you

shouldn't be taking your hatred of *him* out on innocent women."

Drake arched a brow. "Innocent, you say? What about your little bird? Is she innocent?"

Bloody everlasting hell. What the devil was wrong with his cousin? The man was looking for a damn beating. But he refused to rise to the bait. If Drake knew the entirety of the duchess's secret, he could have leveraged it all on his own. But then, Drake also didn't like to dirty his hands except when boxing. And his deuced cousin of his never moved in haste. Everything he did was calculated. Dare began to wonder if he himself had been no more than a chess piece from the very start. Family. A man didn't require enemies while he had family.

He sent Drake a warning look.

"She isn't my lady love or a *little bird*."

Both men chuckled.

Saints, these friends. "Tell me now, you are my enemies, aren't you?"

"I suppose you are correct," Knox said dryly. "Lady Leonora is most certainly not a little bird or *your* lady love."

Dare went on alert. The emphasis . . . "Why do you say that? Do you know something I do not?"

Knox shrugged. "Ran into Heart at White's earlier. Heard he invited Calstone to the theatre."

Dare's brows furrowed. "So?"

Knox picked at his sleeve, responding nonchalantly, "I believe he told Leeds that he is favoring a match between his sister and the duke."

And there it was. The rest of what was left of his good mood plummeted to the floor.

Calstone and Leonora?

He couldn't deny it—they made an elegant pair. One could even say they were both a bit odd in their own ways. Both sparkled in their own ways. Both carried an allure entirely their own. And the duke's title was one that could protect her from any storm. She'd want for nothing. As a duchess, no one would be able to ridicule her or shun her.

This was the best match for her.

It was the best for her, but he couldn't stand the flashing images of the couple that blasted his mind. Her happy laugh as she gazed up at the duke. Them sharing . . .

Dare cursed, destroying that thought immediately. "Are you sure you heard right?" Could Knox be mistaken?

"The man was sitting right behind me," Knox said. "I'm not deaf."

Drake chuckled. "The life of you nobles."

Dare shot a glare his cousin's way. "Back to *your* matters. How did you discover the duchess had a daughter?"

Drake shrugged. "Let's just say there's a madam in a gaming hell who helped aid in the delivery of a child as well as a lady's wedding to the Duke of Crane despite her ruin."

The Lyon's Den, no doubt.

"Remarkable," Knox murmured, but not sounding all that interested.

"Drake," Dare bit out.

"Don't worry," the man said with a smile that Dare didn't appreciate. "The secret has been kept for round about twenty years and it shall be kept for twenty more."

"How reassuring of you to point that out. I'm more concerned with how you plan to deal with the matter."

Drake just smiled.

Dare wasn't so easily fooled. And he hated that damn smile. Drake didn't just have a plan—that plan was already in motion. He inwardly cursed. Just what was his cousin up to? He knew better than to ask. But one thing he didn't need to ask—if it was about the duchess's daughter, then it involved Leonora.

"Don't worry," Drake said, observing him lazily. "I'm not a monster. I just want what is owed to me and peace for my mother."

"That damn Crane." Knox lifted his lips in distaste. "He used and tossed women aside with no thought to the consequences."

Dare flinched. Well, hell.

Did Knox have to frame it that exact way? Though his friend wasn't wrong. It wasn't his fault that the statement stabbed straight at Dare's heart. Dare's black heart, some would call it. And they wouldn't be wrong, either.

Dare didn't care about much. He didn't care about whatever marriage he was expected to make in the future. He didn't care about an heir. He didn't care about *duty*. And he didn't *want* to care. About Leonora. About Calstone. About the damn theatre. Caring didn't do a man any good. Just look at Drake. Caring too much about old grudges had brought him here, though he couldn't exactly fault the man's intentions.

However, life was much easier if one didn't care.

So why do I damn well care?

He glanced at the clock. It was already late. Whatever play Leonora had gone to watch with Calstone should he well underway.

It didn't matter.

He cared but also didn't care. He glanced back at the clock.

Damn it.

Dare leaped to his feet.

"Where are you going?" Knox asked, setting his glass aside.

"Out."

"Out where? Drake promised we were drinking tonight."

That was Drake's problem. "Not in the mood," he said, striding from the room.

The only thing he was in the mood for was seeing with his own eyes whether Leonora was laughing along to a play with another man after she seduced him the night before.

God help her if she was.

God help *him*.

Chapter Nineteen

L EONORA HAD A secret.

A secret shared by only two people in the entire world. And it hung on her lips like a teasing whisper that would never reach the ear of even the most careful listener, and it danced in every step she took. How long would the thrill of it last? The most thrilling part had certainly been the actual moment of being ruined—or rather ravaged—by one of the most notorious rakes that had ever roamed London. But also, the morning after had still been thoroughly thrilling. Even stepping into the splendor of Drury Lane on Heart's arm, walking about the swarming hallway to their box, the thrum of the thrill bubbled through her veins with no signs of stopping.

Until she entered the box.

She started, two lines forming between her brows as she stared at a man she'd never expected to meet here. She glanced at her brother, and his smile sent a chill down her spine.

Something was wrong with this picture.

In a Duke-of-Calstone sort of way.

What was he doing here? She turned to Heart and lifted a brow.

Heart pretended not to notice and nodded at Calstone before retreating a step toward the door. "You will have to pardon me for a bit."

"Heart." Was this not supposed to be a bonding experience for the both of them? "What are you up to, dear brother?" Though a monkey could wager and guess correctly. But nothing could justify him leaving at the moment! "And where are you off to?"

Calstone, who'd had a smile on his face when they'd entered, had also formed a slight crease between his brows, which told her all she needed to know.

He hadn't expected her brother's duplicity either.

Heart, you sly fox.

"I'm not up to anything diabolical, I assure you," Heart said with a wave of a hand. "I merely forgot about a commitment. I'll be back by the second half of the play."

"So you are just leaving me here? Alone?" She pointed at the duke. "With him?" Unbelievable!

"I cannot believe I'm saying this," the duke said, joining her side, "but I share the sentiment."

Heart inclined his head. "My apologies, Calstone. I'm afraid I shall still have to rely on you to keep Leonora company while I see to my commitment."

Leonora's hands settled on her hips. "What commitment is this, exactly?"

"It's business." His chest puffed up. "Nothing to concern your precious head over."

Really? "What *business* can be done this time of night?"

"*Personal* business."

Hah! "Personal business? With a certain duchess, I imagine."

His entire body jerked in response, and Leonora inwardly scoffed. So obvious. So predictable.

"Why the devil would you stay such a thing?" Heart demanded.

"Why would you tell me tonight is for sibling bonding and then leave?" Leonora countered. "It seems to me that you are leaving me to bond with the duke while you are off bonding with someone else."

"Leonora," he bit out.

She stood her ground. She would be raked over the coals for mentioning the duchess later—she could tell by Heart's molten face she wouldn't be able to escape her fate. If she were choosing, she'd much rather be raked over Rake.

And it struck her then—the idea of her fate. This whole matching attempt was one more effort to protect her, was it not? What else could it be? And the attempts wouldn't stop either, not until she married a man her family believed could protect her, too. She saw it then, her whole season, and the next, and next rolling out before her like a carpet of Heart and her family protecting her.

That was not the life—or the sort of marriage—she wanted.

She realized suddenly that it was time—time to stop hesitating and confess she knew the truth. Besides, they would have to include her at some point. Then they could work out the future together.

But first things first.

"This is utterly ridiculous of you, Heart."

The duke coughed delicately off to the side.

"That's enough," Heart said with a warning look. "I will see you later."

Leonora watched in disbelief as he strode from the box, back stiff, leaving her alone with the duke. She glanced at Calstone, her mind racing through ideas for how to escape this situation. She didn't want to sit through an entire play smiling while she inwardly fumed at that rascal Heart!

"Well, this is certainly interesting," the duke said, then chuckled. "I can't say this has ever happened to me before."

"Are you not angry?" Leonora asked. She wanted to throttle the man who called himself her brother.

He shrugged. "Fortunately, I am slow to lose my temper. Shall we make a run for it? I'm afraid, however, if we do, it will do neither of us any good."

Leonora sighed. There was no helping it, was there? Though

the idea of making a run for it did hold some appeal. It would certainly spark a rumor or two. But she also didn't want the duke to be further dragged into whatever plot her brother had concocted.

"Well, since we are here, shall we at least enjoy the first half of the play?" Calstone said, correctly interpreting her silence and motioning to the seats.

"I apologize for my brother's little scheme," she offered, taking a seat. She might as well enjoy the first half as he suggested, though her earlier thrill had all but disappeared. She had wanted to know how long it would last. Well, it had crumbled in the face of Heart's machinations. The only way to rekindle that thrill would be if a certain other lord were to walk through those doors. The cause of her thrill—her fellow secret sharer.

She sighed softly. Leonora rarely ever succumbed to speechlessness. Yet tonight . . . she had no words for the stunt Heart had pulled. Just where had he disappeared to? Had she been right about the duchess? Or was he sitting in some dark corner like a fool and waiting for the first half of the play to end? The man must have lost his faculties. Leaving her alone with Calstone in their booth? While not entirely improper—since they were in full view of the entire theatre—it was the second most calculating thing he'd ever done—the first becoming her brother.

Both ploys spoke volumes about his inner conflicts.

However, who was she if not a moment snatcher? And at present she had a moment with the Duke of Calstone and a play. Unfortunately, while she had no problem seizing the moment, as she stared down at the stage, watching the performers, she could not focus on a single actor's performance.

She cast a sidelong glance at the duke.

"I'm sorry," she couldn't help but apologize to the man once more. "I do not know what has gotten into Heart's head." Or perhaps there had only been air in his head all along. It would certainly explain a few things!

A smile danced in Calstone's eyes as he looked her way.

"Your brother means well."

If only Heart meaning *well* did something other than annoy her. "This is one step too far, in my opinion."

"We could still make a run for it. Though I must admit, I've never had a lady resist the presence of my company to quite such a degree before. Tonight even more so than that day in the boat."

She grinned. "To be fair, it's not that I loathe your presence, but I did enjoy it far more when you were in that boat." At least then he had been a shield between her and Heart.

"Truly? I was but a mere spectator who fervently regretted the desire to spectate."

"Exactly."

He laughed. "I see." He leaned his head in toward hers. "Don't be too hard on your brother. You might not like what he did either then or tonight—it's underhanded to be sure—but he adores you. Of that, there can be no doubt. Also, I'm enjoying myself."

"You are?" Leonora asked incredulously. "Even though you find yourself once again a spectator?"

He shrugged. "Tonight there is no water, so I'd say I'm fairly safe, wouldn't you?"

Leonora shook her head. "Don't succumb to Heart's madness. Will you still be enjoying this if I truly set my sights on you?"

He grinned. "You won't."

"How do you know that?"

"It's just one of those things a man knows."

Leonora cast her eyes heavenward, but she could not prevent a smile from forming, or a chuckle from escaping. "That ducal arrogance alone is enough for me to not set my sights anywhere near you. How long before the interval, do you think?"

"I've never met a woman so eager to relieve herself from my company. It still amazes me."

"Oh? I've never met a duke so eager to be led by the lapels."

"I'm a spectator of life. It's the best cure for boredom."

"How pleasant for *me* that I could relieve your boredom some."

"Ah, well, it's the cost of having a meddlesome brother. I suppose you would much rather be here with your Lord Dare."

Leonora jolted in response to Dare's name uttered on the duke's lips. A tiny sliver of the earlier dwindled thrill shot up her belly and burrowed in her chest. "He is not *my* Lord Dare. Why does everyone assume so?" Because they flirted so much?

"I don't mean anything by the statement, only that the two of you seemed drawn to each other."

"It's called friendship." Or the relationship between the ravager and the ravaged. Did that have a name?

"Friends bat their eyes at each other?"

Leonora cocked her head at the duke, who gazed back smiling at her. Had she batted her lashes at Dare? Maybe. The picture of him batting his lashes at her, however, brought a matching grin to her face. What a delightful picture!

The earl certainly had the face of an angel and the attitude of a devil, but there was also an endearing part of him that could make her laugh despite his harrowing reputation and the chaos that was his past.

The words *infamous* and *notorious* and *rake* all vanished when she was with him. Even when she called him rakish or he himself referred to himself as such, it was more in a teasing manner than anything else. Leonora didn't see the rake. She never really had.

She saw the man.

What did he see when he looked at her? Did he see a foolish flirt or a beguiling woman? Probably a bit of everything.

Perhaps not much of anything.

Now why had that unwelcome thought claimed a spot of torment in her heart?

"WHAT THE BLOODY hell are they laughing at?"

Two chuckles followed Dare's sour question.

He shot a glare to his left, to Drake. "And why did *you* follow me here? You never attend these sorts of events in this part of town."

"For the former, I have my reasons," Drake murmured, his eyes sweeping the interior of Dare's private box. "As for the latter, you have inspired me."

Inspired his arse! The man enjoyed watching him trip over his own damn proverbial boots, that's what.

"Come now," Knox drawled from his other side. "Let's enjoy the play."

There was no way he could do that, he bit out in his mind, glancing back at the box that housed Leonora and her perfect duke. At that moment, she was looking up at the man and smiling at something he'd said. Not one person here tonight needed a looking glass to see her lips curling upward. It was there. Plain for everyone to draw conclusions from.

And Lord, she looked beautiful. Even from this distance, he could tell. And she looked it while not beside him. She looked it beside another man.

"Why don't you just admit you like the chit?" Drake asked, mockery dripping from every word.

"Why should I admit that?" *To you of all people?* Though he had admitted it to himself more times than he cared to count. Every look her way was an admission. Every touch. Every smile. But someone as jaded as Drake—*cough*—would never understand this.

"Leave the man be, Drake," Knox said. "He doesn't fancy the lady, not in the way you are implying."

"Oh, he does."

Dare cut a chilling look to his cousin. "What is *like* anyway? It means horse shite. Whether I like her or not, it changes nothing."

Drake shrugged. "If it changes nothing, it's because *you* change nothing."

"Is this how a pot calls a kettle black?"

"I call it as I see it."

"Then what the devil should I call you as I see you?"

"Me?" Drake crossed one ankle over the other. "You should call me as you *don't* see me. That is usually a better way."

"Cousins . . ." Knox murmured. "This is not the place to bicker like two eleven-year-old boys."

Right. Dare wasn't about to bicker with the arse. He planted his gaze firmly back on the box with the vision in blue so that he could dissect every one of Leonora's small interactions with the duke.

This nonsense with Drake, feeble and fleeting though it was, had turned the already sour taste in his mouth to a bitter one. What did it matter to Drake whether he liked Leonora or not? The one it should matter to was his own self. All these damn feelings belonged to him, not his cousin.

Knox nudged his arm. "Here."

Dare glanced over and let out a foul curse at the lorgnette being offered. He pushed it away with a scowl. "Now you are mocking me as well?"

"I'm helping you." Knox grinned. "While entertaining myself."

Dare rolled his eyes. He didn't have friends. Not a single one. All he had were pigs masquerading as friends.

"Give it to Drake," Dare countered evilly. "He might need a better look at the stage with his lack of culture and all."

"Is this what nobles do to entertain themselves? What godawful play is this anyway?"

"Shakespeare," Knox said. "*As You Like It*. Quite interestingly, it does tend to mock those who fall into the trap of love."

Dare scowled, his eyes never leaving the private box across from him. *Mock me if you must.* One day he would return the favor.

"Nevertheless, I'm rather enjoying the reminder of why I never venture into your world. Such shallow entertainment."

Could he kick his cousin from the box? "Then return to your dark little world in Brighton. No one is stopping you."

"Ah, the intermission," Knox murmured as he rose to his feet. "Thank Christ."

Dare sprang to his feet, his gaze lingering one moment longer on Leonora before he balled his hands into fists and strode from the box. He only had one direction in mind—the path that took him to *her*. He didn't want or need a lorgnette to see she'd gifted another smile to someone who wasn't him. No. What he wanted was a look up close to catch with his very eyes the evidence of what he'd known all along.

She was not for him.

She deserved better than him.

She could snatch herself a duke and never think again about him and all they had shared. He'd taken her innocence, couldn't take more. Could never hope for more. He drew to a halt, finding he had already descended the three flights of stairs that brought him back to the lobby with its sparkling chandeliers hanging overhead.

What are you doing, Dare? He shouldn't even be here tonight. When last in his life had he attended the theatre? He'd always been a prowler of the night. Now what had he become?

He shouldn't be here.

Even his feet knew that, for they had brought him here instead of taking him to her.

A high-pitched screech brought a chill to the very heart of him, and Dare knew—for some reason, he just knew—that this did not bode well for him.

That one screech drew out what sounded like a thousand more.

Run, Dare. Just run!

But he stood frozen for all of three seconds before he turned around—and then wished to God he'd run instead.

Something smashed into him. What in God's green earth?

He stared down at a monkey, who bared its small white teeth

and let out a shriek that tried, but failed, to rival the surrounding cries. One of those cries was his, but thank God that one sounded only in his head!

Why the hell was this damn monkey attacking him? No, why the bloody hell were *animals* attacking him? First the bird. Then the alligator. Now a damn monkey with a red hat on his head.

His hand gripped the fur and yanked.

And tossed the thing, quite accidentally, onto someone else.

Dare's eyes went wide.

A couple had entered the sphere of madness, and the monkey he had tossed aside now clung to a man's head, whilst the woman beside him leaped away with a yelp. What the devil was Calstone doing here? His gaze flicked to Leonora, whose eyes were blazing with laughter, one hand covering her mouth.

"Damn it!" Calstone let out a string of curses. "Get this savage creature off me!"

A portly man rushed forward, yelling, "Monty! Come here, Monty!"

Dare wanted to scowl at the man, but he couldn't drag his gaze from Leonora long enough for his brows to grow solemn enough. In the end, he couldn't help but demand, "How the hell does this happen? Are these things even allowed in the theatre?"

The man bowed while rushing forward, almost resembling that of a rocking chair set into motion. Only this rocking chair jiggled and had sweat dripping from his face like rain. "My apologies, my lords." He dabbed a handkerchief at his face. "Monty is part of the second act, and he escaped."

"*As You Like It* has a monkey in the play?" That was news to Dare.

"Monty was added last minute for a bit of comedic effect."

Bloody hell, don't talk to him about comedic effect! He had never been so humiliated in his life. His gaze flicked at Calstone, who still had the little beast attached to his face.

He instantly felt better.

"Oh, dear," Leonora seemed to finally breathe through her

amusement. She stepped up to the duke.

Dare wanted to protest. He wanted to stop her. Wedge his way in between her and Calstone, but a hand clasped onto his shoulder, keeping him from acting on his impulse and forcing him to watch as Leonora and the portly man fussed over Calstone, finally managing to wrench the monkey off the duke.

"Too many people," Knox murmured, his grip tightening before he let go.

Only then did Dare notice the gathering crowd that had been attracted by the chaos. At some point, Knox and Drake had joined the fray, both their faces remarkably stoic given the ensuing frolics.

Dare turned from their dour faces only to see Leonora with the duke's mug between her hands, inspecting his face.

The perfect couple.

He should leave. If ever there were a time to escape, this would be it. But his legs, for some reason, had changed their mind and instead of heading to the door as per their original intention, they now blasted forward to the pair.

Even his arms had developed minds of their own, for he certainly did not instruct his left arm to reach for her and clasp her wrist gently while the other pushed Calstone away hard.

No adequate curse word existed for this moment.

The drop of a pin would echo through the theatre, such was the silence caused by his shocking action. Even the monkey had gone silent, staring at him with big, confused eyes.

You've gone and done it now, Dare.

Chapter Twenty

ASTONISHING MOMENTS HAD a way of springing out at a person when they were least expected. Sometimes, they might be curated, like when her friends would purposely do something scandalous to shock the *ton*, but more often, they were not. And these moments were the most astonishing.

Like Dare.

She'd seen a lot of faces on Dare before. Sly. Flirtatious. Furious. Exasperated. And most of them, each in their own way, had amused her. However, tonight, she didn't know what was more comedic, the new expressions flashing across his face or the monkey that had attached itself to him. But the monkey and ensuing facial expressions were, arguably, not even the astonishing part of this situation, Leonora thought, as the tension in the air between Dare and Calstone fairly hummed. This moment was more astonishing than all other moments put together!

Her gaze flicked between the two men, settling for a moment on the veins running down Dare's neck and disappearing beneath his cravat. It brought the moment of his bare chest in the warehouse to mind. As well as the night they'd shared. The sense of thrill she had started the night off with returned tenfold.

But she couldn't very well have him take a tumble with the duke.

Leonora grabbed hold of his arm. "Dare."

His eyes found hers, and she shook her head. His lips pulled up in a sneer, but he instantly stepped back, the polished—or rather unpolished, yet refined—rake once more. Even that usual roguish smile hung on his face.

"My apologies, Duke."

Calstone dusted off his jacket. "For Lady Leonora's sake, I accept your apology."

Oh, Lord. While she appreciated the duke's sentiment, she inwardly grimaced at it. It only drew more attention onto her. Whispers and titters already filled the air of the lobby, almost deafening in their simultaneous rise.

"Thank you," Leonora said before Dare could reply. With that look on his face, it would probably be something infuriating. The duke's acceptance was already more than she could hope for. To Dare, she said, "What are you doing here?"

"Am I not allowed to attend the theatre?" He sounded bitter.

She blinked. "Of course you are." But when she had spotted him leaving his box at the interval, and she glimpsed his cousin as well, she'd understood his presence was perhaps not as simple as it might appear.

She even dared, for a second, to believe it might have been for her. And that second had been enough for her to rush from her own box, Calstone in tow, in the hope of intercepting him, which had led to the current moment.

His hot eyes settled on her. She felt them prickle on her skin like heated needle points. "And now you would fawn over the duke but not me? The monkey attacked me first."

Hold on. Was he perhaps . . . *jealous*?

Dare she believe?

No. Certainly not.

But his choice of words—*fawn over*? Was this something a rake ought to say? A smile sprang to her face, followed by a chuckle that turned into a bubble of laughter. Ah, this was no good, but she couldn't stop herself. This could not be considered a moment to rule all moments, but it certainly ranked near the top!

"Leonora? Why are you laughing?" A scowl formed between his brows. "Did the duke give you drink?"

Calston's throat cleared. "I resent that. And also, her laughter is not the issue here."

"Then what, by your account, is?" Dare demanded.

Leonora inhaled deeply and caught the duke's subtle shift in attention, which had lowered to where she still gripped Dare's arm, then down to where Dare still held onto her wrist. No. Her hand. Somewhere in all the chaos, his fingers had laced with hers.

They both froze.

Even the titters had suddenly stopped, waiting with bated breath for her and Dare's next move. She looked up at him, and their eyes locked. Monkey aside, she could just imagine certain other gossip sheets tomorrow. *A Lady and a Rake Hold Hands.* Or maybe *A Touch Too Far?*

Fingers Intertwined, Reputations on the Line!

Heart was going to kill her.

"Hit me," he whispered.

Leonora blinked at him, and not the flirtatious kind. "What?" she said through her own fading smile. Had she heard him correctly?

"Hit me," he repeated with a hiss. "It's the only way out of this for you."

"What about you?" How could she slap that handsome face that had never been slapped by a woman before? She surely didn't want to be the first. And she'd never slapped a man before, either. How hard a slap would be considered good enough to provide a way out? This was just too absurd!

"I don't need a way out as you do."

Right.

Only she would be tainted from this. But who was she if not a walking invisible scandal? Her family had done their best to shield her and give her the best life possible, but that did not take away the hidden truth that had been molding her for the past six years.

Scandal didn't scare her.

Her fingers, intertwined with his, tightened in a clasp.

He jerked.

Her smile brightened again in response.

"That is not how you slap a man," his low voice came along with his fingers slowly unweaving from hers. She deliberated whether she should grip his hand harder.

"Dear God, the two of you are not just flirting, but flirting with scandal," Calstone muttered.

As if his words could conjure catastrophe, Heart's voice suddenly boomed "Leonora!" throughout the hall, causing everyone present to jolt on the spot.

Dare's hands clamped firm again. Out of instinct, Leonora thought, as hers squeezed a bit tighter as well. And how could one's heart take on such a speed so quickly? It almost defied reason.

Calstone suddenly blocked their view to the left—Heart's view—to be exact. However, Leonora's relief didn't last long.

"I already saw everything, Calstone! Step aside."

"It's all right, Your Grace, thank you." She quickly disengaged from Dare, a picture of poise as Calstone nodded and stepped off to the side. Her brother came into view in all his glorious fury.

Leonora lifted her chin, prepared for battle, but stilled—beside Heart walked the Duchess of Crane. She couldn't tell where they'd come from, but it wasn't the front entrance.

Heart had never left.

His personal business *had* been a certain duchess. She had been curious all this time, too hesitant to ask her family directly, circling around and around. Could tonight hold the answers she sought?

He marched to stop before them. "What is the meaning of this?"

"Meaning?" Leonora dragged her gaze away from the duchess, even though she wanted nothing but to stare. "What meaning would you attach to this rather public situation? It certainly cannot be a wicked one."

"Leonora," Heart bit out, stepping up to her, his figure looming like a hulking mountain. "Every single person here can interpret the poorly hidden meaning behind your little romantic display, or whatever you wish to call it. Is this your chaste friendship you told me about?"

Dare chuckled. "Chaste friendship. What a marvelous term."

Leonora's pulse surged. There was nothing chaste about them—not anymore. Perhaps there never had been. Mayhap that had only been her delusion. However, when she had rattled off that phrase—chaste friendship—she had believed herself and Dare to be nothing more than two people who enjoyed each other's flirtations that could never be more.

"Well, the term—" she began.

"Is quite apt," Dare interrupted. "In our previous lives, we must have been brother and sister, so chaste is our friendship."

Low titters erupted once again.

Leonora glanced at Dare. This flat tone . . . yet his smile remained in place. The air of a rake never faltered. The only difference was that those stark, blue eyes refused to meet hers.

"Leonora," a soft feminine voice came as the duchess stepped forward to place a hand on her arm. "Perhaps we should retire to a more private spot."

Leonora stepped back, evading the touch. Clear as day, the woman supported Heart, and she didn't feel like playing along at the moment. "I'm perfectly all right where I am."

"I don't think . . ." the duchess began again, but trailed off when Dare suddenly bowed.

Leonora blinked at him.

"I fear my friends require my immediate attention," Dare said loudly, firmly. "I shall take my leave here. I apologize for any misunderstanding."

Misunderstanding? Was he leaving her here alone at a time like this? A moment like this? Shouldn't he be running off with her over his shoulder and a bellowing Heart chasing after them?

She certainly wouldn't mind realizing such a fantasy. But merely departing like this?

"Rake." She reached out to him, and he evaded *her* touch, just like she had done with the duchess.

"Enjoy the rest of your evening, my lady."

My lady?

"No, I—"

He stepped back. "You should enjoy the rest of your evening with your family."

"But I—"

He didn't listen. He cut her off by pivoting, giving her his back, which, for some inexplicable reason, overlapped with the memory of him walking into a boxing match shirtless, only this time . . .

It didn't feel like he would return.

DARE DESCENDED THE steps of Drury Lane with an urgency he last felt when he was escaping all the hands reaching for him at his father's funeral. There were few days in his life that had been as bad as that one. And few days as good. On the one hand, he had lost his father, who had, for all his faults, been a passable father. On the other hand, a sense of finality, a sense of peace, had settled in his heart.

Both his parents were gone. Along with all their pain.

Damnation. His heart.

He clutched at his chest, dragging his hand up to his throat as his breathing became a graver concern than the pounding in his chest. Both nearly drew him to his knees.

Hell . . .

Damnation . . .

And . . .

The moment he reached his carriage, all elegance deserted him—did he even have any left?—and he launched onto the seat inside. "Home," he barked in a single order. He couldn't say more. He couldn't say it softly.

The driver didn't question him, and the carriage flew forward the moment the door shut. He could find comfort in at least this. He always had a means of retreat ready. That never failed him, and it didn't fail him now.

Christ. Poets always waxed on about love and hope in tortured pieces of meter and rhyme. If his life were a poem, it would surely be a tortured masterpiece.

She told Heart they had a *chaste* friendship. Chaste friendship? Their bloody meanings of "chaste" were *not* the same! If hers was noon, the brightest part of the day, then his was decidedly—flatly—midnight. They couldn't be more opposite.

He could just imagine how every single male ancestor of his was rolling in his grave while every single female was curling up in laughter.

What the hell did you expect, Dare? That she'd confessed to her ruin?

He suddenly burst out in laughter. Why ever would she do that? He had taken her innocence. Could he ever hope for more from her when he himself could never offer her more than what he already was? There was a *reason* she had chosen him to gift her innocence to. There was a reason *she* had never held any false hope about him.

He slammed a fist against the door.

Why the hell can't I be more?

He pressed the palm of his hand against his forehead.

You know why.

Yes.

Darkness shrouded him, and no matter how much of her light pierced through the shadows, the shadows always returned the moment she left. If he were a good man, he'd have done the right thing. He'd have asked for her hand. Taken responsibility. But he was not good. To him, being the better man meant not repeating his father's mistakes—ensuring he never put himself in a position where he could.

How comedic.

They spoke of marriage as being leg shackled, but if that were truly the case—his leg shackled with hers, in a literal sense—perhaps the threat of the past repeating itself would become null and void.

But he knew better. Marriage didn't change a man. It only exposed what was already there. And what was inside him wasn't fit to be bound to someone like her.

She was bright afternoons and warmth, and he was the cold creeping in at dusk, the kind that made people shut their windows and lock their doors. She was the kind of woman who made men believe they could be better—except Dare had spent a lifetime knowing exactly what he was. No amount of fool's hope could rewrite that truth.

Still, those words echoed in his head. *Chaste friendship.*

His mouth twisted. No, there was nothing chaste about the way he wanted her. The way he thought of her, even now, with his pulse still hammering from the sheer *want* of her.

He dragged a hand through his hair and let his head fall back against the seat. The carriage jolted as it hit a rut, but he barely felt it. He had endured worse disruptions. He had survived worse. And yet, for the first time in his life, he wasn't entirely certain he would survive *this*.

Her.

And the damnable burn clawing at his chest.

After some time, the carriage stopped and Dare sighed. He hated nights at home. *Too damn silent.*

"Dare, old fellow! What the devil!"

Dare almost slipped stepping from the carriage and glanced back to see Knox and Drake jumping from the driver's seat of another carriage. A question mark formed on his brow. "Whose vehicle is that?" Had they chased after him?

"Not important," Drake said.

Enemies, I tell you, enemies. What friends would do this at such a time?

"I'm not in the mood for whatever nonsense you bring with you," Dare bit out.

"Then you wish to be alone?" Knox's mocking tone jabbed his ears.

Enemy—and one that read him like a book. Dare sneered and strode to his home, not objecting to their shadows following in his trail. "I don't want to talk about her."

"Wouldn't dream of mentioning her name," Knox drawled.

"Yes, we are more interested in the monkey," Drake added.

Dare clenched his fist and whirled on them "What do you want to say about that damn monkey? Say it now. Because the moment I enter that house," he jabbed a finger at his door, "this night never happened."

"You weren't bitten were you?" Knox asked. "If you were, I shall have my physician summoned. Monkeys are vile creatures."

"No." He glanced down at his clothing and then at his hands. No imprints of bites anywhere. That monkey had merely given him a fright and flashed his teeth at him. *Laughing* at him. He had become the mockery of the animal world.

More irony. He had called himself a man of nothing but animal instinct so often over the years that it wouldn't surprise him if *real* animals now saw through his shite and were deciding to reject his claim. Honestly.

However, that same instinct had cautioned him to retreat from the theatre. But that wasn't saying much, since the same instinct had moments prior caused him to push the duke away from *her* before far too many people who now served as witnesses to what may be the strangest moment of his life.

"You flung a monkey in a duke's face."

Dare shot a nasty look at his cousin. "That's not a question."

Drake nodded. "Did it feel good?"

Did it? A sudden smile split his face. Bloody hell, he had felt so damn rotten a moment before but the mere memory of the monkey clinging to Calstone's face . . . His mood lifted a bit. "I suppose it did."

"If you are happy, we are happy, old fellow." Knox peeked at the house. "Will you allow us in now?"

"Only if you vow no more questions about monkeys, dukes, and *her*."

Two heads nodded.

"Good. Then you are welcome." He would rather not be alone anyway, and even Drake had come along—a man who didn't normally set foot in these parts.

Knox waved a hand. "Just to be sure, we are allowed to discuss your ruin?"

Ruin? *His* ruin or her ruin? Their ruin? What happened tonight was not enough to ruin her, was it? Certainly not him. They had been engaged in all sorts of public flirtations this past season, so tonight should hardly be more than a bit of scandal, a few headlines to stir up gossip. In the grand scheme of things, he should be nothing more than a hint of sour lemon on an otherwise sweet cake.

He could never be the sweetness.

Chapter Twenty-One

FAMILY. FURY. THE two words entwined. The British cavalry couldn't tear these two words apart, so inseparable were they. Just like Leonora could never separate the blood pulsing through her veins from that which ran through her parents'. She could never escape this inheritance. It was in her, forever. Like so many other things. Dare had once said she was smarter than Heart, which meant she must have inherited her mother's cleverness. But she'd inherited plenty from her father—stubbornness chief among them. She could never run from it. Could never hide it.

She turned to face Heart the moment she finished marching into the first drawing room convenient for their confrontation, feeling the heavy burden of silence from the carriage ride home. That silence clung to her like a shadow.

Common wisdom claimed that the ties of family were more important than all others, and Leonora agreed. However, she had reached the precipice of a moment that refused to be contained for much longer. She would suffocate if she remained this way.

"What the devil did you do?" Heart growled. "What the devil happened at the theatre?"

She had lived her life.

"You held his hand! Hand. Palm on palm. Thank God you were wearing gloves. Do you understand how it might still be interpreted?"

Of course.

"How could you allow such a thing?" He dragged both hands through his hair. "You're an innocent lady!"

I'm really not.

"He is a damnable rake!"

Perhaps not damnable.

"The gossip rags will tear you asunder!"

"Heart."

His glowing eyes fixed on her, his breathing ragged and uneven. Leonora strode over and took his hand in hers and placed it over his heart. "Breathe."

He inhaled, exhaled, his eyes on her.

"Dare is not the concern here," she said quietly. Not tonight at least. In the morning, he would become a concern again. The way he had strode from the theatre earlier. The flicker in his gaze in his parting look. She'd dissect it all later. For now, other matters required her attention.

Heart's brows furrowed. "He is every concern—"

"Father."

He jerked back, and her hand fell away. His face lost all color, and even his breathing seemed to stop. Leonora's pulse, on the other hand, threatened to push from her chest and straight into her throat. She had said it. She had finally said it. Finally called him father.

"Why would you call me that?" he whispered hoarsely.

"Because you are my father."

"What are you talking about? I'm your—"

"Father. You're my father."

"Damn it, Leonora." Some color returned to his cheeks, but not much. "What do you think you know?"

Leonora stared at his face, and for the first time, she saw more than the role of a brother he had assumed—a man more at a loss than she could have imagined. A man backed farther into a corner she had ever envisioned. "I know you are my father. I've known for the past six years."

"Christ, I need to sit." He staggered to a chair and plopped down, burying his face in his hands. He glanced at her between his fingers. "How?"

"I overheard you questioning Mama and Papa one evening after dinner about the decision to keep the truth from me. Ironically, that question revealed it to me."

A tense pause. "Why didn't you confront us? Why didn't you ever say anything?"

Leonora shrugged lightly. "Honestly, I cannot say. At first, for about a second or two, perhaps an hour or two, I felt betrayed. But even as I felt that betrayal, I understood that you all had made the decisions you'd made to protect me. To give me the best life."

"Christ." The heels of his palms pressed against his eyes. "This is too much."

Her heart pinched. "Oh, it's not that much. Simply a truth revealed."

His head fell back, hands not leaving his face. "I thought you would hate me if you ever discovered the truth."

Hate him. "I could never hate my family, Heart. I can grapple with what to call you, tease you, argue with you, but never hate you. I didn't tell you because I didn't want to hurt you." She hadn't wanted to open wounds which appeared to be tearing at him now. This was why she'd never felt confident enough to expose him.

"You should hate me. I was a blackguard. I didn't do the right thing when it mattered."

"You mean with my real mother. The Duchess of Crane."

His hands fell away, and his red eyes stared back at her. "How . . .?"

"Honestly, it was Calstone."

"The duke? How . . ."

His confusion brought a small smile to the corner of her lips. "He commented on my uncanny likeness to the duchess. So I suspected, and then you and Mama confirmed my suspicions. And any sliver of doubt I retained, you just dispelled."

"Mother?"

Leonora bit her lip. "Yes, Mother."

He stilled, then let out a loud curse. "Grapple with titles, you said. Understood. This is deuced uncomfortable." He inhaled deeply. "Mother is not in Wales, I take it?"

"You didn't know?" Leonora asked.

He shook his head. "You spotted her?"

"On my last morning ride."

A scowl formed on his brow. "The one you had with that ruffian?"

"Let's not divert from the topic at hand, *father*."

"Christ, don't call me that. My old heart can't take it."

Leonora stared at her father. Her brother. Heart. A man fraught with flaws, demons, mistakes. "I don't blame you for the choices in the past." She lowered her voice to a whisper. "I don't even blame my birth mother."

"Damn it." His face fell back into his hands. "If I had done the right thing, none of this would have happened. She would not have been forced to give you up, forced into a marriage she didn't want, forced to live a life . . ."

"Heart."

His entire body clenched up before her eyes. She stepped up to him, lowered to her haunches, pulled his hands from his face.

His dewy eyes met hers.

"Mistakes don't define your life." Look at her, ruined in a whole other way than what anyone could ever imagine. A mistake? Perhaps. But only if she chose that it be one. "So look forward, and don't dwell in a past you cannot change. After all, you are not the same man you were back then, are you? You've become a much better man since then. At least, that is how I see it."

The hands in hers flipped to grip hers tightly. "Cassandra— the duchess—has been wanting to meet you, talk to you, but I have been pushing against it."

"Because you feared I might discover the truth?"

"That it would be revealed before you made a match."

Oh, Lord. "You should not worry about that." Leonora glanced away.

"Do not tell me it's because of *that* reprobate?"

No, and yes. "Very well, I won't tell you it's *that* reprobate."

Though it was true that she had made her choice with him, with their night together, and didn't regret it. And even though she had never harbored any misgivings about Dare and his character, she would be lying if she claimed there hadn't been a small smidgeon of hope sprouting in her heart for something more. But this was not a discussion she could ever indulge in! This was but a secret hope, one nestled deep in her heart.

No, Leonora. This is not you.

She didn't go through life hoping this and that. She acted. She seized. She chased what she wanted. Her gaze dropped to the big hands holdings hers. She understood why Heart always dragged her away from Dare.

He didn't wish for her to become her mother.

Only it might be too late for that. She'd been ravaged by Rake. Her eyes fell on her belly. She might even be . . . Her whole body went cold as her brother's imagined past flashed before her eyes in a tragic, unfortunate set of events. A fate she might now share.

"You're just as damn stubborn as I," he said on a mutter.

Ah. Heart. He'd be furious if it were indeed the case. "You do know I love you."

His fingers tightened on hers. "I love you, too."

I'm sorry.

I failed to meet your expectations.

DARE STIRRED FROM a restless sleep by a sharp knock at the door.

"My lord?" the butler called.

He groaned, cracking one eye open. Where the devil was he? Oh, right, he'd come home from the theatre, followed by Knox and Drake. Things got blurry after that. But this wasn't his chamber. This was . . . his study? More specifically, the *floor* of his study.

He pushed himself up, his mind sluggish. Drake was sprawled in his chair, feet resting on the desk, while Knox was half-draped over the sofa. What kind of friends were these? Why should he be on the damn floor of his own home?

Enemies, I tell you.

He rubbed his temples and blinked to clear his foggy vision. His eyes fell on one bootless foot—his—and the cravat tossed beside it—also his. This is why he didn't drink.

"My lord?"

"What is it, Brett?"

"The Duchess of Crane is seeking an audience, my lord."

"Send her away." His eyes snapped wide. "Wait. Send her to the room where we receive people. Give me a minute." He at least had to wipe the crust from his eyes and find his missing boot. Bloody hell, his temples pounded. But that wasn't what mattered at the moment.

Leonora's mother had called on him.

He couldn't fathom why. Unless . . . The aftermath of the monkey incident? Christ, he just wanted to forget—all of it. The monkey. Her. The duke.

Dare pushed to his feet, staggering to the door. He swept the room for his boot, but of course, couldn't find it. To hell with it all. He pulled off the one he still had on. He was in no condition to meet the woman, but he also didn't care much about his condition, so he'd just go and meet her to see what she wanted.

She rose the moment he entered the receiving room. Her brow furrowed as her gaze moved over him from head to toe, pausing at his stocking feet, a silent commentary he didn't care to dwell on.

"Your Grace," he drawled, choosing a spot the farthest away from her—the wall—and leaned against it. "Forgive my appearance."

"I'm not here for pleasantries, Lord Dare." The duchess placed a parcel on the table and pushed it toward him.

"What is this?" Nothing good, he'd wager.

"What your cousin desires the most."

The deed? Christ, the throb in his temples worsened. "Why offer me this?"

"It is not for free."

Of course not. She would want payment, and it didn't take a damn genius to guess what. "Do I dare ask the price?"

"Lady Leonora. Never approach her again. Do not speak to her, do not look at her, do not even so much as think about her."

The last would be a little hard. Impossible, in fact.

Christ, what was the time? He needed sustenance. Coffee. Tea. A piss. Anything. Everything.

"And what is your interest in Lady Leonora? What business is it of yours to demand such a thing?"

"That you do not need to know."

If only he could forget. "You did not want to give this *parcel* to Drake before. Why should I be your messenger? And why now? You have always known Drake and I are family."

"Yes, but your family shunned Drake and his mother. I only learned recently that you, now the head of the family, did not."

"You shunned him, too."

"For a reason."

"His birth?"

She averted her gaze. "No. My husband chased any skirt that brushed past him. I know this better than anyone." She met his gaze again. "Your cousin made it impossible to give this parcel back before now, that is all."

Drake, you damn mongrel, what the hell did you do? "How so?"

She pursed her lips, before answering bluntly, "He discovered a secret and made demands."

"Blackmail."

"Such a distasteful word, but correct. However, the demand was difficult and the secret . . . unfortunate. The situation was not straightforward."

What secret could Drake possibly have discovered that would set the duchess on edge and cause her to dig her heels in the ground?

Dare froze.

Leonora. Leonora was the secret.

Drake, you damn blackguard.

His cousin knew.

He'd always bloody known.

"So you offer me this now in exchange for distancing myself from Lady Leonora?" He let out a dry laugh. "Drake gets what he wants, you get what you want, and I get nothing. Convenient."

"It does seem unfair, does it not?"

"But you don't care about that, do you?"

She merely shrugged. "It may not look it, but Heart was once a dear friend of mine. I would hate to see his sister disgraced or ruined because of men like you." Her voice cooled. "As for the matter of your cousin, all I will say about that is that I'm tired of fighting. I'd rather put the past to bed."

"You should have put it to bed two years ago. Why now?"

She paused before answering, "I was angry. Angry for a long time. But I've come to learn that some things matter far more than clinging to hurts you are better off letting go."

Now, why did it sound like she was referring to him and Leonora?

"But you don't just want me to stay away from Lady Leonora, you want my cousin to back down as well, correct?"

She inclined her head. "Once he has the deed, there is no reason for him to keeping fighting. It's in all our interests to let matters go."

"I cannot control my cousin." He could throttle him, however.

"I'm willing to wager you would find a way to do the right thing, to get him to do the right thing." Dare sighed, and she continued. "I shall give this to you, and all I require is your word."

His word that he would walk away from Leonora.

"You must hold Heart in high esteem to go this far for him and his family."

"I am indebted to his family, so yes. Will you accept this offer or not?"

His tongue wouldn't form the word *yes*. Every word associated with resistance fought against that *yes* from rolling off his tongue. It bloody annoyed him, this request, as equally as Drake's damn puppeteering. He pushed, he prodded, he rattled the tree and let others scramble for falling fruit until they were exhausted. But he never *forced* an outcome. An impressive ability Dare might have admired, if he hadn't been caught up in the shake as well.

"Let us dispense with the niceties and come straight to the point. You wish me," and his family, Drake, "to stay away from your daughter in exchange for this deed of property." He was no longer in the mood for pretense and roundabout speech.

Her composure slipped. "Your cousin told you."

"No. She did. Leonora."

The woman's face went as pale as a blank sheet of paper. "I beg your pardon?"

"Leonora already knows you are her mother. Or suspects, at least. She knows Heart is her father. She deduced the rest. I shall keep your secret because I have already been keeping it. For her. I will also take that deed."

She suddenly rose to her feet, rubbing at her sable skirts. "If you know this, then you know why I am asking you to stay away from her."

He did. He damn well didn't want to know, but he did.

He was also curious. "How long have you been wearing black?"

"Twenty years."

Bloody hell.

His gaze dropped to the parcel on the table between them. It shouldn't be a difficult choice. He had no future with Leonora, no matter the stir she caused in his heart. He had already walked away, had he not? That was certainly his intention at Drury Lane. So why did his fingers tremble at the mere thought of accepting that deed?

But he'd taken her innocence. He couldn't take any more. Could he?

No.

He couldn't.

Only pain would follow acting on his stubborn affection. No. It was better for him to bear the pain than her. He would not risk seeing Leonora share the same fate as his mother because he'd failed like his father had. But he *could* accept this arrangement. He could accept this deed and in return never approach Leonora again.

No matter what price love demanded from him, he would pay it.

"Very well." He met the duchess's gaze. "I'll stay away from Leonora."

Chapter Twenty-Two

A FORTNIGHT.

Fourteen days.

Too many hours.

Leonora stopped before the door of the drawing room. Time truly dragged when one had no person to spark life into each moment. And no sparks sparked Leonora's life at the moment. The hours bled into one another, colorless and dull. It felt rather jarring that the world continued while she was utterly devoid of spirit.

Devoid of *him*.

No sharp, witty barbs thrown her way, no stolen touches or intimate moments of ecstasy. None. Gone was being understood in a way that made her feel breathless. Gone was the anticipation, the awareness that somewhere—perhaps around the next corner, perhaps in the next heartbeat—*he* would be there. Well, if she were honest, a smidgeon of that anticipation still lingered, but it carried a more desperate edge rather than the pulsing beat of excitement. This must be what a woman felt being ravaged and discarded by a rake. And yet, at the theatre . . .

Shush, Leonora.

But that moment . . . that moment when he'd grasped her wrist and pushed Calstone away from her . . .

She clutched her breast. It meant . . . *something*. And at the same time, did it also mean *nothing*?

Leonora shook away the thought, inhaled a deep breath, and entered the drawing room to which she had been summoned and stopped short when she came face to face with three figures: Heart, the duchess, and the marchioness—her mama.

"Leonora, dear," the marchioness, Lady Heartly, said. "Please come have a seat."

Her gaze darted between the three people. It didn't take a brilliant mind to understand that certain introductions were to be made today and certain truths were to be revealed. On the one hand, she welcomed the truth. On the other hand, she couldn't help but feel a twinge of wariness, too.

Leonora crossed the room and lowered herself into a chair unhurriedly, flushing as those three pairs of eyes burned into her. Inside, her heart pounded.

The marchioness cleared her throat. "Heart has told us that you overheard a conversation between us when you were a child. I cannot even imagine what you must have been feeling over these past years."

Leonora shook her head, unwilling to add to their worry. "I know why you did it, so please, do not feel any guilt on my behalf." Their burden had been far heavier than hers, and they had carried it for far longer.

The marchioness nodded. "And as you have correctly deducted, the Duchess of Crane is your mother."

Leonora's gaze flicked to the woman in question. Her mother. She had thought once they were officially introduced, she might feel an instant sort of mother-daughter connection. But there was no such extraordinary feeling.

"Leonora," the duchess said, her voice soft but proud. "You've grown into a beautiful young woman. You must have so many questions for me."

Questions? Leonora's gaze dropped to where the woman rubbed one finger over the other before meeting her gaze again. She didn't have any questions, in fact. Perhaps in the past, but not anymore. She loved her family, and the Duchess of Crane wasn't part of it. She hadn't been for the past twenty years. She had merely birthed her.

All Leonora had wanted was the truth, which she now had. As for the rest, she could surmise what had transpired between the duchess and Heart. A rake had seduced an innocent lady, or perhaps the other way around, and when the consequences came in the form of Leonora, that rake failed to do the right thing, which left the lady with limited options.

It was a tale that might be considered as old as time.

The duchess's family might even have had a hand in how it had all played out in the end. Perhaps they wouldn't have welcomed the idea of her marrying the rake who had ruined her anyway. However, it didn't matter to Leonora. In time, they might build a relationship, and she was certainly open to that— would be delighted, in fact—but at the moment her mind was rather stuck on someone other than her real mother.

"Leonora?" Heart said gruffly. "Are you all right? Do you want some tea?"

Right. Leonora cleared her throat and shook her head.

Then she suddenly recalled something that Dare had said at the lake. "I do have some questions, now that I think about it." Not questions that had anything to do with the distant past, rather a more recent past. But first, she turned to the marchioness, "Are you not supposed to be in Wales, Mother? I witnessed your early morning meeting with the duchess that time in the park."

The marchioness jolted. "Oh. That. Yes." She let out a little cough behind her hand. "I heard Cassandra planned to return to London and grew concerned. But now that it has come to this, I plan to travel back to join your father in Wales as early as tomorrow."

Ah. Well, Leonora had suspected as much. Her gaze found the duchess's. "Dare told me you paid him a visit."

The woman's eyes widened. "He told you that?"

Leonora nodded. The duchess seemed oddly surprised. Why would he not? Before she could ask her next question, however, Heart shot a heated glance to the duchess and growled, "I thought you said he agreed to stay away from Leonora if you handed him the deed of that other fellow."

Wait, what? Leonora's heart threatened to stop.

"I did," the duchess murmured. "He accepted the condition without hesitation."

Leonora froze.

The words rang in her ears, hollow and heavy all at once. Accepted the condition without hesitation? Deed? That other fellow? But her heart only latched onto the first part. Accepted the condition. And Heart said Dare had agreed to stay away from her.

The truth settled in her chest like a stone. She knew it as surely as she knew the sun would rise each morning—this condition was their leverage to keep them apart. Heart's reaction had already been a giveaway, but any lingering doubt crumbled at the duchess's pinched expression.

Leonora's breath caught.

And then, her heart moved to the most devastating part of the statement. *Without hesitation.*

That blasted rogue! How could he do this to her?

Drat it. Her heart threatened to burst as everything started to fall into place. Heart and the duchess had meddled in her affairs. They had made a deal with Dare. And the cad had accepted.

Without hesitation.

Leonora rose to her feet, drawing all eyes back to her. "When was this?"

The duchess's brows furrowed. "A fortnight ago. I was only . . ." Her voice trailed off as Leonora balled her hands into fists, pretty certain from the expressions on all three faces looking back at her that the composure in her own had cracked.

This was why she hadn't even caught a glimpse of his shadow at any event. He had made a deal for the thing his cousin was in search of. The deed.

This is what you get for falling in love with a rake, Leonora.

Curse it all!

She'd fallen in love with a rake even though she had never intended—nor even attempted—to reform him. But then, she hadn't intended to fall in love with him either. Yet even if she had set out to reform him, she would have failed, simply because she had no desire to change anyone. She'd understood all this and had still fallen supremely hard.

Her family hadn't made it any easier, either. "How could you do such a thing?" Leonora demanded from the duchess.

"Leonora," Heart warned, his brows scrunching even more.

Hah! "That tone will not work on me today, Heart. You knew about this, too. How could you stoop to such low tricks?"

"Heart didn't know until after the fact," the duchess said. "I was merely trying to look out for you."

"I can look after myself." She sent her a pointed look. "I've been doing it for years."

"Nevertheless, Dare is no good for you, Leonora," Heart said. "The man is a lothario. Cassandra did you a favor."

A favor? How could this be borne? "You ruined the thing that mattered most to me!"

"The thing that mattered most?" Heart sneered. "You mean your chaste friendship with that libertine? He must not have thought it mattered so much, since he walked away from you so easily."

A vise tightened around her heart.

"Heart is right, Leonora," the duchess said, casting a brief, knowing glance at Heart, who responded with a grunt. "A man like Dare will only cause you grief. The last thing we want is for our past to repeat with you. It's better to stay away from him before it's too late."

"You mean before I'm seduced and must give up a child?"

Heart leaped to his feet. "Leonora!"

"What is it, Heart?" Leonora challenged, shoulders set. "You sorely underestimate me. You must know I'm not the sort of woman who bows to convention. If consequences arise from my associating with an infamous rogue, I shall face it the same way I face everything in my life—with boldness and without fear. You have no right to meddle in my relationships."

"When it comes to your reputation, I have every right," he boomed. "I have not protected you from fire and brimstone for twenty years only for it to be ruined by that blackguard!"

"Dare knows," Leonora said flatly. "He knows I am a by-blow. He knows everything."

The marchioness gasped.

"You *told* him?" Heart demanded, his face growing multiple shades of red. "*Him?*"

"I didn't spell it out, but he guessed. How could he not, when the duchess who resembles me so well calls on him to warn him off? Not a fortnight ago—before that. Weren't you there as well? He guessed. I didn't deny it."

The duchess's brows gathered together.

Heart cursed and dragged both hands through his hair. His eyes looked almost hopeless. "Do you know what you've done?"

"That's enough," the marchioness said firmly. "Calm your temper. If the earl knows, he knows. There is nothing to be done about it now."

Leonora agreed. This was enough. She couldn't believe they would do something so underhanded as to try to control her associations in this way. And Dare! Did he truly care for her so little that he would agree without hesitation? She shouldn't be angry or disappointed or even heartbroken at the fact that he didn't love her. After all, she had known what she was getting into when she had flirted with him. When she had seduced him. However, quietly acquiescing like an obedient, well-behaved lady without speaking to the man himself was simply not an option.

Face to face.

Heart to heart.

She turned on her heel and marched off.

"Leonora!" Heart called after her. "Where the devil are you

going?"

She stopped at the door to look over her shoulder. "If it was the past you didn't want me to repeat, you are too late," she smiled as his eyes widened, "for it has already repeated itself."

AH, WHAT HELLISH damnation.

He missed that little temptress.

A fist slammed into Dare's jaw. His head snapped sideways, pain exploding along his cheekbone, snapping him back to the present. The taste of blood filled his mouth.

"You're not focusing, cousin," Drake taunted. Roars went up all around the warehouse, as they circled each other, both shirtless and bloody. The sting of his knuckles registered only faintly. He had lost track of how many punches he'd thrown.

He took comfort in the fact that Drake looked a bit worse.

"You've been challenging me every day for a fortnight," Drake continued, rolling his shoulders. "Aren't you tired?"

"You lied to me." Knuckles cracked. "I'm venting."

Drake spit out blood and wiped his mouth with the back of his hand. "I withheld the truth."

Dare sneered. "Omission might not be an outright lie, but your intention behind the omission makes it one. You used me."

"No," Drake corrected with a smirk. "You are using me. I wish to return to Brighton in this lifetime."

"Then return."

"Then hand over the deed."

Dare's fist flew through the air, aimed straight for his cousin's face. Unfortunately, Drake ducked, and in the next instant, his knuckles connected with Dare's ribs, sending a jolt of misery up his side.

The man had confessed to letting a word slip here, a threat there, all leading the duchess back to London—where she would find her daughter flirting with a rake. His cousin's network, and his damned calculations, were deuced frightening.

He bit out a laugh through clenched teeth. "When I'm satisfied, I shall give it to you."

"You won't be satisfied until *you* return to *her* side," Drake countered. "I did you a favor, cousin."

"Don't speak nonsense."

"Admit it—you made a mistake."

No. It couldn't have been a mistake. Distancing himself was for the best. Leonora would marry the perfect man. A man like Calstone. A man worthy of her. A man the exact opposite of him. He . . . it didn't matter what he did, so long as he didn't hurt anyone like his father hurt his mother. He'd die before he'd do that.

But he also didn't want to let go.

I must.

Another blow from Drake cracked against his jaw. He cursed, ducking to the side before straightening and rolling his neck left and right. He didn't like pain. All his life, everything he had done was in service of avoiding it. And yet, the only thing more tolerable than the throb in his heart that had started to bloom in that secret library and had sprouted roots the moment he took that deed, was taking blows from Drake.

It will pass with time. He had to believe that. Anything else . . .

He dared not contemplate.

In the meantime, while he waited, he would torture his cousin for keeping the truth from him this entire time. That he'd known Leonora was the Duchess of Crane's child with Heart. That he had mocked him from the shadows. That he had tried to blackmail the woman into handing over the deed and failed.

The thought still made him want to reduce all Drake's properties to ashes.

Drake struck again, but this time, he was ready. He countered with a sharp jab to his cousin's gut, sending him staggering back. He didn't stop. The crowd roared with each hit and spat curses whenever one of them missed. It wasn't an official match. There would be no victor at the end of this.

And Drake had the nerve to say Dare had made a mistake? The only mistake he'd made was not beating Drake to a damn pulp.

Admit it.

Dare bent over, clutching at his leg with one hand and lifting his hand with the other. He dragged in several breaths. "Time."

A mocking smile answered him.

Arse.

Drake wiped the sweat from his brow. "Not going to admit it?"

This again. He straightened, clenching and unclenching his fists. "What the hell do you know anyway?"

"You've never been this out of sorts with a bird before."

"That's because she's not a bird, so watch your bloody language." What bird? She was a witch. A temptress. A miracle.

And he had left nothing but dust in his wake when he left.

Had she been worried? Had she been attending balls in the hope of catching him there? Had she been disappointed when he hadn't shown up? How many times had he stood before the doors of a house, the sounds of a ball or party or musicale drawing him forward, light spilling from within, before turning on his heel and walking away?

Admit . . .

Every single time, every single step had been a mistake. However, he hadn't been able to bring himself to step through those doors and into the light.

He hated this.

Hated himself for becoming like this. But what the hell was a man like him supposed to do? Hide his leopard spots beneath a coat of wool? Pretend his infamous reputation did not exist? Don a halo and hope no one noticed the horns?

"Do you know that my mother loved that man?" Drake asked, circling him, interrupting his spiral.

Was he talking about the late Duke of Crane?

"I could never understand how someone could love a monster," his cousin went on. "I still don't." Dark eyes, black as night, landed on Dare. Eyes Drake had inherited from the late duke. The man cracked his knuckles. "Are you a monster?"

What kind of question was that? "You know my father—"

"I'm not talking about your father," he cut Dare off. "I'm talking about you."

"I'm not a monster. My father wasn't either." His failures had just led to his mother's death, but a monster? No. He was a man with tragic flaws.

"If you're not a monster, then stop being so hesitant and go catch the little bird you set free."

"I can't promise I won't betray us." He laid his truth bare across the charged air of the warehouse even though the jeers once goading them to fight had subsided. This was his burden— the burden of his past set in the balance against the bright possibility of her future.

A dismissive snort. "Says who?"

"History."

Drake nodded, walked over to a crate, and sat down. "The sins of the father turn into the flaws of his son." He leaned back, tilting his chin up, eyes blazing with challenge "Or not."

"Spit it out if you have something to say."

"The past repeating itself isn't up to your father, it's up to you. If you don't like it, change it. Forge a new course for your offspring."

Dare's brows furrowed. *The past repeating itself isn't up to your father, it's up to you.* What the devil was he supposed to do with those words? Christ, they pressed onto his chest like a thousand red bricks. They gripped him in such a numbing vise that he stood frozen, torn between the familiar, cold comfort of certainty and the blinding, terrifying thought that maybe—just maybe—he could change things.

Could he change things?

Could he make himself a different man? One worthy of something more than just the burden of his bloodline? More than the shadows of his father's sins? Leonora—beautiful, brilliant, and far beyond his reach—could he be the man she deserved? A man who wouldn't tear apart everything they could build, but would instead be the one to hold it together?

He clenched his fists, pulse pounding in his temples.

No, he wasn't like his father. He couldn't be. And if he was to ever to become the man he could be—a man worthy of her—he had to try.

And try hard.

For her. For himself. For a chance to leave the darkness, to rewrite the future instead of repeating the past.

It was up to him. Yes. But damn it, what if he failed? What if he failed her? His offspring? Himself?

He cursed. *Getting ahead of yourself there, Dare?*

Who was to say she would still have anything to do with him?

But if, by any chance, she felt for him what he felt for her . . . He might not be a man worthy of her yet, but he could start becoming that man. He would continue becoming until his very last breath, and hope to God it had been enough, that he had not failed. That he had succeeded.

A certain parrot's cry flitted through his head. *The earl is an idiot. The earl is an idiot.*

Christ. He *was* an idiot.

"Actually, mate, it seems you won't have to go hunting after all."

Hunting? He swore this mouth of his cousin's was deuced vexing. Birds. Hunting. Why the hell did it remind him of his parrots and alligators? Toss a monkey in the mix, too. Memories he could do without.

Memories that also all . . . included *her.*

Then again, perhaps not so bad at all.

He scowled at Drake. "Why not shut your mouth and prepare to be beaten?"

"Are you sure?" He nodded to a spot behind Dare. "I'd rather not humiliate you."

Dare glanced over his shoulder and then snapped all the way around so fast a muscle in his neck pulled. He ignored the pain. There she stood. Watching him. Her hair tumbled down the way he loved, his jacket draped over her shoulders as though she belonged to him.

Utterly riveting.

Chapter Twenty-Three

LEONORA STARED AT the man in the center of the warehouse, bare chested, his skin marred with bruises, her heart in her throat, pulsing fiercely. She didn't know if he had won or lost, but drat it all—he had never looked more devastatingly handsome. After leaving the drawing room . . . After what she had discovered . . .

She'd fought hard to hold her tongue in that room, to keep from blurting something she could never take back. It was certainly not how she had envisioned her first official meeting with her mother would go. Leonora still couldn't fathom the duchess's degree of meddling. On the brighter side, standing in that stifling drawing room, beholding Heart and the duchess together, the entire array of their life choices had flashed before her eyes.

And she had come to a clear, vivid conclusion.

Their life was not *her* life.

Their end was not her and Dare's end.

Period.

And speaking of that rake . . . his eyes, socketed in a face mottled blue, black, and purple, and streaked with smears of red, stared back at her with an expression she couldn't quite place. When he hadn't been home, she'd set upon his friend Lord Knoxley, who had pointed her here. And now here she was. She'd come to get answers, prepared to accept them.

She stepped up to him. One step. Two steps. Three, four, five, and all that followed until she stood before him. Her gaze touched every battle stain on his handsome face. "It looks worse closer than from a distance."

His lips parted but no words came out.

"Like a parrot," she said, her eyes finally locking with his.

The warehouse quieted, save for a few low snickers from the crowd, and a scowl formed on his brow. "A parrot?"

His gruff voice sent a tiny thrill through her. But she wouldn't allow it to soften her. "All words but no substance."

More snickers followed, but the man before her merely stared, raw and unflinching, taking it all, and not denying her claim. Was he not going to say anything? Would she have to challenge him to a boxing match to get a reaction?

"You took the deed." She couldn't keep a note of accusation out of her voice.

"I did."

Leonora balled her hands into fists. "Do you still have it?"

"Yes."

She paused. He did? Her gaze flickered to Drake and back again. If Dare had made a deal with the duchess, shouldn't he have given his cousin the deed by now? She searched his gaze for any clue to his thoughts, but he gave away nothing except for a flicker of something that looked very much like naked desperation.

"I'll give it back," Dare said hoarsely. "The deed."

Her entire body stilled, rooted to the spot, as her thoughts scrambled to make sense of what he'd just said. Give it back? What did that mean? Did he mean he'd take back what he'd done, what he'd agreed to? Did that mean . . . did she dare hope? Lord, those bruises. She couldn't look at them, and yet she couldn't look away.

"I object to that," Drake called from his seat on a wooden crate. He didn't look any better than Dare, in fact.

Laughter from the crowd registered dimly, but Leonora ignored it, ignored Drake. She didn't give a whit about his deed or his problems. She only cared about the man before her.

"Why would you do that?" Leonora asked. "Why would you give the deed back?"

"I should never have taken it in the first place."

"Why did you?" Leonora whispered. "I ask, because I find myself rather attached to you, Lord Dare, and rather disappointed that my family members conspired against me to keep us . . . unattached."

"What about me? You must be equally disappointed in me. I accepted their conditions."

She nodded. He had. Yet Leonora didn't blame him, not when it came to it. She might want to pummel the man, but blame him she could not. He had his own burdens he needed to unshackle himself from.

"I should be. The truth is, I've never seen you for something you are not." A faint, wistful smile. "But my brother recently reminded me that even on the blackest night, stars still shine." And she'd rather look beyond this mistake than to fixate on it. Everyone deserved a second chance.

"You're the stars," he said hastily, yet he moved not an inch. "Not me."

More laughter echoed off the walls.

"No." Leonora shook her head. "We mere mortals aren't meant to be stars." She smiled when confusion lit his gaze. "They are merely meant to serve as a light in an otherwise darkened void."

"Leonora . . ."

A voice shouted from the crowd, "Kiss her!" followed by a chorus of jeers.

Leonora ignored the crowd and took another step closer to the man she loved beyond all reason. "They have continually and invariably guided me to you time and again. So don't ask me to fight against the stars. I won't."

"But you have no wish to reform a rake."

That's right. She didn't. "I don't want to reform you."

His jaw clenched. "Then . . ."

"I want you to be rake forever," she said simply. "With one woman in mind."

He visibly started before his brows furrowed.

"Is that not what you thought I'd say?" Leonora grinned. "I love you, Rake. No matter who or what are you. I came here to say this."

"Leonora, I—"

"I don't wish to reform you," she repeated, firmer this time, because this was where he would always resist, where the scars of his past would whisper that he wasn't worthy of her love. But she knew better even if he didn't yet. She saw him. "Stay a rake all your life. But only have eyes for me."

She would tell him a hundred times if she had to. A thousand. She didn't mind repeating this all her life.

Dare would never hurt her.

What he had done—accepting her mother's offer, walking away—most women would cry out in fury or retract into a sea urchin shell. Not her. She understood. His actions came from a place of love.

"Do you know what you are saying?" he asked quietly.

"Yes."

Two wounded hands framed her face. "God, for some reason I have no words."

"You could say you only have eyes for me."

He smiled then. "I do. Only for you."

A cheer went up.

"Good," Leonora said with a nod, her relief so great she thought her knees might give way. "There is one thing, though."

His voice was soft, curious. "Should I be worried?"

She smiled at him. "I am searching for a certain sort of love. Unfashionable. A bit ridiculous. The laces-undone sort of love. If you can't give me such love . . ."

His thumbs rubbed back and forth against her cheeks. "You mean a we-can't-part-with-each-other-forever sort of love? Just that?"

Her pulse shattered and weaved back together again.

Was he saying . . .

She'd hunted him down believing she had to face him with her truth, expecting to be rejected by his. She had wanted to reassure him that, no matter his decision, she understood even if every syllable of his response broke her heart. Dare she believe in a different ending to their story?

"Do you love me, too?" Leonora asked.

A pin drop could have been heard in the silence.

She didn't care. If he couldn't say it, she would ask. And if he couldn't respond with words, she would see it in the way he looked at her, the way he had always looked at her. The way he acted. She'd arrived here tonight ready and prepared for everything and anything. Now she was about to find out what sort of anything it would be.

"Leonora."

There it was.

That look. That stark, unguarded look in his blue eyes.

The moment to rule all moments.

Lightning struck, and she suddenly realized—all moments with him were moments that ruled all moments. How could she not have seen it before? When she was with him, time didn't feel empty. It felt whole.

Leonora's smile widened, and she lifted a hand, wanting to trail a finger over a bruise on his face but hesitating. "Do you know, fear can survive any calamity except love?"

A brow arched. "Are you calling love a calamity?"

"Is it not? It has so thoroughly claimed me that I don't know what is left and what is right."

He pressed his forehead against hers, saying, almost begrudgingly, "Ah, you are a tempting witch. Why can't I resist you?"

"You were not meant to resist me." She covered his hands on

her face with hers. "Perhaps you should follow the stars as well."

"I'm still worried. What if I hurt you?"

"And what if I hurt you?" Leonora countered. "There is no guarantee of a smooth partnership, Rake. There is only the promise that we might try. Also, I have my ways."

"Ways?"

"Should you lack in the *trying*."

His voice dropped, turning gruff. "What ways are those?"

"Curious?" Leonora lifted onto her toes to place a kiss on his lips, uncaring whether anyone was staring or not. "Shall we find out?"

The chorus in the warehouse was . . .

Yes.

⊁⊰⊱⊰

DARE COULDN'T BELIEVE his eyes, couldn't believe his ears, and most certainly couldn't believe the hands touching him.

They were a dream. Her love. Her confession . . . everything. A dream. A beautiful, lovely, dream.

And he never wanted to wake up.

In a way, he'd lived his life prepared to let go of everything before it could be taken from him, which was why he didn't get attached. But Leonora Heart was one attachment he hadn't been able to shake free from. Now, he didn't have to.

To think it had all started with a teasing remark, a playful exchange that had spiraled into something far deeper than he could have ever predicted. At first, it had been nothing more than a nightly pastime, a harmless dance of wit. But then he became acquainted with her, became acquainted with himself, in a way that left no hope of recovery. With each teasing exchange, she wrapped another tentacle around him, drawing him deeper into her depths. And he had allowed those tentacles to wrap around him, sinking willingly into that temptress's world, inch by inch.

Another inch.

Another inch.

Until there was no escape. Until he no longer wanted one. Her hold on him was irrevocable. As a result, the direction of his life had changed. Every path after her first smile had always led him back to her.

"Are you going to be a fool all your life?" Drake remarked from the side. "Answer the woman."

Dare shot his cousin a glare.

Leonora squeezed his hands, drawing his focus back to her. "Are you not willing to find out with me?" she asked softly.

Dare started. Find out? He was willing. Very damn willing. "I am. Willing, that is."

"Are you sure?"

He nodded. Confound it! Why was it so hard to string along more words? They sat there on his tongue, heavy as lead and light as a feather. *I love you, too.* Or maybe *I never want to part ever again.* Most definitely *I never want to let go.* "Don't go," he managed—just. Sky-blue eyes blinked at him. "I mean . . ."

A grin followed his failed explanation, and her smile held all the rays of all his sun. "Don't worry, I'm not leaving." A teasing glint entered her gaze. "As long as you hold on, and perhaps even beyond that, I will not go."

Dare wanted to gather her into his arms and kiss her senseless. "Most men are better than me."

"I don't want better. I want you," she said without pause. "But what about me? There are better women than me, too."

No, there weren't. There was only her. Only Leonora.

Forever.

His limbs finally moved, his hands leaving her face as his arms wrapped around her, lifting her up against him. "Just you." His gaze bore into hers. "And this idiot earl who loves you so damn much." The pressure coiled inside him finally loosened completely. "Your tentacles have wrapped around me tight and secure."

"Are you calling me a sea creature? How brazen!"

"A beautiful little tempting one." He nuzzled her cheek. How the hell had he stayed away from her for a fortnight without going mad? "And you will marry me?"

She didn't answer at once.

The longest second of his life stretched between them, and he felt like a man holding his breath at the edge of a cliff. Then finally, her lips split into a grin, stealing the very breath he'd been holding so tightly.

She brushed a kiss over his lips and said, "I hope you can procure a special license."

Dare grinned, starting to walk to the exit with her still in his arms, leaving his cousin and the crowd behind. "Wait. Your brother is now my secret father-in-law and your parents are—" A finger hushed him.

"Just focus on me." Her eyes sparkled at him.

"I can do that."

Drake cursed behind them. "I want my damn deed!"

Dare ignored him.

She laughed. "I suppose all my gathering of moments led me to my dream—before I even knew I had one. And it was you, always you."

He was a dream? He quite liked that. "If that is the case, you can pursue all your moments, as many as you want, just don't ever lose your dream about me. Let me always be your dream. Grow old with me." If that were her dream, she'd surely stay with him forever to reach it.

"Now that *I* can do."

Ah, hell. He was ridiculous. Ridiculously, madly in love with her. And now that she was in his arms, he could never part with her. He could never let go. He wasn't that strong. He doubted he could have lasted much longer anyway. Even if she hadn't come here today, hadn't looked his way again, he probably would have slowly inserted himself back into her light. Like a moth to a flame.

"I suppose my reputation as a rake is shattered."

Her arms moved from his shoulder to circle his neck. "Oh, do not worry that much about it. You are still one part refined gentlemen and nine parts rogue. Only now you shall aim all that roguish charm at me. Just how I like you."

"A rake?"

"Just about . . . a rake." She grinned, planting another chaste kiss on his lips. "My rake."

"Forever."

"Promise?"

"I promise."

It was an easy promise to make. He loved her. Irrevocably. Unequivocally. Without end. The kind of love she had dared to name and he dared to claim. Because this was the kind of love that remade a man, reshaped his very soul. And if she was his dream, he would make sure he was worthy of hers. Every day. For the rest of his life.

Epilogue

DARE'S LIPS LINGERED on Leonora's, the heat of her breath fusing with his as they tumbled onto his bed. The world outside—his cousin, her family, society at large—seemed far removed from this, trivial in comparison. It was just them—his pulse in his ears, the soft curve of her body beneath his, and the promise of everything he thought he could never have.

It hadn't been a dream.

She'd hunted him down to the warehouse.

She'd told him she loved him.

She was in his home. His arms. His bed.

Then—*knock knock knock.*

Dare groaned, breaking the kiss with a reluctant sigh, resting his forehead against Leonora's. She let out a breath of laughter, and he closed his eyes for a moment, willing the interruption to vanish.

The knock came again. "My lord?" a muffled voice came from the other side of the door.

"What is it, Brett?" he called impatiently.

"Sorry to interrupt, my lord, but you have a caller."

He groaned louder, rolling off of Leonora and sitting up on the edge of the bed. "Tell them to go away."

There was a pause, then, "It is Lord Heart, my lord."

Bloody hell.

"Heart is here?" Leonora shot up beside him, her wide blue eyes darting between him and the door. "What do we do?"

He looked at her, his lips curling into a wicked grin. "What any self-respecting rake who has already been ruined would do. Cry foul."

She laughed, the sound bright and carefree. Trusting. "Then go cry foul, my lord."

The way she said it, with that playful lilt to her voice, made him want to stay right there with her. But if he didn't deal with Heart, the man would probably turn the whole damn house upside down searching for him.

He shoved off from the bed and made his way to the door, cursing the fates for being so cruel. Damn Heart. With one last, regretful glance at Leonora, he left his bedchamber to go and deal with his future family-in-law.

Descending the stairs, he slowed before coming to a complete halt midway. Heart stood at the bottom of the staircase, a scowl etched across his sharp features and his hands clenched at his sides. His whole body bellowed righteous indignation.

Heh.

No matter what Dare felt for the man, there was something undeniably *entertaining* about the way they could never truly stand each other. And if he were being honest, there was always a tinge of amusement to be found in watching him squirm.

Their eyes locked, and Heart's face darkened—if possible— even more.

"Do you always greet guests half-dressed?"

Dare glanced down at his attire. He and Leonora had come straight from the warehouse, so he hadn't given it much thought. At least he was wearing a shirt. He shrugged. "I'm comfortable enough."

"Of course you are." Heart's voice was laced with distaste, though it was hard to tell if it was the lack of clothing or simply the sight of Dare himself that irritated him.

"This is my house, is it not?" Dare answered smoothly, taking in Heart's own frazzled appearance with a lazy smile.

"Where is Leonora?" Heart asked, his voice suddenly tightening.

"I'm here."

Dare glanced up the stairs, catching the sight of Leonora standing there, a vision of glorious defiance. Her sandy hair cascaded down her shoulders in soft waves, her gaze trained directly on him, as though she had just stepped out of a dream.

"Leonora!" Heart's voice cracked through the air like a whip. "I am not even going to begin to comment on this behavior. Yet." His tone chilled. "Let's go. Now."

Leonora crossed her arms over her chest in clear challenge, her chin raised high. "I'm not going anywhere," she retorted coolly, every bit as stubborn as Heart.

"You're not staying here either," Heart snapped.

"I beg to differ."

"Dare, you blackguard!" Heart's glare turned even more fierce. "Are you just going to stand there?"

Dare leaned against the banister of the staircase, an amused smirk tugging at his lips despite the tension thick in the air. "I do what the lady tells me," he said with a casual shrug. "You are more than welcome to stay too." He flashed a wolfish grin at Heart. "We are family, after all."

Heart's lip curled. "No, we aren't."

"Dare," Leonora murmured, her voice laced with concern. She moved closer to him, her fingers brushing his arm. "You do realize he's *completely* furious, don't you?"

"You do realize I can bloody hear you!"

"Oh, I'm well aware," Dare replied, ignoring Heart. "Should we reassure him? We are getting married after all."

She laughed. "Impossible rogue."

Heart cursed. "Are you sure this is what you want, Leonora?"

Her gaze settled on Heart, and Dare caught the slight clench of her jaw. "Do not think I have forgiven you yet for your interference. I'm marrying Dare, and you cannot stop me."

Heart's face reddened, and for a moment, Dare wondered if the man might actually explode. But instead, Heart took a deep breath, visibly trying to maintain his composure. "We can talk about this at home."

"This is home," Leonora said softly, so softly that Dare's heart throbbed.

He cleared his throat. The last thing he wanted for Leonora and her family to be at odds because of him. He exhaled and tipped his head toward the hall. "Come to the study, Heart. We can talk."

Heart narrowed his eyes. "Oh? Finally ready to beg for my blessing?"

"I was thinking more along the lines of offering you a drink before you expire from all that righteous fury."

Heart let out a sharp breath, shaking his head as he stalked toward the study. "God help me if we're going to be family."

Dare winked at Leonora. "You say that like it's a bad thing," Dare quipped, guiding his betrothed toward the study as well.

He gave a happy, hearty laugh. Inside his head, of course. *Betrothed.*

The End

About the Author

Tanya Wilde is an Award-Winning author that developed a passion for reading when she had nothing better to do than lurk in the library during her lunch breaks. Her blazing love affair with pen and paper soon followed after she devoured all their historical romance books! In 2020, she won the Romance Writers Organization of South Africa (ROSA) Imbali Award for Excellence in Romance Writing for Not Quite a Rogue.

When she's not meddling in the lives of her characters or pondering names for her imaginary big, white greyhound, she's off on adventures with her partner in crime.

Wilde lives in a small town at the foot of the Outeniqua Mountains, South Africa.

Website – www.authortanyawilde.com
Instagram – instagram.com / tanyawilde
Facebook – facebook.com / groups / 843373666456177
BookBub – bookbub.com / authors / tanya-wilde